EAGLES COVE

A Finders Mystery

ELKE SINCLAIR

authorHOUSE®

AuthorHouse™
1663 Liberty Drive
Bloomington, IN 47403
www.authorhouse.com
Phone: 833-262-8899

Published by AuthorHouse 07/26/2022

ISBN: 978-1-6655-6447-2 (sc)
ISBN: 978-1-6655-6448-9 (e)

Library of Congress Control Number: 2022912754

Print information available on the last page.

Dedicated to *cozy mystery lovers everywhere

*Amateur sleuths, unsuspecting victims ,a quirky supporting cast, a trail of clues and red herrings, a closed, self-contained community, a passion for justice.

---Cozy Mystery Definition.

CHAPTER 1

THE CALL CAME AT 7:32 a.m., when Nan Abbott was just opening her mouth to take a large bite of a slice of toast smothered in a tart marmalade.

"Drat!" she exclaimed, dropping the toast onto a plate before picking up her phone. Her vexation turned to pleasure once she noticed the caller was her good friend Marley Phillips. Placing the phone to her ear, she smiled widely and said, "Hey, Marley. What's up?"

Ignoring any need for a salutation, Marley spoke quickly. "How would you like to visit the Brainerd Lakes area with me?" Her voice was a few octaves higher than usual, reflecting her excitement.

Nan hesitated for a moment before answering. It wasn't that she felt the question's timing was inconvenient or that Marley's suggesting something on the fly was unusual. Rather, she was busily searching for an answer to two questions: Why did Marley, the queen of proper behavior, always forego formalities when excited, and where had Nan recently heard references to the Brainerd Lakes area of Minnesota?

Then it came to her: *Of course! The missing women!* Marley must have been referring to the disappearance of two women from a lake resort near Brainerd.

The case had been in and out of the papers for more than two years, with no resolution. It was a mystery that was fast becoming cold, which meant it was precisely the kind of mystery that lit a fire in Marley and Nan.

Nan felt her pulse quicken. "Are you saying what I hope you're saying? Are we actually going to get involved in the missing women's case?"

"I just got off the phone with Eva," Marley said. "And yes, it appears that after all this time, the particular skills and talents of the Finders are needed on this case."

With her hunger momentarily abated, Nan pushed the plate of toast to one side. "Well, it's about time. I'd given up hope of us ever getting a green light on this one. It's been red for so long that I'd nearly forgotten all about the case, if you can believe that."

Marley laughed softly. "I can't. But I'll take your word for it. According to Eva, Gretchen has given us a definite green light. So you can relax and live another day."

Nan raised her fists above her head and shook them in the air. "Good old Gretchen!" she cried out for no particular reason other than the thrill of it. On the other end of the phone, she could hear Marley laughingly parroting her remark.

Eva's daughter, Gretchen, was a senior commander with the Saint Paul Police Department. She had contacted her mother in the past and involved the Finders in her previous investigations. The fact that Gretchen was once again asking for their assistance was exciting. It strongly underscored their experience and expertise in crime solving—not an accolade to dismiss lightly. The Finders consisted of a group of old friends, five in all, who happened to be senior citizens.

"So I take it," Marley said, "that a trip to Brainerd will not be inconvenient for you?"

Nan hesitated. While the prospect of a trip to northern Minnesota for the purpose of crime solving sounded exciting, her attention had been annoyingly drawn downward toward two demanding felines. They were in the process of twining themselves around her ankles and chirping insistently in the specific way Russian blues did when they wanted someone to think they were starving.

Rumpole and Bailey, her two toms, obviously had finished their soft breakfasts and were now hoping to have a share of hers. She steeled herself to resist their petitions and reached for a crossword-ready mechanical pencil and paper napkin.

"Inconvenient? Not on your life," she told Marley. "I'm taking notes. Tell me everything I need to know. How did all of this come about? What's the backstory?"

"Eva called me early this morning. She didn't want to wait any longer to tell us the news," Marley replied. "And the overall point was, Gretchen feels the department to be totally stymied. I mean, they've hit a wall, Nan. They truly have."

"There's nothing more coming in? No new clues or information?" Nan asked, gazing down at two sets of large, wide-set emerald eyes. The cats were presently doing a masterful job of imploring her to end their pitiful starvation. She would have liked to argue the point that Russian blues' love of any kind of food tended to cause them to put on unwanted weight, and as a responsible pet owner, she felt it was her duty to follow their vet's strict guidelines, but she realized that addressing her complaints to the two sets of twitching ears and lashing tails, while they remained neither fed nor interested, was pointless. She broke off two small pieces of her toast and placed them on the floor for the cats.

"The well has gone dry, I'm afraid," Marley said. "That's not to say the police don't have strong suspicions, because they certainly do. The problem is, they can't probe any further as active law enforcement officers. Certainly, we've learned that the police can't trample on people's civil rights just because they have suspicions, strong as they may be. So the result is, as of today, two women are still missing. And people want answers, Nan. In fact, they're starting to demand them, especially those closest to the missing women."

"Well, of course they want answers," Nan said. "Who wouldn't? And yet from what I've read, even after all this time, the police still have no hard evidence. I mean, when all is said and done, the circumstances add up to nothing more than a missing-persons case. The police reports state the two women are missing. They have every right to fall off the face of the earth if they so choose."

"That's right," Marley replied. "Add to that the fact that the police have absolutely no hard evidence of foul play, no forensics, no crime scene, and no bodies. Well, you can see where they would be frustrated."

"It's got to be exasperating as hell," Nan said.

"I'm sure. According to Gretchen, at this point, she can't see the Finders doing any harm. In fact, she thinks we might provide the shake-up this case needs. We've done it before, you know?"

Nan held her breath. "I'm glad she sees it that way."

"She does," Marley said. "She's getting desperate. And of course, Gretchen is only too aware of all the good we've done for her and the force in the past. We're used to following leads to see where they might take us and asking questions that demand a response one way or another."

"Nothing wrong with stirring up still waters to see what might float to the top," said Nan, who was in the process of sipping coffee that had gone cold. "So we have Gretchen's full support then?" she asked, setting down her mug.

"We do," Marley said emphatically. Then, with less enthusiasm, she added, "As always, she'll keep her relationship with us under wraps."

"No problem. We're used to working that way. As long as she continues to supply Eva with information and helps in whatever way she can to smooth the way between us and the local authorities."

"We can count on it. She'll do all she can in that regard," Marley said.

"That's all we can ask for," Nan said. "So what's the plan?"

"I invited everyone to my place tonight so we can go over all the information concerning the case to date."

Nan smiled. Hearing Marley call it "the case" told Nan that she hadn't come around to owning it quite yet. But Nan knew that in little time, they would all be calling it "our case," and she felt her excitement grow.

She willed herself to concentrate and turned her attention back to Marley, who was still talking: "I told Sean, Ray, and

Eva to come at eight o'clock. We'll have a strategy session, like we always do before we begin a case. You know how Eva is. She insists that all of us have the crucial information and are on the same page. She's convinced following such a practice assures our safety."

"Makes sense," Nan said resignedly.

"Did you know that Eva has been rather obsessed with these disappearances?"

"I didn't know to what extent, but it doesn't surprise me. She did get us all together last February to talk about it, didn't she? And you know Eva—when she gets involved with something, it's only natural she gives it her all. Besides, it's a fascinating mystery. The disappearance of two women precisely one year apart? C'mon."

"I'm not saying it isn't an alluring puzzle. What I meant is, it's been over two years, and Eva has been at it all this time."

"Again," Nan said, "I'm not surprised. When the story first appeared in the papers, I was also totally intrigued. But as time went on and there was no indication of any foul play, I lost interest. To tell you the truth, I thought the women would have turned up by now. Now I'm not so sure they ever will."

"Eva feels the same way, and so do Sean and Ray. They're convinced the women are dead. Eva feels so strongly about it that she's involved both of her blogs to supply answers to her many questions. She has her followers researching overtime in the hope of discovering more information."

Eva's two blogs supplied them with additional brainpower and extended their geographic outreach. The blogs had become so invaluable to the Finders that Nan had almost forgotten why Eva started them in the first place. Eva had started her first blog out of her long love of baking and well before the Finders had retired from full-time work and dedicated themselves to solving crime. The purpose of that first blog, *Knead to Dough*, was to share and collect artisanal bread recipes. However, since her retirement, she at times cleverly changed it temporarily to *Knead to Know* when she was working on a Finders' case and needed her followers to help provide her with information pertinent to the investigation.

Eva's second blog consisted of fellow research librarians who, like Eva, appreciated the opportunity to collect and search out arcane data. That blog was called *Who, What, Where, and When*, and it had become customary for her fellow research lovers to, again temporarily, add the word *Why* during one of Eva's crime investigations.

Followers of the blogs seemed more than ready to shift their attention from baking bread or researching little-known facts to helping Eva solve a crime whenever she asked for their help. Her requests introduced a certain variety and spice into their flour-dusted or bookworm lives. Over the years, Eva's blogs had expanded considerably to include people from all walks of life and many locales. In this way, Eva utilized the many talents, experiences, and insights of her internet followers.

Eva's followers' willingness to work overtime for the Finders never ceased to amaze the Finders.

"Good ol' Eva," Nan cried. "Who better to do a thorough job of sorting fact from fiction than a bunch of retired research librarians with plenty of time on their hands?"

"You do have to admit they're pros at it," said Marley. "And they've certainly come through for us in the past. I hope they do so again."

"I have faith in them," Nan replied. "They've never let us down."

"I have faith in all of us," Marley said, emphasizing the word *all*.

Nan, who had never met anyone more faith-filled than Marley, knew she meant it. "I'd better start packing and taking care of a few errands. I assume, since we're meeting to strategize tonight, you want to leave for Brainerd in the morning?"

"I do," Marley said. "I'll call and make all the arrangements for our stay. Since it's off-season, we shouldn't have any problem booking a cabin at the same resort the two women stayed at."

"What was its name again?" Nan asked.

"Eagles Cove Marley replied. "It's called Eagle's Cove Resort. Oh, and before I forget: Will you pick up Eva on your way over this evening? You know how she hates to drive at night."

"Sure. No problem. How long do you expect we'll be gone?"

"I should think at least a week. Does that sound right to you?"

"Sounds about right," Nan said. "If we don't raise something interesting by then, we might as well hang it up. Besides, we can always stay longer if we need to."

"My reasoning exactly," Marley said. "See you tonight."

"I'm looking forward to it," Nan replied before disconnecting the call.

As Nan gazed across the kitchen table and out the window to her garden beyond and the cloud-filled sky above, she was suddenly filled with the realization that she was happy—truly happy. Her heart was racing, and every nerve in her body tingled, yet she was happy.

As strange as it seemed, she knew that powerful emotion came from the knowledge that she and Marley were about to embark on an adventure that would undoubtedly include an element of physical danger. In the next week or two, all five of their senses would need to be on such high alert that the scourge of Alzheimer's wouldn't stand a chance of invading their little gray cells—and she wouldn't have had it any other way. As Finders' member Sean Finnegan often remarked, "Solving mysteries is the very best kind of mind aerobics there is."

She stared down into her coffee mug filled with dark brew and thought about how often the Finders had tried to explain their addiction to crime solving to friends and family, but to no avail. They could never quite make their loved ones see the coherent sense in it all. To outsiders, the Finders' taking on, at their age, a case that involved a high level of risk and the possibility of danger was foolish, and any rational person would have been persuaded to rethink, regroup, and choose a far safer alternative hobby. How could she and Marley possibly explain that the inclusion of risk and danger was as essential to them as having icing on their cake or a cherry in their Manhattan? An element of risk was as beneficial to their souls as doing a zip line across a deep ravine or taking a balloon ride down the Saint Croix River. All Nan knew for sure was that while working a case, she and Marley felt younger and more alive than they ever had.

Furthermore, she knew the Finders all felt the same way. The five of them worked well together because they all had the same penchant. In retirement, not one of them gravitated toward customary senior activities, such as progressive dinners, water aerobics, beach volleyball, watercolor painting, or golf-crazed country clubs. As beneficial and fun as those activities could be, they were far too tame, ordinary, and status quo for the Finders. With the time retirement allotted them, they could finally cash in on the reputation they'd acquired after solving their first murder while still in their teens.

Between then and now, life had intervened with college; careers; travel; marriages; and, for some, children, divorce, or widowhood. Real live crime was what they all wanted to focus on in their senior years. Not the crimes found between the covers of mystery books they'd settled for when they worked nine to five but real crimes that involved puzzles that had no readily available answers. The Finders didn't care if the case was cold, lukewarm, or hot. They weren't fussy in that way. As long as the crime involved the diligent unraveling of a mystery, they were precisely where they wanted to be. Or, as Marley said, "Solving the grave injustice of murder guarantees we are on the right side of heaven."

The phrase always made Nan wonder, *Is there a wrong side of heaven?*

Nan stared blankly at the items on her kitchen table, which she had mindlessly arranged in a straight line. Salt and pepper shakers, the napkin holder, and a variety of small carved birds she always kept on her kitchen table simply because she liked them there all stood in an orderly row like good little soldiers. She shook her head to clear it and told herself she'd wasted enough time reflecting. She had tasks to accomplish and errands to run before her trip to Brainerd and northern Minnesota tomorrow.

She took a quick mental inventory of the details she would need to address before leaving town. Besides checking the tires on her car and filling the gas tank, she needed to call her next-door neighbors Sylvie and Joe to arrange for them to visit with and feed her two lovable and usually well-mannered cats while she was away. Of course, she could always take Rumpole and Bailey with her. She'd done it before, and they both traveled fairly well. But in this particular situation, she felt it better to leave them at home. Besides, Joe and Sylvie no longer had any pets of their own and enjoyed hanging with and spoiling her cats—or so they continually told her. Not wanting to deprive them of an opportunity to spend time with her two boys, she felt it only right to give them a call.

But since it was still far too early to phone Joe and Sylvie, she decided to take care of an even more pressing matter: her uneaten breakfast. As she drew back her chair and rose from the table, she noticed that one of the two pieces of toast she'd placed on the floor had disappeared, while the other looked as if it might have been licked a bit or perhaps merely touched haughtily by a small black nose. She bent over, swooped up the lone remaining toast bit, walked across the kitchen, and tossed it into the trash bin. Then she poured her cold coffee down the sink.

Rumpole and Bailey were now nowhere in sight; having accomplished their goal of getting her to give in to their demands, they were either pursuing other adventures or curling themselves into their beds for a morning nap.

Nan refilled her mug with fresh coffee from the pot next to the stove and once again seated herself at the kitchen table, where she picked up the now cold toast smothered with marmalade. She opened her mouth wide and took a big, satisfying bite. As she slowly chewed, she thought of some additional tasks she needed to accomplish before she could leave town tomorrow: stop at the bank, clean out the refrigerator, fill the bird feeders, and buy more cat litter.

She took another huge bite of her toast, only this time, she chewed a lot faster.

CHAPTER 2

NAN LET OUT A LONG characteristic sigh. There she was, driving down Saint Paul's iconic Grand Avenue lined with majestic Victorian houses the likes of which wouldn't be seen again that side of the Mississippi, about to pick up her friend Eva and drive her to Marley's house, where the Finders were gathering, and all she could think about was the miniscule amount of leg space between the passenger front seat and the dashboard. It was not a lot of space, and it seemed to shrink the more she stared at it.

The problem was that no matter how hard she tried, her normally talented imagination found it impossible to conjure up a way in which Eva's six-foot-plus body would fit into such a limited space without bending into a human pretzel. The thought of Eva forced to become a contortionist in order to sit in the front seat of her small, low-slung car made Nan wince. Even more painful than the image itself was the knowledge that Eva would be sure to register a strong complaint.

Eva, bless her, was a complainer. She couldn't help it. She was a perfectionist who had a highly organized and methodical mind but had the grave misfortune of living in a world that was anything but. Nan told herself she had only herself to blame if Eva read her the riot act. After all, she'd chosen the car more for its fuel efficiency and inconspicuous, blah color than for any degree of comfort it might provide her passengers. The car included the exact features she'd been looking for at the time: it was small, compact, low to the ground, and of the ideal size to tuck behind a bush, hedge, or row of trees. Plus, its price tag had fit within her always-limited budget as if it were tailor-made.

"I want something totally bland and not the least bit sexy," she'd told Harold, the overly friendly auto salesperson, as the two of them walked the entire length of several used car lots. "A car no one would notice. One that's perfectly content to be shy."

Harold had stopped short and peered down at her. "Did you say *shy?*" he'd asked tentatively.

"Yes, that's correct," she'd replied. "*Shy*. It means having a strong repulsion to drawing attention to oneself. That's the type of car I want."

Harold had rolled his eyes in a way that implied, "It takes all kinds," and under normal circumstances, she would have been highly offended and probably laid into him concerning the importance of giving the customer whatever was preferred. But she had known the long list of must-haves she'd given the poor man didn't make the circumstances anywhere near normal. So she'd tempered her annoyance with a good dash of understanding, and she was glad she had, as in the end, Harold not only had succeeded but had delivered in every respect her many wants.

Since then, her little car had proven itself a keeper

time and time again. In fact, she'd felt it so effortlessly and flawlessly performed the chameleon art of surveillance for which she'd selected it that she'd christened it Agatha after Agatha Christie. Nan, being a solver of mysteries herself, had always felt an affinity toward the famous author. She also thought the humble nature of the car perfectly matched that of Christie, who, having forgotten the invitation an overzealous doorman requested one night at the London Savoy, had been about to turn around and go home rather than name-drop her own name and receive immediate entrance to an event being held to honor her play *The Mousetrap.*

The fact that Agatha Christie, writer of *The Mousetrap*, which would become the longest-running play in British history, had been so self-effacing that she'd almost turned away from an event honoring her famed writing abilities had the lasting effect of endearing Christie to Nan forever. Besides, Nan had always lamented the fact that she had long ago read all of Christie's books and could therefore no longer be entirely blown away by the ingenuity of one of her plots or the genius of her main sleuths.

The only problem Nan had with her Agatha, however, was that passengers too often grumbled at the old girl's lack of comfortable interior space. It was an issue she found hard to relate to. Being just short of five foot two on a good day, Nan rarely, if ever, discovered herself in what others called cramped conditions. Although she would never have admitted it to anyone other than herself, even airplane seats in coach seemed roomy to her.

On Goodrich Avenue, Nan parked Agatha at the curb in front of Eva's painted-lady Victorian home, unbuckled her seat belt, and reached to open the car door. Before she could alight, however, her ears picked up the staccato *tap-tap* of Eva's silver-tipped cane on the slate tiles of her front walk. Eva had obviously been watching at her front door. Nan looked out the passenger window and watched Eva's slow approach.

The oldest of the Finders, Eva, at seventy-three years of age, had once held the position of head librarian at a large Saint Paul library, and she still carried herself in the same authoritarian manner that always had made people think twice about talking among the stacks. There was no arguing that Eva had a professional, even regal, air about her that naturally attracted attention.

At present, however, she was encumbered in her forward motion by an accumulation of personal items. In the crook of her left arm was a bright red, white, and blue sleeve containing her trusty laptop, and looped over the same arm was a medium-sized Longaberger basket containing, among an assortment of items of canine comfort, her Maltese dog, Dewey.

As always, though, even laden down as she was, Eva looked fabulous. Nan had always attributed that fact to the color of Eva's hair. It was a natural silver shade, the kind of stunning silver that fortunate women whose hair turned gray early didn't, in Nan's eyes, fully appreciate. Unlike Nan, whose hair fell in twisted curls about her face as if she were a Raggedy Ann doll and whose natural Irish red had faded so long ago that she could now get easily lost in a crowd, Eva stood out wherever she went. She wore her hair drawn back from her face in the same French roll she'd favored for the past fifty years, which only served to enhance her fine, chiseled features. That day, other than a bright Hermès scarf looped around her neck, she was dressed all in black, with simple pencil slacks, a knit top, and flats. Nan always thought that for Eva to look so stunning at her age, she must have done everything right in her life and then some.

Unfortunately for Nan, she hadn't followed suit.

When Eva drew closer, Nan stepped out of the car and rushed around the hood to assist her. She and Eva greeted each other with a gentle touch cheek to cheek, and then Nan reached to open the passenger door as Eva handed her the basket containing Dewey. Nan waited patiently as Eva placed her laptop on the floor of the car, leaning it against the center console. She then tried her best to help Eva fold her long legs into the compact car.

"I'm so sorry, Eva," she said, deciding to head off what was sure to be a torrent of Eva complaints. "But the seat is back as far as it will go."

But to Nan's surprise, Eva didn't object. "I'm fine, Nan," she said. "It's not your fault I'm a tad over six feet."

Just then, Dewey, not impressed with the current activity, decided to bark wildly at some phantom only he could see in Eva's front yard. Nan tried her best to calm him, but to no avail, so it was not surprising when, as soon as Eva became a pretzel in the front seat, Nan eagerly plunked Dewey onto her friend's lap and slammed the car door. She took her time in walking around the car, and once behind the wheel, she was pleasantly surprised to discover Eva had somehow managed to quiet Dewey, who now sat within his basket as silent as a lamb.

Nan snapped her seat belt into place, started the motor,

depressed the signal lever, and pulled away from the curb with a screech of the car's tires that took both her and Eva by surprise. A sharp yip from Dewey was swiftly followed by an exclamation from Eva.

"Whoa, Nan!" she said, placing the palm of one hand firmly on Agatha's dashboard in an attempt to steady herself. "You may be as eager to get to tonight's gathering as I am, but please tell me you're not planning to drive like some randy teenager all the way to Marley's."

"No, of course not. Sorry about that," Nan said, tapping the brake with the toe of her shoe. "But you're right. I am in a hurry to get to Marley's. I'm curious to discover from you all that Marley and I need to know before we start our trip tomorrow. Also, I know you won't clue me in to any of it until we meet with everyone. So yeah, I'm kind of anxious to get to Marley's."

Eva reached out and gave Nan's knee a sympathetic pat. "I can understand your impatience, Nan. Until now, you and Marley haven't had a role to play in this investigation, have you?"

Nan's sudden feeling of discomfort made her wrinkle her nose. "We've had no role to play. Nothing. Nada. But from what I understand, you've been quite active. And that's wonderful. I'm not complaining."

"Sure you are!" Eva said with a laugh. "Look, I know how hard it is for you and Marley to be sidelined like this. But this case, which my blogs' followers and I have been working on and into which the Finders will now be sending you, like all our projects, is complex. After all, it involves not one but two missing women. And while we don't yet know with certainty, both of them may be dead."

"Do you think they're dead?" Nan asked.

"The point is, we don't know," Eva replied. "And that's the problem. We don't know what you and Marley may be heading into. That's why the time spent in doing research and development is absolutely essential. R&D is immensely important, Nan. Its amount and quality often determine the outcome of our investigations. You know that as well as I. And it also goes a long way to keeping you and Marley safe, which is no small thing."

Nan suddenly realized she'd given Eva the perfect opportunity to deliver her favorite lecture of all time: the importance of executing due diligence.

In the hope of cutting short Eva's sermon, Nan said, "I know, I know. Believe me, Marley and I are grateful for all that you, your blog followers, and the rest of the Finders do to keep us safe. But this case is over two years old now and is becoming colder by the day. We both know the statistics are dire for cold cases, so I want to get my boots on the ground, so to speak. I can't rest until I can actually get into the midst of solving this thing, damn it!"

Eva laughed, and a twinkle lit her eyes. "Actually, Nan, my followers and I want to see this *thing* solved as well."

"Well, the waiting seems like an eternity to Marley and me."

Suddenly, Nan was forced to react sharply by the appearance of a jogger in the intersection. One second, he wasn't there, and the next, he was directly in front of the car. Her heart stopped cold, and both she and Eva yelled, "Stop!"

Nan slammed her foot against the brake pedal, which allowed the jogger to pass with barely a breeze between his life and his death. The force of his scathing look and the brutality of his dirty remark were somewhat lessened by Nan's notice of a set of earbud wires dangling on both sides of his head. "He's listening to music! He's listening to music and not paying attention!" she shouted. "How dare he swear at us, and how dare he call me an old lady, when he just came out of nowhere and ran into the street without looking?"

"He almost heard the heavenly choir that time," Eva said, holding up her thumb and index finger. "He was that close."

The women took a few moments to regain their composure, and once they continued on, Nan rolled down her side window to allow fresh air to clear her head.

After a while, Eva said calmly, as if the jogger incident had never happened and she had searched her brain for a different topic, "By the way, you'll never guess who contacted me the other day."

Nan, who was not fully prepared to concentrate on anything else at the moment other than her driving, frowned slightly. "I can't imagine," she answered.

"Our old dance instructor, Miss Bingham's niece, Rose. Do you remember her from the trial?"

Eva could not have broached a better subject to get Nan's mind off what could have been a 911 call. She was suddenly transported back some fifty years to Miss Bingham's murder trial, and somewhere in the cobwebs of her memory, she saw a quiet young girl with a round face, fringe bangs, and glasses.

"Sure, but just barely," Nan said. "She arrived rather late in the trial, as I recall. Didn't she fly in from out east to be with her mother?"

"Yes, that's right. She was a student in college at the time. She came right after midterms."

"And she called you? What did she want?"

"It seems her mother passed away recently, and while Rose was going through her things, she came across a picture of the two sisters, her mom and Miss Bingham. The image, of course, brought to mind her aunt's violent death."

"Understandable."

"Rose told me she suddenly realized how much information she lacked regarding the murder and the trial, which began to weigh on her mind. So realizing she hadn't asked enough questions, she called me."

Nan nodded knowingly. "I can relate. I know that feeling well—that sense of panic and remorse when you realize a big part of your own life history may be lost to you forever."

Eva smiled and added, "And given our ages, she wouldn't want to waste any more time in contacting us, would she? I think she started with me because she knew I had a background as a researcher."

"Well, if anyone knows that crime, it's us. After all, we cracked the case, didn't we? We fingered the murderer. I take it you filled her in on all the particulars?"

Nan could still easily recall the day Ray had observed a singularly curious detail that had later proven crucial in solving the case: when Miss B's killer came to the dance studio dressed as a woman, Ray noticed that the supposed woman who passed him on the stairway had a twitchy left eye just like the man who had picked up Miss B after class, who they thought may have been a boyfriend. After Eva commented on the fact that she thought the so-called woman was wearing a bad, cheaply made wig, which also was sitting on her head askew, they took their suspicions to the police. Mere suspicion was not enough to allow the police to act, but after hearing that the attack on Miss B had caused her death and that the police had found the murder weapon, they quickly hatched a plan to get the boyfriend's fingerprints. When he showed up at a reception following her funeral, they seized the opportunity. Their cleverness in carefully secreting a glass he used for punch allowed a fingerprint match to be made and eventually brought about an arrest.

"Anyway," Eva said, "Rose and I had a nice long discussion. It was fascinating to discover what she remembered and what she either never knew or had blocked out. She remembered that it was her aunt who gave us the moniker we used at first: the Gaggle."

Nan laughed. "She remembered that? Goodness, I can still hear Miss Bingham yelling at us in that high-pitched, raspy voice of hers." Nan raised her voice two octaves and mimicked Miss Bingham: "Come away from that wall, children. How do you expect to concentrate on learning to dance, when all you do is waste time haggling and gaggling?"

Now Eva was laughing as well. "You sound just like her, Nan. Do you know how upset she had to have been to light into us like that? She was always so prim and proper. Remember the way Marley protested? I can still see Marley, with hands on her hips, standing her ground, telling Miss B that she didn't understand how absolutely imperative it was that we all decide where we were going after the skating party Saturday night."

Nan's laughter became a series of odd, throaty sounds

as she interjected. "And Miss Bingham pointed to the dance floor and said, 'On these premises, Miss Phillips, the only thing that's imperative is dance!'"

"And what about Marley's crack about our being 'defenders of the wall' when Miss B called us wallflowers?" Eva said.

Nan choked on her laughter and had to clutch the wheel to keep from running up onto the curb. "That Marley," she said. "She's always had her own style and way of saying things, hasn't she?"

They had all attended Miss Bingham's Preparatory Dance Class for Gentlemen and Young Ladies because the adults in their lives had hoped they somehow would acquire the social skills necessary to achieve a successful adulthood through dance. To that end, each set of parents had happily handed their progeny over to Miss B.

"It still amazes me that we wouldn't have met each other if not for Miss B's dance class," Nan said. "Sean and Ray went to a private all-boys school, and I was enrolled at the neighborhood Catholic girls' school."

Eva nodded. "I know. Thank heaven parents in those days all thought alike. It still astounds me how they thought proper manners and decorum would somehow be acquired through dance. Via some sort of osmosis, I suppose?"

"Everyone we knew was enrolled in a dance class back then," Nan said with a laugh.

"That's right," Eva responded. "And all any of us ended up learning was how to, despite sweaty palms and shaky knees, approach, chat, and move rhythmically with members of the opposite sex."

"And we all know what good comes from that!" Nan exclaimed.

Eva and Nan were now laughing so heartily they wished they could hold their sides to keep them from aching. Eva drew in a breath and said, "I remember how fascinated I was with Miss B's term *gaggle*. I had never heard it before, you see. I couldn't wait to get home and open my dictionary to look up the word."

Nan gave her a surprised look. "Really? Wow, even back then, you were hardwired for research."

"And then I called everyone," Eva said. "All five of us. Ray and Sean latched on to the dictionary definitions of the word. Ray's remark was along the lines of 'Well, when we're excited, you have to admit we can sound like a flock of geese,' and Sean weighed in with 'And we are far more loose and free-spirited than tightly organized.' We all fell in love with that word, and for a group of teenagers who didn't yet have a niche, what more could we have hoped for?"

Nan then turned the steering wheel sharply and drove onto the street that would take them straight to Marley's house, while Eva gave Dewey another doggy treat from her pocket.

"Such lovely memories," Eva said, and Nan nodded. "You know, Marley's gumption and your courage are what make you such competent investigators. The Finders are fortunate to have you. Especially given that the two of you are willing to venture where the rest of us would rather not go."

Nan suddenly saw the inconsistency between their present laughter and the tragic circumstances and real danger that surrounded their cases. Then she thought again of Miss Bingham. "You know," she said softly, "we may have courage, but kindness escaped us with Miss Bingham, didn't it? Poor Miss Bingham. That dear woman didn't deserve what we dished out."

"No," Eva said, "she didn't. But we were younger then. Besides, you have to admit we made up for it in the end."

Nan looked over at Eva and gave her a wide, knowing smile. "That we did," she said, "That we did."

CHAPTER 3

As Eva returned her attention to Dewey, Nan concentrated on her driving. They were barely making any progress. The traffic was congested and moving by inches. She couldn't make out what was slowing their advance, but she hoped it would turn out to be something more worthwhile than drivers' goose-necking a maintenance truck or a couple of tree trimmers. Finding herself with time to spare, she thought of how their group had, by solving Miss B's murder, acquired a reputation that would come to influence their future.

Besides Nan and Eva, the Finders consisted of Marley Phillips, an heiress and the primary financial patron of the group; Sean Finnegan, a retired college engineering professor; and Ray Ballard, a chemist, who, by common agreement, was the genius of the group. Each member, Nan knew, brought particular talents and gifts that had proven invaluable to their association.

Marley's full name was Marlowe Bentley Phillips. She had been christened Marlowe by her father, a huge fan of Raymond Chandler. Her mom had been unfamiliar with

Chandler's sleuth, Philip Marlowe, but had fallen in love with the name Marlowe when it was suggested for her baby girl. Like Nan, Marley was in her late sixties and thought of as a youngster within the Finders. Although Nan at first had been sure Marley's family wealth and traditional, classic background would conflict with her own nonconforming, bohemian spirit and vibe, she had come to admit that as investigators, the two of them worked flawlessly together, each having complete trust and confidence in the other's daring and judgment.

The traffic suddenly began to flow again, and Nan continued onward, swerving around and passing by the two cars whose fender bender had caused the delay. She wondered if the difficulty of that night's journey could be a bad omen. Was some weird supernatural force trying to prevent them from gathering?

"It doesn't look as though anyone was hurt," Eva said. "Just unlucky or possibly stupid."

Along both its north and south sides, Summit Avenue exhibited an impressive row of Victorian-era mansions one after another, each made of local stone. Each proudly boasted the wealth, power, and influence of a previous generation's social and commercial elite. Marley's house stood dominant among them.

"Tonight's meeting," Eva said, "will give us a chance to review all the details we discussed in February and all my new information." There was a pause, and then she added casually, "I assume Ray is coming to the meeting tonight?"

Nan, knowing well Eva's lifelong crush on Ray Ballard, quickly nodded. "Of course. I can't imagine him not being there. Besides, we need his input."

"He's so clever, isn't he?" Eva asked lovingly.

"Yes, he is. We're very fortunate to have a chemist of his caliber in our group," Nan replied.

Nan turned the car into Marley's driveway as Eva remarked, "I just saw someone with a dark bob at the front door of Marley's house. Could it have been her? We're not late, are we? I know I hate it when anyone's late."

"Late? I don't think so," Nan answered. "Maybe she's just eager to get this meeting started. I'm sure Sean and Ray are already inside."

Nan came to a stop alongside the three-story stone mansion that had been in Marley's family for four generations. She always parked under the porte cochere at the mansion's side entrance whenever she brought Eva, because it made entering Marley's house easier for her. She knew Ray and Sean lived close enough to walk and rarely drove to Marley's, so she felt comfortable in blocking the one lane leading back to the carriage house.

Nan exited first to help her friend out of the little car. Offering Eva her arm, which was swiftly refused, and holding Dewey in his basket, Nan commented on the recent improvements Marley had made to her landscaping. "Look at what Marley has designed, Eva. Isn't it lovely?"

"Elegant woman, elegant house," Eva said as they both looked approvingly at the strip of plantings along the edge of the driveway.

Marley opened wide the side door and called out a greeting. Her silhouette was unmistakably athletic, as revealed in her wide shoulders and long, slender torso. Within the Finders, Marley was the athletic one. She had won multiple trophies in golf, tennis, and equestrian show jumping and dressage in her youth. She had also been a champion swimmer who had trained professionally to swim the English Channel. Nan thought she would have mastered the challenge successfully if a nasty bout of mononucleosis hadn't stymied her well-laid plans.

A wide, somewhat crooked smile played across Marley's face, which leant her almond-shaped gray eyes a welcoming gleam, as she approached her chums. Nan commented on the profusion of newly emergent spring bulbs that bordered the new flagstone walkway; some of the sharp-tipped tulip greens were jauntily wearing comical little hats made of last fall's rust-colored leaves and shreds of cedar mulch.

"Aren't they adorable?" Nan asked, pointing to the tulips. "It's obvious this side of your house is the sunniest. Look how far along these little guys are." Favorable comments on Marley's gardening and landscaping efforts were as pleasing to their hostess as were her friends and family themselves.

"They're doing quite well, aren't they?" Marley said. "They'll become a swath of various shades of lavender, pale rose, and purple when in full bloom."

Nan continued her enthusiastic accolades regarding Marley's landscaping as Eva casually tossed her cane into the car's backseat.

"I believe I'll leave my cane behind," Eva said. "It's not always needed and can get in the way. And the laptop is what is most important."

Nan and Marley both suppressed smiles. They knew Eva was sensitive to the fact that she was two years older than Ray and, therefore, was reluctant to appear old in his eyes.

A waft of fragrant wood smoke suddenly alerted Nan's

nose to the curling gray swaths coming from the nearest of the mansion's tall chimneys.

"You've laid a fire?" she called out to Marley. "I thought we'd be meeting in the sunroom!"

Marley shook her head. "The house has felt chilly all day, so I decided to forego the conservatory and put us in the back parlor."

Nan and Eva entered the side door.

Marley reached over and squeezed Nan's arm, putting into words all that Nan was feeling inside. "I am so excited about our trip tomorrow I can hardly contain myself," she said. "Finally, the two of us can start our work."

Nan, who knew her own blue eyes were already sparkling with the same excitement, smiled widely and nodded her agreement.

Marley noticed Eva wobble slightly, and she reached out to firmly grasp her friend's elbow. Nan took Eva's other arm, and between the two of them, they managed to guide Eva up the few stairs that led to the central hall. Eva then shrugged off any further assistance, and with Marley now holding the basket containing Dewey, who lifted his head and looked about with interest, Eva made her way resolutely toward the back parlor. She was determined to appear before Ray unassisted.

Marley and Nan held back for a moment in order to cover a few details before their upcoming trip to the Brainerd Lakes area. Knowing Nan always wanted to be in the driver's seat, Marley said, "I assumed you wanted to drive Agatha tomorrow, so I told Roadie I wouldn't need any of the cars."

Nan laughed. "Showing up at the resort in a BMW

might raise a few red flags. You're right. I'll drive. Agatha and I will pick you up at seven tomorrow morning."

"That will work for me," Marley said. "We can stop for breakfast on the way. We'll have plenty of time. Check-in at the resort isn't until two o'clock. The only thing is, Daniel left for New York early this morning on a business trip before an important package he was expecting could be delivered." She frowned. "Only moments ago, I was looking for the UPS truck out the front door, when I spotted you and Eva arriving. I want that package on his desk before I leave tomorrow. If it hasn't arrived, I won't be able to concentrate on anything else."

Marley was married to Daniel Halloran, a classical music composer whose work could be heard around the world as well as within the walls of Marley's home, either live or recorded, on most days.

"Then let's hope it's delivered this evening," said Nan. "Both of us need to have all our wits about us tomorrow."

They walked down the hallway and entered Marley's family room. It was cavernous, with a high ceiling. Eva was seated comfortably in a plush wing chair close to both the fireplace and Ray, who had apparently appointed himself keeper of the flames.

Ray Ballard, a retired chemist, was a quiet man of few words but deeply considered thoughts. He still maintained a working laboratory in one wing of his home. A confirmed bachelor, Ray stood straight and tall at six foot two even after many years of bending over test tubes and beakers. His dislike of all things unscientific made him eschew anything "fussy" or "unnatural," as he put it, which led the rest of his friends to believe he didn't color his jet-black locks. Ray was the man the group turned to for such unusual things as a fast-setting gel that Nan and Marley could use to fill, lift, and subsequently make a mold of a boot or shoe imprint. Nan often teased him about his failure to concoct a truth serum for her and Marley to use when they confronted a suspect they knew to be lying. His response to her request was always the same: he would look away, rub the lobe of his right ear, and say, "I'm working on it," which was something Nan never doubted for a minute.

As Nan and Marley entered the room, both Eva and Ray looked up and smiled.

"Sean's not here yet?" Nan asked. Sean Finnegan was the jokester of the group. Always looking for a laugh, he was a longtime amateur inventor and tinkerer who supplied the group with any number of ingenious tools of their trade.

"No," Ray replied. "But I talked to him earlier, and he's definitely coming."

After bringing Dewey in his basket to Eva's side, Nan and Marley seated themselves, and Nan slowly took in the room and its contents. Because Marley's family were descended from ancestors whose fortunes had been made in Minnesota's early days of shipping and lumbering, Nan had expected to see delicate Sheraton tables and exquisite embroidered fabrics on antique furniture in every room of Marley's home the first time she visited. Not so. The realities of the Phillips-Halloran household, which previously had included the highly energetic activities of a son and daughter and their many visiting friends, had caused Dan and Marley to choose more practical sofas, chairs, and tables. They also had employed ingeniously designed cabinets to be rolled in front of the long windows in the family room to protect the delicate and ancient curved glass. The cabinets had once held a variety of board games, art supplies, and vinyl records. At present, however, awaiting the return of grandchildren, the cabinets had been rolled back against the interior wall and now served as liquor cabinets and consoles.

Marley, recognizing the difficulty Eva would have in trying to juggle a laptop and a cup of coffee, called over her live-in domestic aide, Sharon, and asked her to bring Eva a small table.

"I expect everyone wants coffee?" Marley asked as she moved to one of the cabinets, upon which sat a Belleek porcelain coffeepot next to cups and saucers and two plates containing ginger cake and shortbread cookies.

When she received affirmative answers from Nan and Eva, Marley poured coffee for them and additional cups for herself and Ray.

Eva opened her laptop, thanked Sharon for the table she'd set before her, and stroked a few keys. Then she beamed across at Ray, thinking how handsome he looked that evening in a conservative blue-and-white-striped shirt and navy cashmere sweater.

"I hope Sean comes soon," Eva said. "I have many more details than I had in February, when we last met. Both blogs have been going crazy with hits from people giving me, and us, tons of information about this case. Really, you are going to be bowled over when you find out how much I have to contribute tonight."

"We are always constantly amazed by what you and your followers come up with," Ray said. "We couldn't do what we do without you or this input."

Before Marley could second Ray's statement, everyone's

attention was drawn to a slight tapping sound coming from somewhere above. They all lifted their heads and looked up at a small, square window, one of a pair that flanked the fireplace.

Eva stiffened in her chair. "What is that? Is it a tree branch?" she asked.

Marley shook her head. "It can't be. I don't have a tree growing that close to the house."

Nan squinted up at the window and said, "It looks like a big moth to me."

Eva suddenly gasped, and her eyes opened wide. Marley swiveled her chair sharply toward the window. As they all stared upward, they observed a hand appear behind one of the stained-glass panels in a window.

"That certainly is Sean Finnegan. He's up to something!" Nan shouted, relieved to see that not a drop of coffee had spilled from the delicate cup she held in her hand.

Ray, still looking up at the window, rubbed the back of his right ear and said, "How can it be Sean? He could never reach that high. That window has to be twelve feet off the ground."

As suddenly as it had appeared, the hand disappeared, which had the effect of forcing Marley to call out, "Sharon, please let Mr. Finnegan in by the breakfast room doors. It seems he's coming around the side of the house."

Ray reached down and used the poker to jab at the logs, causing the fire to blaze up and the logs, muttering, to settle into new configurations. "He's a bit overdue," he said curtly.

Sharon, who seemed to have a bias against foolishness, pursed her lips disapprovingly as she led a chortling, white-haired, freckled-faced gentleman into the room. Sean, looking like a jolly elf who delivered on days other than Christmas, bounded into the room, carrying a briefcase in one hand and what looked like a collection of thin frames and poles in the other. More short than medium in height, he had the broad shoulders, chest, and bowed legs of his Irish sailing ancestors. In addition to his open personality, Sean was a ball of energy, always in motion and always with a trick up his sleeve.

"It's demo time, my friends," he announced heartily. "Merlin has arrived with his bag of tricks!"

Marley held up a hand to shush him while she turned to Sharon. "Sharon, thank you for your help, but you don't have to stay any longer. I'm sure you have other plans since I promised you extra time off this week. Roadie will watch the house while I'm away, so you have several days to come and go just as you please."

Roadie, the longtime family chauffeur, who was into his eighties now and still maintained the cars, although he no longer drove them, lived in the carriage house above the garage. He was the only household help besides Sharon to live on the premises.

"I'm on my way," Sharon replied, and being without the curiosity that gripped the room's other occupants, she turned and angled through the foyer toward the back stairs.

"Now," Marley said as she eased herself into an overstuffed chair, "we are all present and accounted for. So let's get started. Sean, tell us about this contraption you've brought into my house."

Sean moved to the left of the oak-framed archway that led into the back hall. He took what looked like a few haphazardly selected thin tubes and aligned them in such a way that they formed an artist's easel. Sweeping his arm before him in a dramatic fashion, he said, "I know how often Nan uses her ability to paint as a cover when she's doing a stakeout, so I thought, *Why not give her an easel that is a bit more multifunctional?*" He gave another theatrical sweep of his arm. "Now, what you see before you may appear to be a basic artist's easel, right? But look. With a few simple adjustments—"

Sean made a few quick changes to the lightweight easel frame, and suddenly, the four of them were looking at a sturdy ladder, which he positioned to lean against the back wall. But he was far from finished. He then disengaged one of the poles from the ladder easel's steps and extended it in a telescope fashion to its full extension: a length of eight feet or more that was now somehow highly flexible and maneuverable. Lifting the pole, he quickly flipped open small metal flaps on each end, which included mirrors. One end of the pole resembled, of all things, a moth.

"This easel, if you can call it that, is made of titanium. Ray gave me the idea!" exclaimed Sean excitedly. Motioning to Ray, he said, "Ray, come help me demonstrate how easily anyone can raise this frame to look through a building's second-story window or over an eight-foot wall or any obstacle that might be in the way of a person's view. You can even use it at an angle if you need to." Still holding everyone's attention, Sean continued. "You're going to love this easel, Nan. As you can see, it's very versatile."

"It does appear to work," Ray said, sounding impressed, as he placed the moth end of the pole against the same window where Sean, from outside, had earlier startled everyone and peered through the lower end. "I can see most of the garden and beyond."

Everyone gathered around Ray to take turns looking through the pole.

"This is great, Sean," Nan said when her turn was over. "Marley and I will put it to good use."

"It's all done with mirrors," Sean said. "But that's not all. There's another hidden surprise." Sean stepped forward as everyone drew back. Then he unscrewed the flat bottom end of one of the easel's three upright legs, and in the next moment, he withdrew a long, thin, sharp object.

"What is that?" Marley asked.

"It's a stiletto," Sean replied casually.

A deep silence fell upon the room and its inhabitants. No one spoke. Then, after a few moments had passed, Nan asked tentatively, "What's it for?"

"What do you think it's for?" Sean replied.

"I don't know. Protection?" Nan asked uneasily.

Noticing her deep level of discomfort, Sean said, "Well, yes, primarily. But I suppose you could use it for any number of things."

"Of course." Ray interjected. "For example, say you're doing surveillance, and you've packed a picnic lunch. You could use it to slice cheese or a baguette."

Ray's levity managed to ease the tension in the room. Everyone laughed. But Nan couldn't quite shake a feeling of foreboding. She didn't want to think of a time when she might have to use Sean's stiletto, mainly because she couldn't imagine herself ever actually using it. She was, and had always been, what others might have called a *peacenik*. The very idea of using a weapon seemed preposterous to her as she recalled the many times she'd marched with her peers or stood shoulder to shoulder with them on some breezy freeway overpass, holding signs that protested the current century's many wrongs. A tendency toward any kind of violence was simply not part of her DNA and not on her radar. She supposed, however, she could use the stiletto as a deterrent to prevent an attack if she had to. Yes, that she could probably do.

A bit peeved that her contribution to the group was being eclipsed by Sean's theatrics, Eva twisted in her wing chair and said dryly, "I guess mere facts and information can't compete with Sean's bag of tricks. Apparently, what I have to contribute is a bit too dry."

Nan laughed and made a face at Eva. Then she turned toward Sean and said, "Thank you, Sean. I love what you brought today. Especially the case it comes in."

Sean's smile widened. "It's tailor-made by me with custom pockets and additional stabilizers. I've made it big enough to carry your paints and supplies as well." He began to give himself a pat-down as his hands sought out each of his jacket pockets.

"Don't tell me there's more!" Eva cried.

Sean ignored her and withdrew a small clamshell-style compact that, upon opening, was seen to contain a hearing aid. "Now, you have to pay attention to what I'm telling you," he said, picking up the device and holding it out in front of him for all to see. "This isn't a hearing aid at all. It's a listening device. It's a dummy, and I've marked the case to reveal that. One of you needs to wear it in her ear at all times."

"Oh great," Nan said, turning to look at Marley. "We get to fight over which one of us seems to be hard of hearing."

Sean laughed, shrugged, and said, "An advantage of being a certain age is that if you're seen wearing a hearing aid, no one thinks twice about it. That way, as long as you're consistent in wearing one, when you wear this one, which is enhanced to allow you to hear something being said thirty to sixty feet away, no one will know the difference."

"Is that so?" said Ray. "Thirty to sixty feet away? You've really been exerting yourself in that workroom of yours. How is that possible?"

Sean held up a thin, round metal disk smaller than a penny. "With these guys! They work not unlike a baby monitor. Being a bachelor, Ray, you wouldn't know about those things. But you can take it from me: they're a necessity for today's parents." No one doubted that Sean, the father of seven children, knew what he was talking about.

"How do we use them?" Marley asked.

"Well," Sean replied, "think of them as bugs that you need to put in place. It's easy. One side is coated with a thin adhesive, and when you peel back the paper, you can stick them almost anywhere. Of course, you'll want to conceal them as much as possible. Once you get within proper distance and turn the monitor hearing aid on full force, you'll be able to hear everything you need to hear."

"How many disks do we have?" Marley asked.

"I gave you six," Sean said. "And that should cover it. But I have to warn you."

"Warn us?" Nan frowned.

"Yes. The aid is only effective when you wear it at all times. Otherwise, you're going to draw attention to yourself.

Also, you need to be sure to always wear it in the same ear, so no one, especially anyone who may be bent on doing you harm, becomes suspicious. Do you think you can remember all that?"

"Sure," Nan said. "Piece of cake."

Sean smiled and again reached into his jacket pocket.

"What else do you have?" Nan asked, leaning back and looking around in amazement.

Obviously proud of his useful and well-designed gadgets, Sean drew out his next sure-to-please offering. "Now, this is not the manicure kit that it resembles but a set of lock picks. Almost any lock can be picked, and I have placed these in the order of difficulty, so please maintain the order they're in now. OK?"

Marley interjected. "Are you going to show me how to use them, Sean? I'd feel better if both of us knew how to use them."

Nan nodded. "I agree. I may not always be the one who needs to pick a lock; besides, these picks look more fine-tuned than the ones you designed for us last time."

"They are, and fear not," Sean said. "We'll have a lesson before I leave tonight." He then stretched out his arms and said, "That's all, folks."

Eva, to no one's surprise, clapped enthusiastically.

"Great work, Sean," Nan told him. Then, turning toward Eva, she said, "Eva, before we return to you, would you let us go over for a piece of that ginger cake and some more coffee?"

Eva graciously agreed that nourishment was in order, and Nan rose from her chair and headed toward the serving counter. She wasn't surprised to see everyone else follow suit.

As she cut herself a slice of cake, she thought about Sean's recent offerings and the likely scenarios she and Marley might encounter in the near future. In the past, their cases had often included hair-raising moments requiring nerves of steel, a trust in each other's abilities, and enough nimble thinking to escape dangerous encounters. She glanced over at Marley and thought about the first time she'd met her. She'd read her all wrong. At present, she was glad there had been no lasting consequence of that initial read, because she couldn't imagine going to Brainerd with anyone other than her good friend.

CHAPTER 4

WHEN ALL HAD REPLENISHED THEIR coffee, had acquired whatever they wanted to nibble on, and were once more seated comfortably, Marley made sure all attention was directed entirely toward Eva. She couldn't help but feel a great deal of respect for her friend, who, despite her obvious eagerness to share her latest research results and even despite the few times she'd been snappish in displaying her impatience with Sean's antics, had shown considerable forbearance during her wait.

"OK, Eva," Marley said. "It's finally over to you. Please tell us all about your findings."

Eva straightened her shoulders, cleared her throat, and began to speak in her customary pedantic manner. Her crisp delivery, and what she had to say, sent a shiver down Marley's spine even more pronounced than the chill she'd felt when she first heard details of the missing women's case at their previous meeting in February. She glanced over at Nan to discern her feelings. As usual, Nan's expression didn't reveal any signs of unease. Instead, she was leaning forward in her chair, appearing more eager than anyone to hear all that Eva had to report.

Last February, all of their information had come from Eva's own research, from various newspaper accounts regarding the two women's disappearances from a resort in northern Minnesota called Eagle's Cove, and from details given to Eva by her daughter, Gretchen. Now, however, Eva had additional updated information garnered from her two blogs.

"It's important to summarize what we know so far," Eva said. "To make sure we all have the same information and that there are no misunderstandings. But first, I want to share with you two important facts that have come to light only recently." She paused to raise an emphatic eyebrow. "The first fact is that the two missing women knew each other."

"Did that information come via your blogs?" Ray asked.

"No, it came from my daughter, Gretchen," Eva replied. "The police inquiry discovered that the younger woman, Lynn Parker, was a former student of Professor Engelmann's. She'd taken a creative writing course from her when she was still in high school."

"Well, that's interesting," Nan said reflectively. "And it opens any number of possibilities."

Eva nodded. "The second fact came from a follower of my blog *Knead to Dough*—after I changed its name to *Knead to Know*, of course. One of my fellow bakers, who happens to be a lifelong resident of Kansas City, is a friend of an acquaintance of the current owners of Eagle's Cove Resort, Dale and Christy Chapman. As you know, the Chapmans are persons of interest according to the police and previously lived in Kansas City before they moved to Minnesota and bought the resort. Anyway, this fellow baker told me that when the state of Minnesota was specifically mentioned as the locale of the two women's disappearances, her friend recalled having seen Dale and Christy Chapman in the company of a man with a strong Minnesotan accent while they were still living in Kansas."

"She was able to recognize a Minnesotan accent?" Marley asked.

"Well, it is fairly distinctive," Eva replied. "My blogger assured me we could rely on her friend's ear because that woman attended the University of Minnesota for a number of years."

Ray asked, "Did she describe this man in any more detail than his accent?"

"In fact, she did. She said he was a big guy, tall and burly, with dark hair, and he wore his bad attitude like a businessman wears an Armani suit."

Marley was taken aback by the vivid description. While she appreciated the phrase and hoped it might turn out to be useful for her and Nan, she was experienced enough to know that as great as the description was, it might prove to have no connection whatsoever to the case or the missing women.

"What is important, though," Eva said, "is that this man was seen with the Chapmans the same week that two armored vans were held up at two different locations in Kansas City, with an undisclosed amount of cash being taken."

Ray broke in to say, "If there was any question regarding how the Chapmans were able to afford to buy Eagle's Cove

Resort when they moved to Minnesota, these robberies could be an answer."

Sean nodded in agreement. "Armored vans only visit high-end businesses, which means they usually carry a hell of a lot of money. Combined, the two vans—and I don't think I'm exaggerating here—could have been carrying half a million dollars or more."

"The facts I was able to gather reveal that the previous owners of the resort were highly motivated sellers," Eva said. "So I wouldn't think the Chapmans needed a very high down payment, and they may have even been able to purchase in a contract-for-deed arrangement."

Eva then gave a summary of what was known about what they had come to call the Missing Women's Case so far. She went over everything her daughter, Gretchen, had told them earlier regarding the two mysterious disappearances from Eagle's Cove Resort in northern Minnesota's Baxter and Brainerd Lakes areas. She reminded them that they had decided to send Marley and Nan to the resort right away because the two women had disappeared at that exact time in late April, one year apart.

"Run these women's vitals past us once again," Sean said. "Just to make sure we don't forget anything."

Eva was glad to oblige. "The first woman, Suzanne Engelmann, was a recently divorced forty-two-year-old college professor who taught English and creative writing at Metro Area Community College in a Minneapolis suburb. And the second woman, Lynn Parker, was a twenty-two-year-old aspiring writer who had told friends she was in need of a getaway to deal with her writer's block." Eva turned her head to take in the entire group before resting her final glance on Marley. "Through Gretchen, Marley was able to discover that both women stayed in cabin number eight while at the resort."

Marley interjected. "And just so you all know, I had no problem reserving that exact cabin at Eagle's Cove. So Nan and I will be staying in cabin number eight as well and will be exactly where we want to be."

"As I said earlier," Eva said, "the two women knew each other, so we should think of the possibility they might have more in common than literature or writing."

Ray held up a hand and asked, "Suzanne, the professor, vanished first—is that right?"

"Correct," Eva said in her crisp, precise style.

Sean said, "So they both just drove out of the resort and were never seen again? Is that the final conclusion of the sheriff's office? Has anything new been reported on that count?"

Eva shook her head. "No, and Gretchen says the sheriff's office is frustrated. They have done everything they can legally do. They interviewed the owners of the resort where the two women stayed, of course, and every likely establishment between there and the Twin Cities where either of the two women might have stopped. That included the nearby towns just to the south and all the way down to the metro area on all the major routes. And they came up with nothing. Searching north, east, or west didn't seem a reasonable expenditure, given their limited resources and the reasonable assumption, based on their interviews, that both women would have been heading back to the Twin Cities."

Marley's attention was drawn to Dewey, who had been curled up in a bundle, fast asleep before the hearth, but now raised his head and perked up his ears at the sound of his mistress's voice. She watched Dewey slowly rise and then stretch, yawn, and shake himself before beginning a slow, tail-wagging amble about the room so he could nuzzle and sniff at various hands and feet.

With Dewey's attention to each of them in turn providing a slight distraction, Marley brought her attention back to Eva, who was still reporting facts.

"Since the authorities had reliable eyewitnesses willing to testify that they had seen Suzanne and Lynn each drive away from the resort, the two women seem to have disappeared into thin air sometime after leaving. Although they questioned everyone at the resort because of the strength of those eyewitness reports, the Crow Wing County police were only able to get a warrant to thoroughly search cabin number eight," Eva said. "When their search turned up no evidence, they were restricted from further searching the resort."

"That's where we come in," Marley said. "We'll go where the police can't." She turned toward Eva. "Remind us once again of the details regarding the personal backgrounds of these women."

"Well," Eva replied, "we know that Suzanne Engelmann was an avid birder and that she had just come out of a divorce. And she was using this time of the year, spring, when birds are most active and nesting, to serve as a distraction from her recent personal issues."

"What do we know about her ex-husband, the guy she recently divorced? Is there anything more there?" Sean asked.

Eva shook her head. "Gretchen says he has a solid alibi.

He owns his own business, and six employees swore to his being at the office working twelve- to fourteen-hour days while frantically trying to wrap up quarterly reports that were already overdue at the time his ex-wife disappeared."

"He could have hired someone," Sean said. "Was the divorce final, or was it still ongoing and possibly acrimonious? In other words, was there a financial motive for the ex to have Suzanne disappear?"

Eva frowned. "No, I did the research, and I couldn't find any motive there. Gretchen and my blog followers said the divorce was settled a few months before Suzanne Engelmann went to Eagle's Cove Resort. From what the police learned, she came out from the legal proceedings quite well financially, and my blog followers all second that. Her ex was the one who wanted the divorce. He had a girlfriend. But it was Suzanne who had the money. And perhaps due to a great deal of guilt over his unfaithfulness, Suzanne was able to obtain a reasonable settlement. She did live well, unlike some divorcées."

"There's still a motive as far as I can see," Sean said. "If the ex was the one who had Suzanne disappear, he wouldn't have to pay the settlement, would he? Do we know if the amount was set up to be paid out in a lump sum or in monthly alimony payments?"

"Good question, Sean." Eva stopped to take a sip of her coffee and a bite of cake.

Marley thought she was feeling a bit vexed over the possibility that even one detail might have escaped her notice.

Lifting a napkin to the corner of her mouth, Eva

continued. "But the settlement wasn't to be paid out by the ex. He's the one who received it."

Sean drew back his head, blinked, and then, with a twinkle in his eye and an upturned smile, turned and looked straight at Ray as he said, "Well, that's one for progress, aye, mate?"

Ray, who was vigorously rubbing the lobe of his right ear, as was his habit when perplexed by something, took over the discussion from Eva and Sean. "We know from your previous report that Lynn, the second missing woman, was a novice writer who had started a mystery novel a few years back. And she'd booked herself into the resort because, according to her friends and family, she hoped the solitude of the resort would unblock her creative juices."

"She had been suffering from a severe case of writer's block," Nan added.

"Or so she said," Ray replied, leaning down to pet Dewey, who had decided to wander a bit farther into the Halloran home and had only now returned to the group after a thorough sniffing of Sean's appliances in the hallway. "We need to ask ourselves: Did she specifically ask for cabin number eight, the same cabin Professor Engelmann stayed in? And if so, why? What was she up to? There might be a connection there."

Eva looked up from her laptop. "I can help with that. There is some speculation among my bloggers that Lynn Parker's renting of cabin number eight was more than a coincidence. She may have hoped to investigate Suzanne's disappearance in order to write a true-crime story. A blogger brought up this possibility when she was able to ascertain the fact that Lynn had mentioned to a friend that the genre of true crime might be easier on her muse."

Nan leaned forward in her chair. "Now, that is a surmise that sounds likely, to me at least."

"Yes, a worthwhile little nugget of information for sure," Marley said. "If Lynn Parker was blocked in one genre, why not try another? She might have thought a change in approach would be just what her muse needed."

"So the idea is that Lynn might have been trying to solve her teacher's disappearance or crime and write a book in the process?" Nan asked.

"Yes, and that may well be what put Lynn herself in danger; she may have asked one too many questions," Eva replied.

Ray, still rubbing the lobe of his ear, grimaced and turned to stare at Eva. "Let me get this straight. Are you telling us that Lynn Parker may have disappeared because she did exactly what Nan and Marley are about to do?"

Marley answered for Eva. "Well, yes. But don't forget, Ray: Nan and I are experienced in what we do. And Lynn, if that's indeed what she was up to, wasn't. Besides, two older ladies asking questions are not seen as anything unusual to most people. As we all know, women are nosy by nature," she quipped. "Especially elderly women. They're just naturally drawn toward gossip."

Sean nodded. "Yeah, like moths to a flame. But when you have a young, healthy twenty-two-year-old suddenly asking a lot of questions, it's another game entirely. For one thing, people would pay attention to that."

The Finder members reflected on what they had just heard by turning their focus inward while purposely avoiding eye contact with one another. They all knew the compensations that being a certain age brought to their chosen trade. Far too many people saw the elderly, especially women, as invisible, as having no conceivable value or significance other than knitting or attending church. However, as they had come to accept, those attitudes helped Nan and Marley transform into inconsequential nonthreats in the eyes of others. Their age's invisibility gave them a cloak of protection, a factor that none of their band would ever come to love but would always use to their full advantage.

After a while, Marley stood up, brushed a few crumbs from her lap, and began to collect the others' coffee cups and plates, raising the room's decibel level with the rich *clink* and *ting* of silver and fine china.

"Don't let the fact of your know-how cause you to drop your guard," Ray warned, addressing Marley and Nan. "Stay vigilant, you two; experience may not be all the protection you'll need."

Sean rose to his feet and began to pace back and forth. "I want to know more about the owners of this resort. Is there anything new to report on them? I hate to see Marley and Nan heading down a blind alley without sufficient information."

Eva clicked a few keys on her laptop and said excitedly, "Here's where my bloggers really came through for us, especially the ones presently living in Kansas City. This is what we know so far about Dale and Christy Chapman from what my contacts tell me. Back in Kansas, Dale Chapman had a series of odd jobs. He was sort of a jack-of-all-trades."

"And yet they somehow accumulated enough money to move to Minnesota and buy a resort?" Marley asked. "In this economy, why would they even want to buy a resort? Most of them are being split up and parceled out to individuals because that's where the profit lies."

"Well, they didn't inherit it—that's for sure," Eva said. "My Kansas City bloggers tell me both sets of parents have been dead or gone for years. By *gone*, I mean that Christy Chapman's father abandoned her and her mother when she was two years old. Neither she nor her husband came from families that had more than a penny to their names."

"Still, they needed enough money for a down payment, even a small amount. One of them could have had a long-lost aunt or uncle who never married and had accumulated a nice nest egg and then suddenly up and died. You never know," Nan said.

"Yes, you do," Sean said firmly. "What about Christy Chapman? Was she employed?"

"Not at anything that was lucrative," Eva replied. "Supposedly, she did service work. Her last employment was at a store that sold computers and other high-end electronics. She worked a register."

Sean placed his hands in his pockets and shrugged. He looked from Marley to Nan and then said, "I apologize in advance, but this is the time when I get that queasy feeling in my stomach."

Not one of them responded to what they all knew to be an obvious truth, but more than one pair of eyes focused on the fire in the fireplace rather than looking at Sean. It took Ray to break the impasse. With a sudden jump from his chair, he said, "I almost forgot to give you the knockout drops." He reached into his right pants pocket and drew out a small black-capped glass bottle. He held it out to Nan who eagerly took it in her right hand. "Now, you have to be extremely careful with these. In fact, don't use this at all unless it's absolutely necessary. The dose is one drop for those weighing up to one hundred twenty pounds, two drops for anyone weighing up to two hundred pounds, and three drops for a really heavy person. But never use more than three drops. More than three, and you're getting into the dead zone, so be careful."

Sean smiled, and a twinkle lit his eyes. "Yeah, remember, above all, our overall goal is to solve crimes, not commit one."

CHAPTER 5

N AN STEERED AGATHA ONTO INTERSTATE 94 and let out a big sigh as she glanced over at Marley. "Well, we're finally on our way up north," she said, placing particular emphasis on the word *finally*. She'd arrived at Marley's that morning at seven o'clock, raring to go, only to be made to sit at a breakfast service of cinnamon-raisin toast, fruit, yogurt, and coffee at Marley's insistence.

"No reason to rush. We have plenty of time. Check-in isn't until two o'clock, and besides, I'm not going anywhere until Dan's package has arrived." Marley's statement had been delivered so decisively and in such a firm, no-argument tone of voice that Nan had quickly obeyed by seating herself at the breakfast table.

With breakfast over and Dan's package received and sitting on his desk in the den, Nan and Marley had wasted no time in jumping into Agatha and beginning their trip.

Once they were well on the way, Nan glanced over at Marley to see why her friend had suddenly become so quiet. Although Nan nudged Marley's knee, she realized Marley had not so much as turned toward her, and all Nan could see was the back of her head.

Minutes passed, and then she heard Marley say dreamily, "I was just thinking about what this trip was like when I was a child and how the three and a half hours seemed to absolutely fly by. Back then, in the stretch between the Twin Cities and the Lake Region, there were so many more single-family farms, each with its own scattering of cattle, horses, or sheep in fenced pastures. There would be row upon row of various crops ripening in flat fields, with their precision broken here and there by jumbled piles of rock. I remember there always seemed to be a small stream or pond within walking distance of a wood-framed, whitewashed two-story farmhouse that was bordered by a windbreak of either tall evergreens or poplars planted in a long row along whichever side of the house the worst weather came from."

She turned and gave Nan a look that revealed in her eyes and her face the child she had been back then with such an intensity and clarity that Nan's heart melted.

"And I still recall," Marley said, "the many small, picturesque towns along the route, each a unique little hamlet in itself, and every church featured a distinctive steeple that reflected the origin of the village's settlers. And I remember how many times, our dear Roadie would point out a pheasant at the side of the road or a meadowlark on a fence post as he drove Grandmama's big old Buick."

Marley turned once again to look out her side window. "But today, all I see are strip malls and sales lots one after another. Nan, I don't mind admitting to you that I miss the way it was."

Nan felt no compulsion to comment, so Marley continued her nostalgic recollections.

"Eventually, when we get farther up north, there will be places where it looks almost as if time stood still, and it will begin to feel more like the way it used to be. Suddenly, we'll be thrust into the wildness of the rock-strewn meadows and forests, where the atmosphere is magical—truly magical— like nowhere else in the state."

Nan gave Marley a knowing look. "Mysterious too, you might say?"

Marley nodded. "Well, it is a place where anything can happen."

"And apparently did!" Nan added.

Marley drew in a deep breath and, as she slowly exhaled, asked, "What do you think happened to those women, Nan? You seem so certain they're dead."

"I am certain. And I think you feel the same way. Isn't that why we're on this trip?"

Marley didn't answer. Instead, she searched among the CDs in Agatha's glove compartment and popped a CD into the player, and in no time, the two women were singing along with Willie Nelson: "On the road again. Just can't wait to get on the road again …"

An hour later, Nan signaled her turn onto northbound Highway 10, which, for reasons known only to itself, the highway department had designated as 10 West, thereby causing confusion for many a driver headed north to the lake while dragging a fishing boat or enduring a backseat filled with overexcited children asking, "Are we there yet?"

Just beyond the town of Becker, Marley told Nan that a turn onto Highway 25 would take them through Foley and then on to Pierz. "It's so worth going this way," she said as Nan signaled a right turn and followed Marley's directions. "These little German settlements have such beautiful churches. And just up ahead in Pierz is Thielen's Meat Market, which is a must-stop. Wait until you see their sausages, and after you taste their bacon, you'll look for an excuse to come back here!"

Nan smiled at the marvel that was memory. She knew that for Marley, the particular meat market she mentioned held a score of scents and tastes that unlocked a million memories of family meals and discussions, and those memories, warm and plentiful, added as much, if not more than anything else, to the burst of flavor she experienced today whenever she bit into a certain sausage or strip of bacon. Nan wondered what influence a lack of association with Thielen's meats would have on her own taste buds. Would she also find the sausage and bacon so delectable?

At the next turn, the market Marley spoke of came into view. Sided by a parking lot filled with cars, Thielen's was both a meat market and a longtime family enterprise. Looking about her as she exited the car and inhaling the wafting cloud that swirled up from a metal smoking bin, Nan could almost anticipate herself making a return trip after just one taste of their product.

Once inside the store, the two made their way through the aisles, looking into glass cases that displayed cheeses, salads, and meats of every kind, and finally made their way to the cash register located on a counter near the exit. They purchased jams, jellies, and more and then packed their cooler with ice, homemade cheese, and what seemed to Nan to be an excessive collection of meat. As Marley and Nan resumed their drive, they began to talk strategy.

"The moment we get to the resort and into our cabin, we need to plug in the laptop so Eva can send us any documents she thinks we might find useful," Marley said.

"Are you sure they even have internet access at the resort?"

"I asked about Wi-Fi and got an ambiguous answer," Marley replied. "I have a feeling it's spotty and not very reliable."

Nan frowned. "Let's hope cell phone reception is good, so one way or another, we can stay in touch with everyone. I don't like being cut off from the rest of the group."

"I agree," Marley said. "By the way, we'd better decide which of us is going to wear the hearing-aid listening device."

"I suppose," Nan said. "We could toss a coin."

"Do you have any objections to wearing it?" Marley asked.

"Well, the thing is, I just don't want to look old."

"Oh, for Pete's sake!" Marley said. "Vanity, thy name is Nan."

A chuckle from Nan sent Marley to the clamshell-style compact so she could insert the dummy aid into her right ear. "All right," she said. "I'll wear it. Looking old doesn't bother me."

"If I look as good as you when I'm your age, it wouldn't bother me either," Nan said with a smirk.

"My age? I'm older than you by only a few months!"

Nan laughed. "In my school, a few months still makes you older than me. Where did you go to school? Besides, time is important, isn't it? Did you know the entire life span of a worker bee is a mere five to six weeks?"

Marley rolled her eyes at Nan. "But think about all they accomplish in that amount of time." When Nan didn't reply, Marley raised a hand to the side of her head, saying, "Since you're not going to give preference to my age, will you do an old lady a favor then and help me remember that this appliance always needs to be in my right ear?"

"Sure," Nan replied. "Here's a tip: we'll simply think of the *right* ear as the *correct* ear."

"Sounds like a plan." Marley smiled.

Then, changing the subject, Nan asked, "Are we going to stop in Brainerd? Wouldn't that be the best and most economical place to get the rest of our groceries and a few bottles of wine?"

Marley nodded. "Yes, and it's also the best place to pick up that map we were talking about. GPS is great, but I'm old-fashioned. I like to see the whole layout spread out before me. I'd specifically like a map of Merrifield if possible."

"Is that the town nearest the resort?"

"Hardly a town," Marley answered. "I think of it as just a bait store at the Y where two roads meet with a gas station."

"If it's that small, I can't imagine it having a map of its own. Maybe we can get a regional Crow Wing County map anyway," Nan said. "Do you think there'd be a map of the lake the resort is on?"

Marley cast a fond glance over at her best friend. "The DNR sent me a detailed fishing map of the lake. We'll know everything about it—depth, shape, marshlands, tributaries, peninsulas, and islands."

It was Nan's turn to smile. She knew Marley to be

intuitive and to have trustworthy instincts, but one of her most outstanding attributes was that unlike Nan, who was inclined to wing it most of the time, Marley always planned ahead.

"I was just thinking," Nan said, "of one of your strong suits—the ability to anticipate our needs—which then led me to think of having a strong suit in a poker game and, from there, to recall how many casinos there are in the northern part of the state."

"I confess to not having given a single thought to casinos," Marley said. "But you're right. I believe, if I'm not mistaken, there are three of them clustered up in those parts. Are you thinking that the gaming industry might be involved in these cases? Do we know if either of the missing women might have been into gambling?"

Nan replied, "No, how would any of us know that? Why? You're not thinking they ran up against henchmen or hit men or whatever enforcers are called these days, are you? Isn't that a bit dramatic for our Native American–owned casino operations here in Minnesota?"

"You're the one who brought up gambling, Nan," Marley said. "Not me. And remember, not every gambler comes by bus from the Twin Cities clad in polyester and clutching a bag full of nickels. Some are hard core and, because of addiction, close to being criminals themselves."

"Oh, you watch too many movies," Nan dismissively responded.

The two women fell silent, and Marley, feeling sleepy, leaned her head against the side window and settled down for a nap.

She must have dozed for a half hour or more, because

when she awoke, they had arrived at the east edge of Brainerd, where Highway 25 merged with 210, and Nan was pulling into the parking lot of a popular truck stop called the Roadside Café. Marley sat up straight, yawned, and said, "Are we there yet, Mom?"

"Almost," Nan answered. "I thought we'd get a bite to eat. I could use some coffee."

"Good idea," Marley said. "I could use a stretch."

Nan parked Agatha in a spot where a van had just pulled away. She stepped out onto the lot, looking about, and then started to walk toward the front door of the café, when Marley called out, "Before we eat, we need to walk down two doors to Warehouse Liquor Store to select some wine for the cabin! They have a good selection and excellent prices."

Nan turned on her heel and followed Marley to a beer-ad-emblazoned glass door. Once inside, she took in the compact space. Unlike at wine shops in the Twin Cities, the owners of this establishment had thrown decor to the wind in lieu of a bottom-line practicality. Cartons were piled high, sorted by general categories: beer, wine, vodka, gin, and so on. One glance at the listed prices of familiar vineyards and brands convinced Nan of the value of such a system.

Nan turned toward Marley. "With these prices, most people probably buy by the case. I bet many of these boxes go out the door full, with each bottle still in its cardboard sleeve."

As if to prove her right, a clerk pushing a dolly loaded with cases of gin and vodka passed by, heading toward an open back door through which Nan could see a late-model luxury car waiting with its engine idling just outside.

The clerk, obviously overhearing her remark, chuckled

and said, "You sure got that right. And this isn't the first trip I've made to that automobile this afternoon either. They enjoy our wines too."

Marley, who had grabbed a cart and was presently placing into it her initial selection of bottles of wine, replied, "Well, we also enjoy wine. Don't we, Nan? See anything you like?"

Nan made her choices, including some cabernets and a malbec, and then she and Marley walked toward the register at the front of the store.

The man behind the register seemed too young to be working in a place selling alcohol. He grinned in the uncomfortable way of all young men who were too self-conscious for their own good and asked the classic cliché of every store clerk: "Find everything you were looking for?"

"Yes, thank you," Marley replied. "Unlike many of your patrons, we don't plan on being here the entire summer, so we passed on selecting a case or two. We only have a few bottles. But we would like some help carrying them out to our car if that's possible."

With the willing help of a clerk whose name tag said, "Tim," they fit their purchases between their suitcases and the cooler that held Thielen's meats. Nan slammed the trunk shut as Marley turned toward Tim and slapped a bill into the palm of his hand that made his eyes widen.

"Not supposed to take this," he told her.

Marley ignored him. Instead, she grasped Nan's elbow and urged her forward. "Onward toward lunch, please," she said. "I'm more than ready."

The two women walked a few doors down to enter the eatery and immediately encountered a long line of people waiting to be seated. Nan glanced about, noticing that the Roadside Café seemed to attract a mixture of customers ranging from a large number of seniors to neon-vested workmen and jeans-clad women. Dotted here and there, she could see a few men in overalls and ball caps—local farmers, in all probability, she thought. The café appeared to attract a smattering of all sorts of people.

"Shouldn't take too long," Marley said. "The line seems to be moving along fairly well."

Because they knew that the place was a favorite stopping spot along the road and that the food would be good, they waited patiently, shuffling their feet along and discussing their need for a more detailed map of the lakes area. Nan noticed a woman standing in line ahead of them who reminded her of someone they both knew, and she was about to comment on that fact, when Marley was suddenly roughly shoved backward into Nan by an arm that seemed to materialize out of nowhere. She then saw that the arm belonged to a man who was rudely butting into line ahead of them. Nan, taken by surprise, saw Marley's stunned look and saw that she stepped back away from the burly individual, who gave every impression of someone not to be trifled with.

Without thinking, Nan instinctively reached around Marley and grabbed the man's arm. "Hey!" she said sharply, giving the man's arm a firm backward tug. "There's a line here, and we are in it."

The man shrugged off her grasp without as much as a glance in her direction or any sign of acknowledgment. His act was so lacking in compassion that she might as well have been an inconvenient irritant, such as a pesky gnat or fly, the way he brushed her off.

Nan felt the blood rush to her face as her temper rose. She hadn't been blessed with a curly mop of red hair most of her life for nothing. Before Marley could stop her, she moved out of the line and stepped in front of the man, twisting her neck to look up into his face. The eyes that met hers were watery, red-tinged, and cold. They would have been hard to dismiss in any case. But the man was extremely tall compared to Nan's petite height, not to mention the menace he telegraphed while looming over her with shoulders, chest, and arms that indicated a line of work involving physical exertion. The man's entire form reinforced his steely gaze and impressed upon Nan an intimidating memory she'd never forget.

Frown lines etched deep within the sagging gray flesh on each side of the man's nose had a look of permanence about them, telling her that the principal way he chose to deal with his world was through anger. In any other circumstance, she might have recognized his pathetic lack of empathy as a disability and felt sorry for him but not when he was treating her friend in that manner.

"What makes you think," she hissed, her voice rising, "that you can just cut in front of us? You need to go to the back of the line. Now!"

People started to notice the altercation, and a buzz of concerned voices traveled up and down the assembly of would-be patrons, alerting the café workers to the existence of a possible problem: a younger man of considerable size was about to attack a little old lady.

Reading the crowd's reaction, Marley was ready to call

out for help, when another man, equally as tall as the first but considerably thinner and dressed in a Harris tweed jacket, interjected: "The lady said something important, Mr. Sykes, and you need to pay attention to her."

Nan didn't know if it was the man's authoritative tone of voice or the rapidly rising alarm of the crowd that caused the big fellow to give way. He threw Nan a look that was framed in a snarl and then turned abruptly, headed for the exit, and threw open the door. As he left the café, an audible sigh rose from the crowd.

"Oh dear," Nan said with a sudden giggle. "I think I've made an enemy for life."

The man who had come to their rescue said dryly, "Well, then so have I."

Nan was about to introduce herself and Marley, when a waitress signaled to the man that a place was available, and he swiftly walked away. The women watched as he crossed the dining room and was taken to a table for two next to a window, where, upon sitting down, he immediately pulled out a notebook and a pen. Then, after looking upward as though seeking inspiration, he lowered his head and began to write.

"Gee," Nan said, "we didn't even get to introduce ourselves or properly thank him."

"He looks like a professor," Marley said.

"You think so? Why would you say that?"

"Oh, I suppose the way he's dressed. The way he speaks, the jacket, the beard—it all fits."

"Our first victim was a professor," Nan said. "Do you think your mind might be making a connection somewhere?"

Marley didn't answer because the waitress had now

hailed them and was already walking across the room. Nan hurried to catch up. Once the women were seated, they quickly ordered chicken salad and fruit cups and concentrated on eating and people-watching, avoiding any more strategizing for the moment.

Eager to be back on the road, they made only one stop on the way out of the café: they made a point of approaching the table where the man who had graciously assisted them earlier had been seated. But they were disappointed to find his table empty and a waitress busily engaged in wiping it down.

"Darn," Nan said. "Just our luck. He's a fast eater as well as our hero."

They took their leave and paid their bill at the cash register near the café's front door.

Once they were back in Agatha and on the way to Merrifield, Nan said, "Marley, let's not do our big grocery shopping this afternoon. We can get whatever we need later when we visit Brainerd. Tonight I'd be fine with a sausage or two from that big sack in the cooler. The wine we purchased was a must, but a big shopping expedition? Nah, let's put it off until tomorrow, OK? I really want to get to the resort and the cabin as soon as possible!"

"I'm fine with that plan," Marley said. "We might get to the cabin a bit early, but I'm sure it will be all right. Now, let's talk about that big lout at the restaurant! What did you make of him? I know you could tell he scared the daylights out of me. But you, Nan—you didn't let his size and belligerence faze you one bit."

Nan could still easily recall cousins Hal and Cubby endlessly harassing her during their twice-yearly childhood visits. Because of their antics more than anything, she had formed a firm and long-standing conviction that bully-boy behaviors needed to be addressed firmly. In her experience, the sooner a response followed an offense and was emphatically delivered the better.

"I've told you about the bullying cousins who loved to terrorize me throughout my childhood," Nan said. "So you really shouldn't have been surprised at my response."

Marley shrugged. "Well, I didn't grow up with a lot of confrontation, so unlike you, I don't know how to handle it. I tend to back down."

"Who knows, but your response isn't the best? If not for the crowd and your so-called professor, that guy might have killed me."

The two fell silent, as they often did, each lost in her own thoughts. Nan took in the scene outside Agatha's windows, observing the flatness of the land around her. She could see fields ringed in scraggly jack pines and other features of the landscape that held no particular point of interest for her, other than a dilapidated windmill that called out to be memorialized in a painting.

Never having visited a farm or harbored an inclination to do so, Nan had always felt most at home in a city—any city. She was a true urbanite who relished the diversity of a metropolitan population and whose interests, with the possible exception of painting a rural landscape, found their soul in art galleries; museums; theaters; and city restaurants featuring well-chosen wines, creative cuisine, and stimulating talk.

"Speaking of eating light this evening," Marley said, "we should be able to pick up all we need—the necessities at least—at the Y Store in Merrifield. When we're there, as you said, we can also get gas."

Nan, who had always been interested in the origin of words, said, "I wonder where they came up with the name Merrifield. What on earth could be merry about a field?"

"It's interesting how places get their names," Marley responded reflectively. "For instance, for all we know, the first part of the name, Merri, might stand for Merribeth or Merrianne, a woman's name. So the field may have at first been named after someone called Merri or even Mary. Long ago, it may have been referred to as Mary's Field, and then later it was shortened to Merrifield."

"That makes sense," Nan said. Knowing they were still some distance from their destination and recalling Marley's love of storytelling, she suggested they think of other origins for names.

Marley laughed. "You're just trying to keep us both awake now that we've driven so far and had such a satisfying lunch. You're hoping I'll forget about the CDs, and you won't have to listen to my singing. But since you asked, think of how some of the neighborhoods in Saint Paul have names reflecting the national origins of their early settlers. Like Swede Hollow and, in the past, Little Italy and such."

"Yes, of course. That is quite common."

"Well, when I first heard mention of Frogtown, the neighborhood along University Avenue in Saint Paul, I suspected a slur on French immigrants. But I was eventually informed that the area had been reclaimed from an actual swamp that had held scads of real live frogs. And that's how it got its name."

"I didn't know that. How interesting," Nan said. "Now

I can't help but wonder how many basements in Frogtown have water problems."

Marley groaned. "Get serious."

"You're right," Nan answered. "We really ought to concentrate on the case we came to solve. What do we know about the resort we're going to? C'mon—let's review the details we have to date."

Marley threw Nan a tired look and said, "You sound like a professor giving an assignment."

"I am a professor," replied Nan. "Remember? I taught art all those years at a university. I need to focus on the resort. You know I'm entirely unfamiliar with these northern resorts. So tell me what I can expect to find when I get there."

Marley raised a hand and ticked off each point on an uplifted finger. "Well, let's see. It's a small mom-and-pop resort. It consists of ten cabins. And if it's at all similar to the resorts I've heard about and visited in my lifetime, there will be a resort lodge surrounded by a series of small two-, three-, and five-room cabins set along a picturesque portion of a lake. Some of the cabins will directly face the lake, and some will be tucked farther back among the woods."

"Does it make a difference where they're located?" Nan asked.

"Only in price," Marley said. "But then, what do I know? I've only visited these resorts. I've never actually stayed in one."

Nan didn't lose the opportunity to smirk. "Not fancy enough for your folks?"

Marley didn't flinch. "It's not that," she said. "We simply had other abodes available to us." Upon that remark, she continued her descriptive recitation of what one might expect to find at a typical northern Minnesota resort. "We can assume that some of its regulars have been coming each and every summer for generations, renewing their reservations for the same week or two year in and year out."

"Great," Nan said. "Let's hope there will be someone staying there now who may have been at the resort when one or both of the women stayed there."

"That's what we're counting on," Marley said. "Unless, that is, the disappearances may have caused people to cancel their yearly reservations."

"Traditions are hard to break," replied Nan.

"True. Unless you have a strong emotion involved, like fear. Then it's easy." Raising another finger, Marley continued. "Some renters at the resort bring their own boats, and others use the boat that comes with their rental cabin and is owned by the resort. We know that Eagle's Cove is primarily a fishing resort rather than a swimming or family sort of place. We know that the cabin we reserved, which both of the women rented, was at one time an actual house and was dragged across the ice one winter when the owners planned to build a larger and more luxurious lake home and were willing to sell their first place to the resort's owners."

"Was it the Chapmans who ended up buying the house and towing it across the ice?" Nan asked.

"No," Marley said. "It was the previous owners, the Tillers. The Chapmans found the house already on the property when they bought the resort. I suspect the earlier owners wanted a building on their property that had all the amenities of an actual home—you know, such as a dishwasher, a chef's kitchen, AC, and a soaking tub. So they have those amenities available for people who want the same comforts they have at home when they are getting back to nature at a resort."

"And the Chapmans?" Nan asked. "What do we know about their purchase of this resort?"

"Not enough," Marley replied. "As of now, we have three facts. The Chapmans bought the resort two and a half years ago from the Tillers. They lived in Kansas City previously. And the most important fact of all as far as we are concerned, they were the owners at the time when the two women disappeared."

"And," Nan added, "we know that Mr. Chapman is good with his hands."

"We do?" Marley said. "Why is that?"

"Because I can't imagine anyone owning one of these small resorts without having a very close acquaintance with hammers and wrenches."

Marley tossed back her head and laughed. "We're coming up toward the Y Store, where we can get a few necessities and put some gas in Agatha. There are larger supermarkets along Highway 371 in Baxter and Brainerd, but the few things we really need right away we can get here to avoid a lot of traffic."

"I'm all for saving time," Nan said, "and driving less."

Marley smiled. After all these years, she knew Nan. She knew Nan couldn't wait to get to cabin number eight, and once there, she would insist they search the place from top to bottom that evening in the hope that some clue, however small, might have escaped notice. Past experience had taught them that a police search might not have turned up the kind of discoveries she and Nan possibly could uncover.

Finding things that were hiding in plain sight had become an essential part of their skill set.

Marley was also counting on guests staying at the resort and some of the staff to be able to provide new information or insights not already garnered by the authorities. That was another skill set the two of them possessed that had helped them in previous situations: their ability to get people to relax and disclose information they didn't know they had. Nan had always attributed it to the amount of comfort people felt when talking to them, and Marley knew she had a point; an official interview wasn't the same as a friendly conversation. Unlike that of a brisk young police officer, their nonstressful, laid-back, and what some would have called grandmotherly demeanor helped people relax. In most cases, this approach brought to light the information she and Nan needed. Now, like her friend, she grew impatient at the long drive, knowing they couldn't acquire any information the resort held without being there.

CHAPTER 6

WHERE TWO ROADS DIVERGED TO form a Y, Nan saw a store with a large sign declaring it to be the Merrifield Y Store. She let out a whooping holler and, in her rush to angle-park, practically ran Agatha into one of the building's large plate-glass windows. Nan turned off the ignition, and she and Marley hopped out, slamming the doors behind them. Marley took time to stretch, but Nan, eager to be in and out, swiftly approached the store's screened door. Before entering, she couldn't help but notice the variety of advertisements for everything from fishing contests to meat raffles, all displayed low in the front windows, and she marveled at the efficiency of it all. Locals would have had little need to subscribe to a newspaper in order to discover current events or happenings if they frequented the store regularly, which, from the number and breadth of advertisements posted, they undoubtedly did.

By the gas pumps and in the right-hand front window were prominently placed large signs promising live bait.

Nan wrinkled her citified nose at the thought of bait of any description in conjunction with groceries. She stepped through the store's front door and noticed, top to bottom, on her left, a section of shelves backed by pegboard displaying a colorful assortment of lures, hooks, sinkers, and other fishing supplies.

Nan then noticed a woman seated by the cash register behind the counter directly to her right. To Nan, who was inexperienced in anything up north, the woman looked exactly as she expected someone to look who lived and worked in the bounty and beauty of the Brainerd Lakes area. She had a wide, open expression and eyes sparkling with good cheer. Her weather-worn face, Nan imagined, had spent many days working in a field under the heat of a raging sun, yet in actuality, she was probably more accustomed to hours spent in a fishing boat or working in a backyard vegetable plot. The woman's short brown hair was streaked with gray and had been made curly by a perm. She wore an oversized, unbuttoned gray-and-black-checked flannel shirt over a bright yellow T-shirt that read, "The Merrifield Y Store." Although Nan was unable to see for herself, she imagined the shirts were worn over a pair of faded blue jeans.

Nan heard Marley enter right behind her. The two of them exchanged greetings with the woman as they passed by her, turning toward the grocery section of the store. As they approached the shelves filled with many sorts of mixes and packages, they heard the woman call out that she would be happy to assist them if they needed help in finding anything.

Nan was surprised to find that the goods displayed in the section before her were a considerable notch above those at an average convenience store, and she was surprised by how many items she saw on the shelves. They each grabbed a basket, took an aisle, and began to quickly collect what they would need for hearty breakfasts and evening snacks, having earlier decided to eat their larger midday meals out.

Nan shouted across the aisle to Marley, "Don't buy any of that microwave popcorn! Buy the real stuff and some oil. We can use a saucepan, or better yet, maybe we'll find a cheap popcorn popper at a flea market up here."

"Flea market?" Marley murmured. "I can't help but wonder if our missing women visited some of the year-round flea markets. We might want to check on that."

"We're going to need to check on everything and anything," Nan said. "Do you want bananas? How about some almonds?"

Nan paused in her gathering of foodstuffs to look down at the checkerboard tile floor that ran toward the back of the store. Drawn by curiosity toward the colorful Live Bait sign posted on a closed door there, she ambled in that direction. "See you in a bit!" she called out to Marley as she placed her basket on top of a shelf and opened the Live Bait door. Upon hearing a gurgling sound that would have caused her to expect to see scrabbling live green lobsters in a glass-fronted aquarium back in town, she went in.

Directly before her and to her right were a series of faucets. Each was continually running water into a separate square holding tank. The entire L-shaped aluminum structure was divided by panels so that each type of bait had its own pool. Labels above the spigots identified the contents. Nan saw that people who came up north for fishing could choose from pike shiners, light northern minnows, night crawlers, leeches, and many more. Mesh scoops sat on the edge of every tank for ease of collection, but she was most amazed at what was not present: there was no fishy smell.

Nan took a step closer to the tubs and noticed a series of flexible white tubes sending oxygen from tall tanks into the bubbling water. She now knew what accounted for the lack of fishy smell: the tanks' water was being oxygenated. With her curiosity satisfied, she scooted out the door to collect her shopping basket and joined Marley at the cash register near the front door.

Marley had apparently asked the woman about the store's previous location and was being told that she was correct in recalling that a smaller building still at the site, though now positioned closer to the intersection, had been the Y Store when Marley was a girl. Now the smaller building served as a bar. Because of the growing number of year-round residents and tourists, an expansion in the variety of merchandise offered at the site had been sorely needed.

"Folks use us so much more now," the woman said as she eyed them curiously while ringing up their purchases. "Stayin' hereabouts?" she then asked with a smile.

"Yes, as a matter of fact, we are," Nan said. "We're on our way to Eagle's Cove Resort. "For a week, maybe more."

The woman's eyes widened. "Oh? Just the two of you? All alone then?" she said with a look of unabashed curiosity.

"That's right," Marley replied. "Why do you ask?"

"Well now, I don't want to spook ya any."

Marley made a point of looking at Nan and then back at the lady. "Spook us? Why? Is there something we should know?"

"Well," the woman said, "it's about those women, you see. The two who went missin', ya know?"

Nan felt her mind leap to a greater level of alertness. Careful to temper her excitement, she said, "Yes, I recall hearing and reading about that. It happened about a year ago, didn't it? At about this same time of year?"

"That's right," the woman said. "And the other woman, the first one, disappeared the year before that. Scary, isn't it, the two of them disappearin' that way and no one knowing what happened to them?"

"There's no doubt that it's strange," Marley said, motioning toward Nan. "But I don't think we need to be concerned with staying at Eagle's Cove Resort. From what I recall, the women disappeared after checking out and leaving the resort. Weren't there witnesses who testified to that fact?"

Their new acquaintance gave a slight shrug. "Sure, but people don't just disappear off the face of the earth."

"No, they don't," Nan said.

"Did you happen to know either of the two women? Did they ever shop here?" Marley asked.

"Sure did," the woman said with a firm nod. "Everyone shops here sooner or later if they're stayin' in these parts."

"So you remember them?" Nan asked.

"I do."

"Did either of the two women stop at your store on the day they vanished?" Marley asked.

The woman shook her head. "Nope. And that's what I told the sheriff when he came in and asked me." She then set the bag she had just filled aside and reached for another. She placed a few items in it and then paused. Looking up at

Marley, she said, "But you know what? Ever since that day, I've been thinkin' a lot about those two women."

Nan felt her pulse quicken. "Good for you," she said encouragingly. "Come up with anything?"

The woman leaned forward and tapped a finger on the counter. "I did. I'm convinced that not only did they not stop here, but I swear neither one of those two women ever drove by this store on the days they disappeared. Nope, not at all!"

The emphasis on her concluding phrase was strengthened by the way she drew her body stiffly upright while a smug look of satisfaction settled upon her weathered, well-tanned face.

"No sirree!" she added. "They didn't drive by at all. And I feel sure saying that because I'd have known if they did." She made a wide sweep with her arm through the air before her. "Look where I'm sittin' behind this counter here. Do you see the view I have out those windows? Why, it's a perfectly clear view of the road. Now, a big part of my day is me lookin' out those windows, watching the world go by. See, I would have noticed those women if they had driven by."

"But what if you were busy?" Marley said. "What if you were waiting on customers, as you are now?"

The woman shrugged and began to pack the rest of the few items left on the counter. "I can still see the cars go by, can't I? It's not as if traffic ever gets too heavy. Why, just a few seconds ago, while I was talkin' to you two, I saw Bob Kravitz go by in his Ford truck, and I noticed he had his sweet little grandson, Billy, with him."

The woman finished packing their bags, and Marley

paid for their purchases, including a fill-up of gas. As the woman handed Marley her change, she gave her a meek smile and said, "I'll admit to having wondered myself, *Is it possible I missed them?* I did ask myself that question. Yes, I did! But after thinkin' on it a lot, I decided that while I might've missed seein' one of those women if I were crazy busy, the odds would have to be very low for me to have missed seein' both of them."

"I believe you're right," Marley said. "And thank you for bagging our items. We have to be off now. But we'll be back again, I'm sure."

"You can count on it," the woman replied.

Marley and Nan each grabbed a grocery bag and left the store. Once they were back on the road, Nan glanced over at Marley. "So what do you think of the store lady's theory?"

"Believe it or not," Marley said, "I found her to be very convincing. It would be inconvenient for anyone to leave the resort and head for Minneapolis without driving by her store. Not if they were taking the most direct route to the main roads."

"I agree," Nan said. "Which means if our two women didn't drive by her store the day they disappeared, then they both disappeared somewhere between Eagle's Cove Resort and the Y Store. How much distance are we speaking of here?"

"Two or three miles, maybe a little more," Marley said.

Nan let out a low whistle. "That would certainly shrink the parameters of our search, wouldn't it?"

"Yes, it would," Marley said. "If, that is, what the woman believes turns out to be true. However, we can't count on that."

Nan wasn't about to have her hopes dashed. "No," she said. "But it's a good place to start, don't you think?"

Marley wrinkled her brow in thought. "Are you suggesting we get a district map and focus our investigation on a three-mile radius from the resort?"

"Yes. At least in the beginning," Nan said. "We can always broaden our search later if we need to. But for now, let's concentrate on the farms and people within that three-mile radius."

"Fine," Marley answered. "Let's do it."

Nan smiled. Marley hated to be without a plan, and Nan was always happy to help supply her with one.

Suddenly, Nan noticed her knuckles were white and realized she was gripping the car's steering wheel in anticipation as she made the turn onto the narrow two-lane county road that she knew led directly to Eagle's Cove Resort and what they believed to be the opening scene of two crimes.

CHAPTER 7

THE NARROW, WINDING GRAVEL DRIVE that led into Eagle's Cove Resort would allow two cars to pass each other just barely if one of the cars drove onto its grassy shoulder. It was bordered on both sides by white and jack pines. The white pines towered majestically over the scraggly jacks, with their dark shadows falling across the road. As the car approached the first small cluster of cabins to the left, they saw a chain-link fence. Beyond the fence was a privately owned home that was not part of the resort. Smoke curled from the chimney on its peaked roof. Marley rolled down the car window, and a pungent smell of wood smoke entered the car's interior. She took a deep breath, savoring memories of the pleasant wood fires on cool evenings at her grandmother's lake home.

Nan, however, breathed deeply and said, "Ah, reminds me of the good old days when I smoked."

Marley laughed but then made a face that revealed to Nan her disapproval of the description of anyone's past smoking history as "the good old days."

Just ahead and to their left, the trees thinned out,

and the road opened onto a wide grassy area containing a community fire pit, a shuffleboard-marked strip of concrete, and a volleyball court sans net. Just before the road curved sharply to the left, they saw a collection of overturned rowboats lined up in a row like beached whales; each wooden frame undoubtedly once had sported bright and cheery primary colors, but now the paint had faded to lackluster pale greens, blues, and reds, with strips of bare wood showing through heavily peeling hulls. Each boat was marked with the number of its designated cabin stenciled in black.

Beyond the boats, two long aluminum docks stretched into the wide, sweeping expanse of the lake. One held a wood-slatted bench at its deep end, and the other was T-shaped and had a few fishing boats tied up to it that, given their relative size and condition, may have belonged to renters.

About as far as two football fields, some six hundred feet out into a bay, they could see a small island. Back from the lake's pebbly shore, in the center of a deeply shaded cluster of trees, stood a log structure with a door sporting a sign above it: Resort Office. The structure appeared to be little more than a glorified log cabin that had been added on to; one side was used as an office for checking guests in and out of the resort and served as a place where they could gather local information and supplies. As Nan and Marley would discover in the days ahead, the amenities available within the resort office included a public telephone, ice and soda pop machines, and racks of brochures advertising area attractions. The addition, slightly larger and also made out of logs, they would come to discover, held the resort's bar-and-café combination.

Nan parked the car in the small lot next to the rental office, and she and Marley got out, taking a moment to stretch their cramped muscles and enjoy the crisp, pine-scented freshness of the air. Marley raised a hand and swept her hair behind her right ear to ensure that Sean's hearing aid was visible. Then they both climbed the three wooden steps that led to the resort office's faded green screen door. Nan held the door open as Marley and a few hopeful flies entered the office.

"Oh, it's bigger than I thought," Marley said in surprise as she looked about the room that had suddenly opened before her. The space, though large, looked anything but inviting. In her estimation, it was horribly dated and just plain dreary.

To her left, against the wall, was a large oak desk, upon which a variety of glossy brochures sagged in a wire display rack that stood next to a dusty lamp and a tired-looking fake flower arrangement that drooped sadly in the middle and displayed colors far more reminiscent of fall than spring. Directly ahead was a faux-marble laminate counter, and behind the counter stood a wooden chair, a high-backed metal stool, and a combination fax machine and printer on a small table. Farther beyond were two multipaned glass French doors, through which she could see a living area furnished with various sofas and chairs lacking in any particular decorative scheme. "The Chapmans obviously have their living quarters back there," Marley whispered. "I wonder if our cabin will be so nondescript."

"We can't expect luxury," Nan replied. "But it should be

better than most of the cabins we've seen so far, all of which look pretty basic. Why don't you ring that bell over there on the top of the counter? Someone must be here."

Marley approached the counter and tapped the bell twice. Then she stepped back to wait.

Nan rolled her eyes, took a step forward, and gave the bell six solid slams with the palm of her hand, putting some strength behind the action.

Although the bell chimed a tinny demand for service, no one came. They saw no movement in the living quarters behind the counter, nor did they hear any sound.

"Ring it again," Marley said.

Nan obliged. However, although she struck the bell even harder this time, there was still no response. Marley let out a sigh and was about to say, "No one's at home," when Nan walked to the end of the counter, rounded it, and rapidly approached the French doors that led to the living quarters. Then, cupping her hands on each side of her eyes, she peered through the window. In the next instant, she grabbed the door's handle and turned it, and to Marley's surprise, the door gave with a jarring click.

Nan looked back at Marley and said breathlessly, "Quick, Marley. Stand by the screen door, and keep watch for me. I'm going in here to plant one of Sean's bugs somewhere. Whistle if anyone comes."

Before Marley could say, "I can't whistle," Nan was through the French doors. Marley wasted no time in turning and making a quick dash for the screen door, where she earnestly took up her post. All she could see without opening the door and leaning out was the wide expanse of the office's parking lot, with Agatha as the lone vehicle.

With her heart racing, she continued to look left and right, stretching forth her neck, in the hope of seeing anyone's approach. But she didn't see anything. Instead, she heard something: the unmistakable crunch of someone walking on one of the resort's gravel paths. As the sound grew closer, she sprang into action. First, she swiveled around to stare at the two doors Nan had disappeared behind, pursing her lips. Before she could attempt a lame whistle, the French doors flew open, and Nan reappeared. Nan hurriedly closed both doors behind her, and as Marley gestured wildly, she slipped around the counter again and came to a dead stop. Marley quickly joined her, standing close by her friend's side.

Nan, breathing a little heavily, reached out a hand, but before she could touch the bell again, a woman's voice came from behind them. "A new cleaner today," the voice said in a tone that implied the statement sufficed as an explanation.

Marley and Nan turned on their heels and stared at the woman who had just entered the resort office. Nan, still struggling to calm her nerves after her little escapade, tried her best to hide her shock at what she saw. The woman before her was strikingly attractive. Young, mid-to-late thirties, she stood about five feet eight or so, with a thin, willowy, figure. She was clad in faded, skintight jeans and a neon-pink halter top presently stretched tightly across her ample breasts. Although her makeup seemed to Nan to be far too heavy for the time of day, it was, nevertheless, flawlessly applied. Her face was a series of sharp angles and well-proportioned features that any camera would have loved, but it was her hair that Nan found most striking. The woman's hair was lavishly thick and seemed to fall about her face and shoulders in an abundance of rippling, shiny dark auburn waves. Nan was aware that her mouth was likely hanging open, and she tried her best to stop staring. In return, the striking individual was staring back appraisingly at her and Marley. But Nan couldn't stop staring. It was hopeless. The woman simply didn't belong. She didn't fit. Nothing about her seemed right in that primitive, all-about-nature environment. On the contrary, the woman looked as if she belonged on a stage, under a set of bright lights. Above all, she didn't come anywhere close to the Christy Chapman Nan had previously imagined.

As usual, when Nan was tongue-tied, Marley came to the rescue. "Good afternoon," she said in a voice every bit as cool as her demeanor. "Are you Mrs. Chapman?"

The woman nodded and replied with a mumbled "Yes" but offered no welcoming greeting of her own. Instead, she skirted around them both and approached the counter, where she raised the hinged section in order to gain entry to the work space behind. Reaching under the counter, she produced a large book, and she plopped it open before her.

"You're here for cabin number eight," she said, making her words a statement rather than a question. "They've just finished cleaning it. Two o'clock is our official sign-in time. You're early."

Nan was taken aback by the underlying hint of surliness in Mrs. Chapman's voice and the lack of any welcome on the woman's part. Her first inclination was to put the woman in her place, and her mind was even then forming an appropriate retort, when she decided to cool it. *Better to build a bridge than a wall*, she told herself.

Marley, glancing at her wristwatch, was way ahead of Nan. "Yes, we're aware of the check-in time," Marley said.

"And we're sorry for coming early. But it is almost two now, and well, we're tired from the long drive. Since the cabin is clean and ready, if we could have the key and the directions to find our way, we'd be very appreciative."

Mrs. Chapman opened a drawer behind the counter and produced a key. She set it on the counter before her and motioned toward the open book. "Sign in first," she said.

Marley signed the registration book, and Mrs. Chapman handed her the key along with a small map of the resort grounds. After taking a pen out of another drawer, she circled one of the cabins on the map. "You're at the far end of the gravel path, east of here," she said. "Right along the bluff. It has a nice view and is a good distance from the other cabins. Very private."

"Thank you," Marley said, pocketing the key. "I believe you have a small café here that serves beer and—"

"Bar food," Mrs. Chapman said. "Burgers, pizza, hoagies—that sort of thing."

Marley smiled. "Yes. And that will certainly suit us for lunch. But I wonder if you might be so kind as to direct us to the closest place for dining in the afternoon or evening?"

Mrs. Chapman closed the registration book and once again placed it under the counter. Then she took out two brochures and practically tossed them across the counter at Marley. "There are a number of choices," she said. "Ojibwa Point is just down the road to the east and has a popular restaurant, although nothing fancy. Two miles north, on Highway 9, is a larger and more popular place. It's called Majestic Oaks. It's a full-service resort with a golf course and restaurant, including a jazz club and spa. Then, of course, if all else fails, there's always the casinos."

"That's what we're here for." Nan piped up, pointing at herself and then Marley. "We're here for the casinos. We're taking a girls' time-out—a little gambling holiday, you might say. Just the two of us, without the hubbies."

The bare hint of a smile touched one corner of Mrs. Chapman's mouth. "I was wondering what brought you to our resort. You don't seem the type to spend the day fishing. And fishing season hasn't started yet."

"Fishing? Us? Goodness no," Nan said with a laugh. "No, you might say we have bigger fish to fry." She broke into an inane giggle at her lame joke.

Marley motioned toward her and said, "Besides gambling, which we both enjoy, my friend Nan here is looking forward to painting a few landscapes. She's quite an accomplished artist, and the scenery up here is so breathtaking."

Nan, who was still smiling like a besotted schoolgirl, nodded in agreement. "I especially like the early spring, when the leaves are just emerging, and I can work on my Monet technique."

Mrs. Chapman seemed satisfied with those rationales, for she looked away and motioned toward the metal racks. "You'll find information about our nearby casinos among those brochures. There are three within close driving distance. Each has a restaurant and an all-you-can-eat buffet."

"Thank you, Mrs. Chapman," Marley said. "That's very helpful."

Mrs. Chapman's smile faded, but Nan noticed her mouth soften. "Call me Christy," she said. "My husband's mother died a long time ago." With that, she took her leave of them, heading toward the living quarters through the French doors.

Marley and Nan exited the office, and only when they were a safe distance away did they turn to each other, each with a look of amazement on her face.

"Well, what did you think?" Nan asked. "She wasn't very welcoming, was she?"

Marley concurred. "No, she wasn't. At first, I was totally confused. I couldn't understand how she'd ever expect any repeat business with an attitude like that."

"It was almost as if she didn't care if we ever came back."

"I know. But I felt it was more than that. It seemed she didn't want us to be here at all. Which I found interesting. At the end, though, she seemed to be less antagonistic."

"I picked that up too. That was after I threw in the part about our supposed gambling vacation. I was hoping to ease any suspicions she might have had regarding why we wanted to be here at this time of year. It seemed to work. Her attitude definitely changed."

Once outside and ensconced in Agatha, they took that sheltered environment as the ideal space to continue an assessment of their encounter with Christy Chapman.

"Did you notice anything unusual about her hair?" Marley asked.

"Only the fact that it was gorgeous, and I should be so lucky," Nan replied.

"You didn't notice anything else? You didn't notice the cut, for instance?"

"The cut?"

"Yes, her haircut." Marley turned to look at Nan, whose blank expression told her Nan didn't have a clue what she was referring to. "Nan, hair doesn't just naturally fall in layers that way of its own accord. No, those layers have to be meticulously cut. Christy Chapman has a precision haircut that was exquisitely executed by a true craftsperson and artist. I'd bet my trust fund on it."

"So?"

"So where would a person get a cut like that in these parts? A stylist with that kind of talent would be a rare find anywhere, but I would think he or she would be a lot easier to locate in the Twin Cities than up north."

"But not entirely impossible," Nan said.

"I suppose," Marley replied. "Nevertheless, I have my doubts. Why would such a talent stay way up here?"

"You can be a real snob at times. You know that?" Nan teased.

"Nonsense. I'm speaking of reality," Marley said. "The point I'm trying to make is, such a haircut doesn't come cheap, Nan. They're damn expensive. I should know. So what are we to think of an owner of an anything-but-exclusive mom-and-pop resort walking around with a hundred-dollar-plus haircut?"

Nan let out a low whistle. "That much?"

"Without a doubt," Marley replied. "So one has to wonder, how does she afford a cut like that?"

Since neither had an answer to that question, they both treated it as rhetorical.

They consulted the resort map Christy Chapman had given them, and once they were belted into Agatha, Nan started the engine and maneuvered the car along the gravel road toward cabin number eight.

"Where did you plant the bug?" Marley asked.

Nan ran a few fingers through her curls and replied, "Well, I knew I didn't have much time, so I placed one under the dining room table. It looked like a good spot because it was centrally located in the apartment, and I figured it was a reasonable place for any discussion we might want to overhear."

Marley nodded. "I'm just glad we had the opportunity to plant something. And that you were quick enough to take advantage of the situation."

"We can't let any opportunity pass us by, Marley. We always need to take the risk, and if we're discovered, well—"

"I know. We use our creative ingenuity to get ourselves out of a tight spot."

"That's right. I could have always said I was simply searching for someone to help us check in."

They continued driving along the resort road, passing unoccupied cabins along the way, which inclined Nan to remark on what appeared to be an obvious shortage of guests staying at the resort. "This place looks utterly abandoned. Look—there are no cars parked next to any of these cabins."

"It's still early in the season," Marley replied. "I did see a car parked next to that private home as we were coming in. And if I'm not mistaken, there's a car up ahead."

Nan looked where Marley was pointing and noticed a dark SUV parked next to a cabin a short distance up the road. As they passed it, they saw an elderly couple sitting at a picnic table next to their rental. Both she and Marley waved at the couple as they drove by, and the two made an enthusiastic and energetic effort to wave back.

"Well, at least they're friendly," Nan said. "It's nice

to know we're not entirely alone up here and that there's someone else around."

Once they passed the last cabin, there was still a distance to go, and it was all uphill, until they came to a dead-end cul-de-sac. "Home at last," said Nan as she parked Agatha behind cabin number eight.

They stepped out of the car and stood still for a few moments to assess the small house and the surrounding environment.

"This place, being on a bluff, has a higher elevation than the rest of the resort. It should provide a good vantage point for us," Nan said. She cocked her head to one side. "Do you hear water running?"

Marley nodded. "Yes. There's a little bridge over there. Do you see it? It must be spanning a creek that runs into the lake."

As Marley strode toward the cabin to unlock the door, Nan walked toward the bridge to get a closer look. At the bluff's edge, she peered down at a narrow creek that flowed out into the lake. The bridge that spanned the creek was no wider than a footpath, and Nan noticed, on its opposite side, a clearing consisting of a small grassy hill, upon which a wooden picnic table stood. Beyond the table, she could just make out a narrow dirt path that headed into a dense wood.

As she stood there, she thought about how welcoming the little bridge appeared and how bridges were just meant to be crossed. She was telling herself she'd cross it someday soon and would also take the narrow path through the woods to discover where it led, when she heard Marley come up behind her.

"Wait until you see the view from our deck," Marley said with a happy smile.

They both turned then and, in a soundless but mutual decision that they had put off their work long enough, headed back toward Agatha to collect their luggage and shopping purchases, which they then carried to the modern two-story cabin painted a soft coral color trimmed in green. The back of the cabin, the side that didn't face the lake, had a small open stoop covered with a portico, and Marley climbed a few steps and pushed open first a screen and then a back door that led into the kitchen.

Before exploring the cabin any further, they began to unpack the groceries. Nan unloaded the paper bags as Marley dealt with the food in the cooler that needed to be refrigerated.

"So why do you think Professor Engelmann chose to rent this particular cabin? It's rather large for one person," Nan said.

Marley thought for a moment and then said, "Any number of reasons. She was recuperating from a divorce. She could well afford it, and she wanted to treat herself. It's also more isolated than the others, which, given what she had recently experienced, she would have appreciated."

"And Lynn Parker? Why would she choose this cabin?"

"That question is more difficult to answer. Why would a young woman of Lynn Parker's age want to rent this particular cabin in this particular resort? Nothing about this place would seem to appeal to a young woman. Besides, it's too big. What would cause her to choose a place with three bedrooms and a cabin this size? Though, according to one of

Eva's bloggers, she may have been writing a true-crime book about the disappearance of her former teacher."

"Now that I've seen this resort," Nan said, "I'm beginning to think that answer is as good as any. It's the only one that makes sense. Look, I'm a creative person, but I can't come up with one good reason a woman of Lynn Parker's age would ever want to book a cabin here."

"I know," Marley said. "And I agree with you. What reason could she give if someone were to inquire? She couldn't very well say, as you did, that she came up here for the gambling or to frequent the casinos. Could she? Young people don't do that. They party in groups—the more the merrier. They'd rather die than go anywhere as a party of one."

Nan had finished putting her portion of the groceries away and was now busy looking through all the cupboards. She opened one filled with glassware and dishes. She gave Marley a big smile. "They may not be Waterford or even Riedel, but this cupboard contains real wineglasses of the glass variety. In fact, the cabin appears to be very well equipped with whatever a person would need."

The women finished checking out the cabin's supplies, opening every cupboard and drawer, before they picked up their luggage and walked toward the front of the place, where they entered an expansive living space with tall ceilings and an open center stairwell. One entire side of the living area held a screened-in porch that overlooked a densely wooded scene consisting mostly of birch and pine.

"Lovely," Nan said. "That screened-in porch will be a great spot to have coffee in the morning and watch for deer."

"Or birds," Marley said. "Don't forget Professor

Engelmann was an avid birdwatcher. I've often wondered at the number of people who find so much enjoyment in the hobby and what makes it so addictive."

"Beats me," Nan said, slowly surveying the cabin's living area. "Perhaps it's akin to the charm some people might find in all this log furniture."

Marley took in the overly heavy furniture constructed of honey-colored peeled logs. The chairs and sofas seemingly had been crafted by woodsmen with an additional fondness for cushions sporting animal motifs. "I have never seen so many wolves, bears, and eagles in my life," she said. "Not all in one room anyway."

"It is quite a menagerie, isn't it?" Nan said, walking forward to slide open the doors that led onto the deck.

They both stepped out onto a faded gray cedar structure that ran the entire length of the front of the cabin and jutted out beyond the bluff before them and to their left. On the deck stood four weather-resistant chairs and a round table, and off to one side, two lounge chairs were available that, although they were perfect for sunning, had seen better days.

Cabin number eight stood on a ragged bluff overlooking the rocky shore of a wide bay that led to a channel extending into the larger expanse of the lake beyond.

Directly ahead some six hundred yards or so, in the middle of the bay, stood a small island with three towering white pines.

"This is the same view Professor Engelmann and Lynn Parker would have seen every day," Marley said.

"I was thinking the same thing," Nan said. "You can see a lot from up here." She walked to the edge of the deck and leaned over the railing. "There's a very narrow strip of sand down there that I'd be hard-pressed to call a beach." Turning her head to the right, she peered down the bluff. "I can see both of the docks and the path leading to the resort office from this spot," she said, shading her eyes with her hand. She then turned her head to the left. "From this side, I can see the ravine that contains the creek. Oh, and I also have a view of the little bridge." Returning to the center of the deck, she stared intently at the scene before her. "And you're right, Marley. This is a fabulous view. We can see every inch of the bay and much of the big lake beyond."

Nan made no objection to Marley's taking the largest of the three bedrooms, which she took to be the master, not only because Marley was financing the trip but also because Nan knew Marley had left behind in Saint Paul a bedroom three times the square footage of any the cabin had to offer.

After they were unpacked and settled in their rooms, there was one more necessary trip to the car to collect Sean's and Ray's contributions and the computer. Marley placed the laptop on the dining room table, connected the fittings, and plugged it into an outlet. She opened it and pushed the power button. Meanwhile, Nan leaned Sean's spying device, in the form of an artist's easel, in a corner of the living room and put the night-vision binoculars and the zippered case containing the lock picks on top of a bookshelf.

Then Nan gave Marley a questioning look. "Well?" she asked hopefully.

"Nothing so far," Marley said. "It may be that we'll have to rely on our cell phones after all."

CHAPTER 8

MARLEY REACHED UP, TOOK THE fake hearing aid out of her ear, and put it back in its shell case. "You can get tired of having something in your ear all the time," she grumbled. "I wonder if Mrs. Chapman even noticed I was wearing a hearing aid."

"I doubt it," Nan replied. "She didn't give either of us a first look, let alone a second."

"According to Sean, I turn it on when I need to hear something at a distance," Marley said. "Now I just have to remember to wear it. Try to help me with that, won't you, Nan?"

"Sure," Nan said, opening a bottle of cabernet. "Grab some glasses, Marley, and let's go out and sit on the deck."

They settled into chairs opposite each other near the table. After a swirl of the glass to look for legs, a sniff or two, and an appreciative sip of the dark red wine, they began to relax. The taste of a familiar brand of cabernet helped to take down some of the tension engendered by a long journey, the odd meeting with Christy Chapman, their nonfunctioning laptop, and their expectations and plans for the week ahead.

Nan asked, "Are you going to carry Ray's knockout drops, or am I?"

"You may do that," Marley answered. "To tell you the truth, they scare me. Especially after Ray mentioned they can be lethal. I hope we never have to use them."

Nan shrugged. "He warned us they could be lethal if we weren't careful with the dosage. So we'll be super careful and use them only in an emergency."

"What would an emergency entail?" Marley asked.

"Oh, you know, if someone was about to kill us or something."

Marley gave Nan an incredulous look. "Of course," she said. "Because in that case, we could always plead self-defense."

Nan stared at Marley to see if she was serious, but Marley tossed her head back and laughed so heartily that Nan found herself joining in.

Dabbing at tears in her eyes, Marley said, "What's wrong with us? How can we find humor in such a subject?"

"There's humor in every matter, Marley. Didn't you know that?" Nan replied. "It just needs the right environment and context."

They decided to take a small break from discussing the case, and as they sipped their wine, they talked about all the insignificant little nothings that held no meaning in the world at large but were nevertheless essential to the nurturing of a friendship. When their glasses were empty, they returned to the living room and the task at hand.

Looking around her, Marley asked, "Where do we start?"

"I know what I want to do," Nan answered. "I want to

take a really good look at the books on that shelf over here." She pointed toward a bookcase that stood about three feet tall and was positioned against a side wall. A variety of romance, suspense, and mystery authors could be recognized among the various paperback and hardback books.

Marley smiled. "Now you're getting creative. So what do you expect to find? Suzanne or Lynn's diary?"

Nan rolled her eyes. "I should be so lucky! No. I'm sure a diary would have been noticed and carried away by the police. I'm looking for the little what-nots the police might have overlooked."

Their past experience had convinced them that nothing would ever be handed to them. Standard operating procedure might have solved cold cases for the police, but for Nan and Marley, imagination and ingenuity were the special gifts they brought to the solving of crimes.

"I'm hoping for a book that may have been left behind by either of the two women. In it, I'm looking for what you might call marginalia," Nan said. "You know, oddments, inklings, omens, notions jotted in the margins, or doodles in the books themselves, for that matter. Or perhaps something placed between the pages to be used as a bookmark and then forgotten and left behind. You'd be surprised at what people use. Postcards, letters, ticket stubs—you name it. Any of that kind of thing might lead us to a better understanding of those two women."

"Well, good luck with that," Marley said. "Meanwhile, since I'm certain each of our missing women would have slept in the master bedroom, I'm off around the corner to make a thorough search of that room."

"Have fun," Nan said as she lowered herself onto the

floor in front of the bookcase and began to peruse the various titles. As she examined the contents of each shelf more closely, she found a surprisingly eclectic assortment of books, including navigational aids; hunting and fishing advice; a couple of volumes on the practice of meditation, both spiritual and transcendental; and tattered copies of various spy, science fiction, and western novels. All the assorted genres, she knew, spoke to the different interests of vacationing visitors who had left them behind after toting them to the resort in the hope of benefiting from a dose of summer escapism, personal knowledge, or further learning.

As she ran a finger over the titles, one in particular caught her eye: *Positive Thinking at a Time of Loss: Divorce and Its Aftermath.* She slid the book gingerly from its place, lowered herself into the nearest chair, and began to slowly scan its pages. Sometime later, she earmarked a page and placed the book on the top of the bookshelf. Then she continued her search.

She held her breath when she noticed a bird field guide that, unlike the other books on the shelf, looked relatively new. She slowly drew the volume toward her and opened it to see an ex libris label identifying the book as belonging to Suzanne Engelmann. Slowly, as if any swift movement would break the connection the universe had just opened for her, Nan lowered herself once more into the chair and, with a trembling finger and a prayer on her lips, turned the first page. This book, she told herself, she would take the time to go through page by page. She closed the book only when she heard Marley come around the corner from the master bedroom.

"Well," Marley announced, "my search wasn't entirely futile. I found a button."

Nan looked over at Marley, who was holding a small brown tortoiseshell button above her head as if it were the Davis Cup for tennis. "Where did you find it?" Nan asked.

"On the floor in the bedroom closet, along with a few dust bunnies the cleaners obviously overlooked."

Nan smiled back. "Well, come see what I discovered," she said excitedly. As Marley approached, Nan rose, quickly retrieved the book from the top of the bookshelf, and then once again seated herself. With Marley peering over her shoulder, Nan ran a hand over the book's cover and said, "This book is all about facing one's life after divorce. I think it may have belonged to Suzanne Engelmann, and she left it behind when she checked out of the resort."

Marley nodded. "Knowing her reasons for coming to the resort, that makes sense."

Nan opened the book to the page she had earlier dog-eared and pointed a finger. "This chapter is entitled 'Loneliness,' and on this page, the author has quoted John Donne's poem 'No Man Is an Island.' Look what someone did with the word *Island*!"

Marley glanced down at the page indicated and noticed writing in the margin, along with a drawing. Someone had underlined the word *Island* and had drawn an arrow from the word to a question mark in the margin next to a rough drawing of what looked like three straight lines that had been partially squiggled out. "What does it mean?" Marley asked.

"I think it's pointing us to the island in the bay," Nan said, pointing to the three squiggled lines. "See? These represent the three giant pine trees that are such a prominent feature of that island."

Marley turned to gaze out the glass doors toward the island beyond. "Do you think so?"

"Yes, I do. What else could it mean? Especially given that someone connected these three squiggly lines with the word *Island*."

Marley pursed her lips. "I don't know. I suppose it's possible. But why the question mark? Do you think Suzanne's intention by underlining the word *Island* and drawing that picture was to leave a clue?"

"Not consciously," Nan said. "I think she was merely doodling. The way people do when they're bored or pondering something and in deep thought. I don't think she was even aware of what she was doing."

"If she were in deep thought, that could explain the question mark," Marley said. "Something might have been puzzling her."

Nan shut the book and placed it aside. "My thought exactly. Now all we have to do is discover what it was about the island Suzanne Engelmann found puzzling."

Marley laughed. "It may turn out to be nothing more than trying to decide whether to go back to her old life following her divorce or move to a remote island somewhere in the South Pacific."

"You could be right," Nan said. "But then again ..."

"You might be onto something," Marley said. She turned to gaze out the glass door toward the small bit of land and its trees out in the bay once more. "Do you know what I was thinking earlier?" She sighed and turned back toward Nan. "I know it sounds crazy and is a wish that's impossible to achieve, but it's important to me that this resort and everything within it and surrounding it be exactly the same as when Suzanne Engelmann and Lynn Parker stayed here. I feel it is very important that the two of us are able to see and experience what they saw and experienced."

"I know. I feel the same way," Nan said. "It's like coming upon a crime scene that's been altered or compromised in some way. You start at a disadvantage." She picked up the bird guide and handed it to Marley. "Take a look at the inside cover of this book, and prepare to be amazed."

When Marley opened the book, her eyes grew wide. "Well, we don't need any more proof than this, do we? This book absolutely belonged to Professor Engelmann."

"Yes. At first, it didn't register as anything of importance that I could see. I went through it page by page and could find nothing of interest. No marginal notes or underlining of any kind. However—"

Marley smiled. "I love *howevers*."

"Well, here's the question I had to ask myself: Knowing what we know about Suzanne Engelmann and her love of birds, would she have willingly left this book behind?"

Marley thought for a moment and then shook her head. "No. She would never have left her field guide behind."

"Unless," Nan said, raising a finger in the air, "she had so many field guides at home she decided to leave this one for future resort visitors."

"I can see where that might make some sense," Marley said. "Most, if not all, of the books on this shelf have been left by former guests. But the problem is, that's not the only bird guide I see on the shelf. So why leave her copy, when there were others available for future guests?"

"Right," Nan said. "And what also seems odd to me—"

"Is the fact that she left her book on divorce behind, as if she didn't feel a need for it anymore?" Marley said, finishing Nan's thought.

"That's right. A person doesn't get over a divorce that quickly. Believe me, I should know. I've had two of them."

"Then why leave that particular book, along with the field guide? One would think she planned on coming back."

"You mean back to the resort and to this cabin at some later date?" Nan asked before shaking her head. "No. I highly doubt it. I think it may well be the opposite. I think rather than planning on coming back, Suzanne Engelmann was in one hell of a hurry to leave this resort the day she disappeared."

"And you think that in her rush to leave, she overlooked packing her books?"

"Well, it's one explanation."

"So what would make someone be in such a big hurry to leave somewhere?"

"Off the cuff, I can think of three reasons: if the person was skipping out on the bill, if there was an emergency elsewhere, or if the person was in danger."

"Well, we know through Gretchen that Suzanne allegedly signed out and paid her bill and that there was no emergency anyone knew of back home, so—"

"She felt herself in danger," Nan said firmly.

"It's all speculation, of course, but since we are certain something happened to her, I think it's safe for us to assume she was in danger, whether she knew it or not."

*   *   *

After conducting a thorough search of the rest of the cabin, which revealed nothing of interest, and enjoying a light supper consisting of Thielen's sausages and a tomato salad, they decided, since it was such a mild evening, to take an after-dinner stroll around the resort grounds. Nan grabbed a jacket, Marley tossed a cashmere sweater over her shoulders, and they left the cabin to begin their walk down the hill toward the resort office and main buildings.

As they walked along, they were surprised to see the elderly couple they'd noticed earlier still sitting at the picnic table outside their cabin. Since they had hoped to have a chance to visit with them, they made a point of stopping long enough to introduce themselves to the pair, whose names turned out to be Ed and Ione Graham. Marley found herself wanting to linger. She thought them delightful. They were the kind of married couple who easily joined in each other's laughter—and there was a lot of laughter. In fact, the couple bubbled over with it—a true testament to their relationship and their cheery personalities.

When Ione told them she and Ed wouldn't keep them any longer from their walk but invited Nan and Marley to return in the morning for coffee, they immediately accepted. They'd hoped for a chance to question the other preseason visitors at the resort, and the invitation would provide the perfect opportunity.

Farther down the road, they continued to pass cabins that showed no signs of occupancy, which caused Nan to draw her jacket snugly about her shoulders and say, "I'm noticing the amount of business this place doesn't seem to have. There's nobody here to speak of. It's spooky. Do you think the disappearances have affected the resort's business?"

"I can't imagine they haven't," Marley said. "But the lack of visitors probably has more to do with the time of year. Remember, the fishing season hasn't opened yet."

They continued to walk on, and as they approached the resort office, they observed a few cars and trucks parked in the lot next to the small bar-and-restaurant addition.

"I think these vehicles belong to locals," Marley said. "It appears a person doesn't have to actually stay here to frequent this bar."

A couple of men were slowly entering the bar, and Nan and Marley stopped for a few minutes to watch them. Then their attention was suddenly drawn to a white pickup truck that came roaring down the resort's dirt road and made a swift, sharp turn into the lot. It came to a hard stop near the entrance, and they saw the driver's door fly open as if the driver were in a hurry. In the next second, Nan and Marley were astonished to see the same man who had treated Marley so rudely at the Roadside Café jump out of the truck and rush into the bar without looking right or left.

Nan, with mouth agape and eyes wide, turned toward Marley. "Was that?" she stammered.

"Yes, it was," Marley said. "I'd recognize that bully—that big lout—anywhere. He's the same brute we encountered earlier today at lunch."

"Well, isn't that just great?" Nan exclaimed, throwing up her hands. "He's back in our lives!"

Marley walked up to the white pickup and stared down at the vehicle's license plate. Nan knew that she was memorizing the first three characters and that it would be her responsibility to memorize the last three. It was a system they'd worked out between them long ago to ensure, given their age, the most reliable way of capturing the data on a license plate. They were more likely to accurately recall the plate that way than if only one of them tried to remember the entire number.

"I have a feeling this guy is going to prove to be important," Marley said.

Nan raised a hand and rubbed her forehead as if trying to erase a niggling thought. "Darn it, so do I."

CHAPTER 9

THE NEXT MORNING, MARLEY ROLLED out of bed, shoved her feet into her slippers, and padded into the kitchen, where she saw Nan, with steaming cup in hand, standing next to a percolating coffeepot.

"I've made coffee," Nan said, turning toward her, "but that's all. I thought we'd have a cup of coffee and a really light breakfast before walking over to visit Ed and Ione."

Marley poured herself a cup of coffee, got a container of yogurt from the fridge, and then motioned toward the windows in the front room. "Let's have our coffee out on the deck and enjoy the view of this lake that was such a draw for the two missing women," she said, starting for the living area.

They both donned warm jackets, and Nan refilled her coffee cup. She also grabbed some yogurt and followed Marley out onto the deck that fronted the cabin. The bay lay directly before them; its surface was marked by a series of small waves that glistened in the morning sun.

Marley walked over to the edge of the deck and stretched forth her neck, peering left at the small bridge that led to a grassy area beyond. To her right, she could see a row of five cabins, including the resort office. In front of the cabins was a pebbly beach with tufts of tall, spiky grass. She could also see the two metal docks, one longer than the other. A coil of thick neon-orange rope and a white life preserver with the name Eagle's Cove Resort written in faded block letters were attached to a tall metal pole at the end of the longer dock. The shorter dock, seemingly used for swimming or sunning, had, at its far end, a metal ladder extending into the water.

Marley and Nan dug into their yogurt while enjoying the expansive view before them and the gulls soaring overhead. At times, a fish would jump with a splash, and eventually, a pair of loons swam lazily into view. Marley and Nan watched them dive under the surface and then reappear.

"You know," Nan said, "it would be nice to have a boat and be able to get out onto the water."

"I was thinking the same thing," Marley said.

"Doesn't a fishing boat come with this cabin?"

"I think so, though I never actually inquired."

"If it came with a motor, we could always take it out for a spin. If it didn't come with a motor, you could always row."

"Thanks," Marley said with a laugh. She looked out at the small island in the bay, with its prominent three tall pines. "I've been thinking ever since your discovery of the book on divorce last evening with that drawing in the margin. And I've been wondering what it is about that island that so intrigued Suzanne Engelmann to cause her to make that drawing. Except for those three tall pines, it doesn't seem to have any remarkable features."

Nan sighed. "You know this may all be conjecture, and that book may not have belonged to her at all."

"C'mon," Marley replied, dismissing such a notion. "You don't believe that any more than I do."

They finished up their coffee and, knowing the elderly visitors nearby were expecting them, headed back inside to shower and change. "Let's have our second cup of coffee with Ed and Ione," Nan said. "No time like the present to start digging."

"It's not digging," Marley said. "The word is *interrogating*."

As Nan headed for the stairs leading to her bedroom, she said over her shoulder, "Interrogation is a police thing and not what I do. So you interrogate if you want to. I'll dig."

Marley simply groaned.

When the two women met up once again, this time properly dressed and with hair combed, just as they were about to leave, Marley asked, "Is it a good idea to turn off the coffee? If we should happen to get into a lengthy conversation, we might be gone for a while."

But Nan, eager as always, was already two feet beyond the door. Marley sighed, unplugged the pot, and took the time to place their coffee mugs in the dishwasher before bustling out the cabin's screen door after her pal.

Nan was the first to approach the Grahams, who were once again seated at the picnic table next to their cabin and chuckling over something one of them had just said.

"Hello," Nan said in greeting. "Isn't this a beautiful morning?"

Ed and Ione beamed up at her from their accustomed places.

"Splendid. Simply splendid!" Ed bellowed.

"But just a wee bit on the cool side, wouldn't you say?"

Ione asked. "We were just sitting here waiting for you two. Is your friend coming? There's hot coffee and muffins waiting for us inside."

"Here she comes," Nan answered, motioning toward Marley, who was approaching at a fast jog.

"Good morning," Marley said, coming to a sudden stop.

"You're a good runner," Ed said with delight. "Do you run often?"

"Almost daily when I'm at home," Marley answered.

"She runs marathons," Nan said. "She's done Boston's and others in the past, and she still does Grandma's Marathon in Duluth every year. However, in the last few years, she has limited her participation to the Minnesota Mile." Nan felt perfectly free to proudly boast of her friend's accomplishments because she knew Marley would never have done it herself. "Last year's winner was seventy years old, and she did it in under five minutes, with Marley right on her heels. I know because I was there cheering them on."

Ed's eyes crinkled with his smile. "Impressive!"

"You've heard the expression 'Strike while the iron is hot'?" Marley said. "Well, I run while I still can."

Ed and Ione laughed, and Ione rose to her feet. "All right," she said. "Everyone inside."

Marley and Nan followed Ione and Ed into a cabin that, although it was considerably smaller and more primitive than the cabin they were presently staying in, offered a cozy, warm, comfortable atmosphere in its rustic simplicity. They seated themselves at a round table that had been set with four coffee cups, a sugar bowl and creamer, silverware, paper napkins, and a plate of what looked like cranberry-nut muffins.

As Ed poured the coffee, Ione passed the muffins.

"Is it the fishing that brings you to this resort?" Nan asked, taking a muffin and placing it on the small plate before her. "Does one of the boats along the dock belong to you?"

Ione shook her head. "Oh no. We don't come during fishing season. Too crowded, and you won't find me putting any squiggly worms on any hooks." She then nodded at Ed, who was seated to her right. "And you won't find this one putting them on for me either."

"I do fish some," Ed said. "But the main reason we come here is for the peace and quiet and the beauty of the area. Besides, unlike home, I don't have to do any chores when I'm here."

The couple threw back their heads and laughed in a way that Nan recognized as a pattern of their relationship.

"I see you're renting the real-house cabin. That's what we call it. Don't we, Ed?" Ione said, and Ed nodded. "We've often thought of upgrading to that one, but we're pretty used to this place. It's where we always stay."

"Old habits die hard," Ed replied.

Marley smiled and leaned in. "So it sounds as though you're regular visitors to this resort."

"Thirteen years so far," Ed said. "We're old-timers in more ways than one."

He and Ione laughed heartily again, and Marley took the opportunity to throw Nan a look that said, *Now the interrogation begins.*

Ione took a sip of coffee and then cradled the steaming mug in her hands. "We've been coming here long enough to see some serious changes in this place," she said.

"I can imagine," Marley replied.

"No, you can't!" Ione exclaimed, shaking her head. "You can't imagine how much things have changed since they came."

"Are you referring to the current owners?" Nan asked. "The Chapmans?"

"Of course I am," Ione said. "Who else?"

Ed leaned across the table and, placing the palm of one hand on one side of his mouth, said, "Ione doesn't cotton much to the Chapmans."

"With good reason, and you know it," Ione said, slapping his arm. "When the Tillers owned this place, there wasn't a year that Ed and I didn't notice some improvement each time we came. A new dock, a series of new paths through the woods, new fixtures in the bathrooms—there was always something. The Tillers treated this place with the care and concern needed to make this resort a pleasure to come to. With the Chapmans now, it seems as if they don't care at all. The place is getting run down, and it's just a crying shame!"

"We're considering not coming back next year," Ed said. "It just isn't the same."

"Things change," Ione said sadly. "And that's to be expected, but—" She shook her head and looked at them as if to ask, *What can you do?* Then, with a slight shake of her shoulders, she shook off her sadness and smiled brightly. "Your cabin, being on the hill, must have the best view of the lake in the entire resort," she said. "In fact, I'm surprised the Chapmans didn't select it for their personal use. But then, it's almost always been rented when we've been here in the past, and I suppose they didn't want to give up the money."

Ed poured himself and Ione more coffee. He would have filled Nan's and Marley's cups also, but theirs were still more than half full. "I may as well warn you now," he told their visitors. "Ione and I are heavy coffee drinkers. We drink coffee all throughout the day."

"Don't tell them our secret faults!" Ione chortled gleefully. "You'll scare them away."

"They don't look like folks who would scare too easily," Ed said, looking from Nan to Marley.

"I guess not," Ione said. "Seeing as how they rented cabin number eight."

Ed poured cream into his coffee and stirred it with his spoon. "Good thing there's two of you instead of one of you alone. It seems a woman alone in that place just plain ain't healthy."

Nan decided to play dumb. Looking from Ed to Ione and back again, she tried her best to sound calm, though her spine was tingling. She asked, "Are you saying the two women who disappeared from this resort both stayed in our cabin? At cabin number eight?"

"Now you've done it, Ed," Ione said with a sigh. "You've scared them good."

"No. No, we're interested. Really, we are. Tell us more," Nan said, hoping they would oblige. "We thought the two events or the people might be connected, but we never thought a particular cabin, or even this exact resort, would have anything to do with the disappearances."

Marley nodded. "From everything I've read, whatever happened to those two women happened away from this resort. They were on the road, heading back to the cities, when they vanished, weren't they? So wouldn't the fact that they just happened to stay in the same cabin be a mere coincidence?"

Ed shrugged. "Me? I don't put much faith in coincidences."

"Neither do I," Ione said. "I've always said there's no such thing as a coincidence. No. That cabin you're staying in is the key to the whole mystery. I'd bet my life on it."

"But how?" Nan asked.

Ione pursed her lips and scratched her head. "Well, I haven't figured out the *how* yet, only that it is."

"Were you able to meet both of the women who disappeared?" Marley asked.

"We got to know the younger one quite well," Ione said. "Didn't we, Ed? Her name was Lynn. She was real young, friendly, and talkative. The first woman, the older one, was much quieter. She liked to stay to herself."

"You never spoke to her?" Nan asked.

"Ed spoke to her once," Ione said. "He went over to the cabin and invited her for coffee. But she told him she didn't drink coffee."

"She was real nice about it," Ed said. "She wasn't rude or anything. But she left me with the definite impression that she wanted to be left alone."

"Of course," Ione said, "as she was just up the road and hill from us, we would see her from time to time. She liked to take early morning walks along the paths, and well, she just naturally had to pass our cabin."

"If you don't mind my asking," Nan said, "what's your take on all this? You must have a theory."

"Good Lord Almighty," Ed said. "Don't get Ione started. After interviewing us two, the police seemed more than a little annoyed that she'd already solved the entire case for them. I mean, she thinks she has it signed, sealed, and delivered."

Ione reached over and slapped one of his hands. "Now, you just stop that. I don't have anything sewn up. But I do have my suspicions."

"Care to elaborate?" Nan said, drawing out the question.

"Well, since you asked," Ione said excitedly. "Here's what I think. First, we had the woman writing teacher up here, with the bird-watching and the binoculars at all hours of the day and night."

"And those weren't any tiny go-to-the-theater-type binoculars she used either," Ed said. "The ones she had could see clear across the bay to the whole of the big lake. I know because I've used that brand of binoculars before."

Ione took a bite of her muffin and chewed slowly. She raised her napkin to the corner of her mouth, lowered it back into her lap, and said, "She brought her own bird feeders to the resort. And she brought her own seed too. Ed saw them. He saw them hanging in the trees next to the cabin's screen porch. It was all birds with her. She didn't seem to have any other interests that we could tell."

Marley looked across the table at Ed. "Did she attract a variety of birds with the feeders?"

Ed shrugged. "I don't know about variety, but she sure attracted a flock of them. In fact, it was their noise and fluttering about that made me notice her feeders in the first place. Funny thing is, the birds she was most interested in were the eagles."

Ione laughed. "That's right. And who ever heard of an eagle visiting a bird feeder?"

"Oh, are there eagles around here?" Nan asked. "I've always thought they preferred rivers rather than lakes."

"Lakes, rivers—it doesn't matter," Ed said. "They both

have fish in them, don't they? Open water and fish—that's all an eagle needs to be happy."

"There used to be a big eagles' nest in the cove, you know," Ione said. "It was on that island in the bay, and it was huge. You couldn't miss it. It was perched at the very top of one of the island's three pines."

Nan and Marley looked at each other, and each knew what the other was thinking. "The nest was at the very top of one of the three pines on the island?" Nan repeated.

"That's right."

"Oh, I would love to see an eagles' nest again," Marley said. "I haven't seen one in years." Turning to Nan, she asked, "Did we bring a set of binoculars, Nan?"

Nan, knowing Marley knew as well as she did that they were equipped with Sean's night-vision binoculars, lied. "Afraid not," she said, shaking her head.

"Wouldn't do you any good if you had," Ed told them. "The nest's no longer there. It's gone. The eagles too."

"Gone? Isn't that unusual?" Marley said in surprise. "I thought they used the same nest year after year."

"They do," Ed said. "And those two eagles did use that nest for years. But well, who knows what happened? Ione and I figure there must have been a big storm. One that destroyed the nest so entirely they moved on rather than rebuilding."

"So the eagles only recently left the island?" Nan asked.

"Yeah. This will be the first spring without them," Ed said. Looking at Nan quizzically, he asked, "Are you interested in eagles?"

"Not really," Nan answered, "but disappearances are always interesting, aren't they? Whether they concern people

117

or birds." She turned to Ione and said, "I'm sorry, but I'm not following you. It seems to me that we've wandered from the original subject. Earlier, you were going to share with us your theory regarding the disappearances of the women."

"And I am," Ione said, reaching out to give Nan's arm a patronizing squeeze. "I needed to bring up the first woman and her love for birds before anything else because, well, where her disappearance is concerned, the two go together. The first woman's disappearance is the key to the second's disappearance, you see. It all has to do with the cabin and the birds. That's where it all started."

Nan blinked hard and, in an attempt not to stare, shifted her gaze from Ione to Ed and back again. "It all started with the cabin and the birds? That's the key?"

"But once again, how?" Marley said, leaning across the table. "How is that the key?"

Ione threw back her head and laughed heartily, and Ed joined her. "Well, I told you. I haven't figured that part out yet. All I know is, you can count on it. It's as good as solid gold that you can take to the bank."

Ed, still chuckling, said, "Talk about facts. Here's another interesting fact for you. Although that teacher woman was good at drawing birds to her, she sure didn't attract male attention like the other one."

Ione gave Ed a sharp look. "Now, don't go spreading gossip about Lynn. There's nothing strange about a young girl liking sex."

"Did I say there was?" Ed replied. "You're the one who made a big deal out of seeing Lyman sneaking out of her cabin at five in the morning."

"I told you, Ed. He wasn't sneaking," Ione said. "He was simply returning to his own place after spending the night."

Nan gave Marley a knowing look. "Who is Lyman?" she asked.

"Professor Lyman," Ione answered. "He lives on the other side of the ravine and frequents the resort's restaurant and bar at times. That's where Ed and I first met him. He's a nice guy. Well spoken, intelligent, and handsome as all get-out. I can see why Lynn took to him."

"And you saw him leave Lynn Parker's cabin at five o'clock one morning?" Marley asked.

"More than one morning," Ione said with a little smile.

"Do you usually get up that early?" Marley asked.

"Well, we bring our own coffeepot, and I set it to come on at a quarter to five. If I'm up and happen to smell that coffee, I pad out and have myself a cup. Then I usually go back to bed. But while I'm having my coffee, I like sitting in the dark and looking out the window. I don't turn any lights on, because that way, if I'm lucky, I might see a fox or a deer or even a falling star or two."

"Or some guy sneaking out the back of a cabin while holding his shoes in one hand and zipping up his pants with the other," Ed said with a smirk.

Ione swatted the air in front of him. "Stop it, Ed! Stop making it sound much worse than it was. It wasn't like that, and you know it."

But Ed wasn't backing down. "What about you-know-who with the pickup? Didn't you tell me he also visited Lynn Parker?"

Ione shook her head. "You mean in her cabin? No! I never saw any such thing. I never said that. I told you that when I visited the small store here at the resort, I saw Lynn in the bar, chatting that man up and drinking a beer with him in the afternoon."

At the word *pickup*, Nan perked up. Thinking of the man she and Marley had seen on their walk last evening, she asked, "This guy in the pickup—does he have a name?"

"Sure he does, but I don't want to repeat it," Ed said. "And I'd advise you not to ask."

Ione gave them both a little, apologetic smile. "You'll have to forgive Ed. He doesn't have anything good to say about the guy. He's a bad one."

"Is he a local? Does he live around here?"

"He lives close enough so he feels he can hang around the resort a lot," Ed replied.

"He sure seems to like his beer," Ione said. "I think he might be friends with Mr. Chapman."

"What makes you say that?" Marley asked.

"Well," Ione said, "besides seeing him with Mr. Chapman around the resort, Ed and I have noticed the two of them at that café just outside Brainerd. What's it called? The Roadside Café?"

"That's right," Ed answered. "Handy place for lunch when you're shopping in Brainerd. Great food too."

Marley raised an eyebrow. "We happened to eat at that café on our way to the resort. I wonder—does this man drive a white pickup truck?"

"Why, yes, he does," Ed said. "Don't tell me you know him."

"I don't know him," Nan answered with a frown. "But we may have come across him. What does this pickup-truck guy look like?"

"He's not your typical, run-of-the-mill fellow," Ed said. "I mean, you can't miss this guy. He's tall, with shoulders on him like a moose, and he's got a way about him that's a mite off-putting."

"I suspect he's just plain mean," Ione said. "He always looks like he's ready for a fight, if you ask me."

"That's him," Nan said, looking at Marley. "He's the guy who butted in line in front of Marley at the café and practically knocked her over."

"Sounds like something he'd do," Ed said. "I'd stay clear of him if I were you."

"Yeah, better to give someone like that a wide berth," Ione added.

"Don't worry. We will," Marley said.

After a few pleasantries when the coffee was drained from their cups and their muffins had been reduced to nothing more than crumbs on their plates, Nan and Marley rose from the table.

"Thank you so much for the coffee and muffins and for the interesting conversation," Marley said. "Feel free to stroll up the hill and visit us at any time. We'd love to have another chat. You can sit on our deck and judge for yourself how great the view is."

Nan smiled and nodded. "Speaking of Brainerd reminded us that we need to take a drive there to do some shopping of our own."

"Go to Super One," Ione said. "It's big, well stocked, and reasonably priced."

"Thanks for the tip," Marley replied. "We'll be sure to look for it."

Ed and Ione rose, and as Ed gathered cups and saucers,

Ione walked them to the door. As Nan and Marley walked up the hill to their so-called real-house cabin, they made a point of turning to give Ione, who was still standing at her cabin's door, a parting wave.

"Well, that was informative," Marley said.

"Very," Nan responded. "So are we driving into Brainerd, as we told Ed and Ione? Or do you have something else entirely in mind?"

"Forget Brainerd for the moment. Right now, we need to write down everything we've just learned from Ione and Ed. And I want to call Eva to give her the latest information, including the license plate number of the fellow we saw last night. As I recall, the man who came to our rescue at the Roadside Café called him Mr. Sykes."

"I wish the man had given us his full name, but even so, Eva should be able to discover it from the license plate. He has to be the same guy Ione said she saw Lynn with at the resort bar, drinking beer," Nan said excitedly. "Are you thinking what I'm thinking?"

"That if Lynn was interested in him, we need to be interested in him as well? Yes, of course. And I'm sure Eva will be able to supply us with not only a name but a location for the lout as well. We need to know the answers to both."

"While you're calling Eva, I think I'll try to reach Sylvie and Joe to check up on how well my boys are settling in," Nan said.

"And once we finish with all that," Marley said, "then we'll drive into Brainerd. Remember, we still need to get that map and more food."

"Sounds like a plan," Nan replied.

CHAPTER 10

As they drove into the shopping centers in town, Nan regaled Marley with an account of Rumpole and Bailey's dirty trick on her kindly neighbors.

"Remember when those two scamps pulled that disappearing act on me?" Nan turned slightly toward her friend with a chuckle while steering Agatha along the country roads. "I was frantic. To this day, wherever they managed to hide that I could not find in my own house is a mystery! Just wait; I'll eventually get a call when those naughty boys return to the kitchen or living room. Poor Sylvie and Joe."

"I'm sure they are likely more than a bit upset, just as you were," replied Marley.

It did not take long to complete the errands that had brought them into Brainerd, and after those few necessary stops, they drove back to cabin number eight for a short nap before taking a leisurely stroll down one of the many paths winding throughout the resort. Since they had yet to encounter their host Dale Chapman, they watched for anyone working about the place. But Eagle's Cove continued to be a quiet place with little to no activity.

Later that evening, they agreed to change and eat dinner out. The option they settled on, one of several possibilities for meals at night, was about a mile and a half down the road from the resort. They picked it more for its convenience and its location right on the lake than any expectation of gourmet cuisine. It was called Ojibwa Point. From the outside, it appeared to be a casual, boxy place, the kind that offered glorified bar food, such as pizza and calzone sandwiches. But in fact, once inside, they could see it featured more upscale decor and offerings that included the house special: a lightly battered, deep-fried piece of walleye that came either in a sandwich or as a fillet with fries.

"Do you think there's a possibility they serve a decent house wine?" Marley whispered to Nan as they entered the front door.

"I haven't the foggiest idea," Nan whispered back. "But I'm sure they have at least thirty different kinds of beer."

Although it was close to eight o'clock, which they considered prime dining time, the restaurant was nearly empty. Obviously, the dinner crowd came and left between five and seven. A smiling hostess approached and directed them to a table where she told them that since the restaurant was west-facing, had they arrived earlier, they would have been able to watch the sun set across the big lake. Marley and Nan, now realizing why the dinner crowd chose to eat earlier, made a note to come back again another evening to view the sunset.

They both ordered walleye with fries and slaw rather than a green salad. Since the restaurant served unsatisfactory red and white wine options according to their preferences in vintage, both women opted for a Sam Adams Light.

After the waitress departed with their order, Marley leaned back in her chair and took a closer look around the bar and restaurant. She was surprised by the place's interior, admitting to herself that it was a cut above the typical up-north beer joint. The walls were of knotty pine, with exposed rafters above and hanging glass-shaded lights with etched Native American designs. Taking up almost the entire east wall was a natural stone fireplace with a raised hearth, displaying split logs of wood stacked within arched alcoves on each side. The fire appeared to be from a gas burner, but the flames flickered beautifully, lending a warm appeal to the room. Above the alcoves containing logs were built-in bookshelves lined with leather-backed books. Hanging above the mantel was a gigantic sculpture of an eagle in flight, with its wings spread out wide and its wingtips upturned.

While Marley surveyed her surroundings, seemingly lost in thought, Nan watched the restaurant's entrance. The door opened, and suddenly, she glimpsed a familiar form. Touching Marley's hand, she leaned over and whispered, "Look. There's the man who came to our aid the other day at the Roadside Café."

Marley turned, and Nan noticed a look of surprise cross her face. "Well," Marley muttered, "I never expected to see him again. I wonder if he has a summer home nearby or, better yet, actually lives here. Should we ask him to join us for dinner?"

"Sure," Nan said. "If he's from around here, maybe we can learn something."

Marley waited for the man to seat himself at the bar before she rose and walked over to him. "Hello there," she said, smiling widely and holding out a hand. "My name is Marley Phillips. Do you remember my friend and me from yesterday?" She turned and motioned toward Nan, who smiled widely and lifted her water glass toward them as a form of salutation.

The man glanced past her toward Nan and smiled. "Of course I remember," he said, reaching for Marley's hand and giving it a firm shake. "I'm Lyman Haynes."

At the mention of his name, Marley felt her mouth begin to open but was able to catch it mid-drop before the man could notice. *This must be the Lyman the Grahams were speaking of earlier,* she thought. *The one who made nocturnal visits to Lynn Parker.*

"How are you two ladies getting along?" he asked. "Not still being bothered by Mr. Sykes, I hope?"

"Not presently," Marley replied. "But we were wondering, if you haven't already eaten, whether we might buy you dinner as a way of thanking you for your help at the Roadside Café."

"There's no need to buy my dinner," Lyman said. "But I'd be glad to join you and your friend. Actually, I'd appreciate the company."

As they crossed the room toward Nan, Marley tried to send a subtle sign to warn her to be on her guard. However, although she made a sideways roll of her eyes as she tipped her head toward Lyman, Nan didn't seem to pick up on the message she was trying to send and only looked quizzically at her.

When they were at the table, Marley looked up at

Lyman and said, "This is my friend Nan Abbott." Then, turning toward Nan, she quickly said, "And, Nan, let me introduce you to Lyman Haynes. He was kind enough to accept our offer to join us for dinner."

Marley noticed Nan's eyes widen slightly at the name Lyman but was relieved to see how quickly she gained control of herself. Nan held out a hand. "Hello, Mr. Haynes," she said. "It's great to finally get the chance to meet our hero."

"Please call me Lyman. And as for the hero thing, it was nothing. Believe me."

Marley and Lyman seated themselves, and Lyman pulled out Marley's chair in a gentlemanly fashion. Once seated, Marley spread her napkin across her lap and asked, "Are you visiting the area like us, Lyman, or do you live here?"

"I live here. I have a house on Eagle's Cove."

"You live on Eagle's Cove?" Marley said, sounding pleased. "Well, isn't it a small world? Nan and I happen to be staying at Eagle's Cove Resort."

"Are you now?" Lyman said. "And what brings you up to Eagle's Cove Resort? You do know its history, don't you?"

"Oh my," Nan said lightly. "There's a history? You mean besides the fact that the resort has been established since the 1930s?"

Lyman smiled. "I wasn't talking about its historical significance. I'm referring to another sort of significance entirely."

"And what would that be?" Marley asked, feigning ignorance.

"Why, the mystery, of course," Lyman said with a groan.

"The blasted everlasting mystery that never seems to go away."

Nan frowned. "Mystery? Why, Eagle's Cove Resort, with its fire pit, shuffleboard court, and badminton net appears to be the least mysterious place I've ever seen. It's pure Americana. Nothing Gothic about it."

Lyman brushed a lock of hair from his forehead. "Don't be too sure about that. The disappearance of two women from that very resort is, in my opinion, mysterious."

Marley drew back her head. "Oh, you're speaking of the two women who failed to return home, aren't you? The two women who are still missing? But from what I read in the newspapers, their disappearances had nothing at all to do with a particular place. They were said to have disappeared after leaving a resort up here, not from the resort."

"That's right," Nan said. "We certainly wouldn't have booked at the resort if we thought something had happened to them on its premises. And who knows? It just may be that they'll both show up someday safe and sound. They're adults, after all, and people have been known to disappear of their own accord."

"Some people simply feel the need to get away, to take a needed break," Marley added.

"And some," Nan said, "have a temporary mental breakdown or a sudden bout of amnesia, much like what happened to Agatha Christie at a stressful time in her life. Back then, everyone thought something tragic had happened to her, and it turned out she was staying at a posh hotel all the while."

At the appearance of a waitress, their conversation came to a close. She carried a small tray in her hands, upon which three glasses clinked together. Setting their drinks before them, she said, "Two Samuel Adams Lights for the ladies, and I brought you your usual Sapphire and tonic with a lime twist, Lyman."

"Thanks, June," he responded, flashing his handsome smile.

She turned to Marley and Nan. "Your meals will be ready shortly, ladies." Then, turning back to Lyman, she asked, "Should I bring your usual sandwich to the table, Professor, or are you going to eat at the bar?"

"Here is fine. Thank you," Lyman answered.

She lingered for a moment and then said, "Couldn't help but overhear you talking about the disappearances. Seems like everyone has a theory."

Marley smiled up at her. "Do you have one?" she asked. To her surprise, the waitress didn't answer and instead turned and headed toward the kitchen but not without first giving her a wink.

Nan, who had missed the wink and wished the waitress had hung around to continue her comments, turned her attention back to Lyman. "You're a professor?" she asked with delight. "What and where do you teach?"

"I teach American history at the nearby community college. But you sound surprised. Why? Don't I look like a professor?"

Nan blushed. "It's not that. It's just, well, I'm in the same line of work. I taught for many years in the metro area. I taught fine art and some theater."

Lyman raised a closed fist for a bump of solidarity. "Always pleased to meet a fellow professor. Are you as poor as I am?"

"You know it," Nan replied with a laugh.

As Nan and Lyman began to trade stories about the rigors of academia, Marley noticed the flirtatious nature of their exchange. Given their age difference, she was amused but disregarded it, until she heard the swish of the waitress's uniform as she brought their meals to the table. The attractive young server set their plates before them and addressed a general question to the table of whether there was anything else they might need. At Lyman's request, she turned and headed back toward the kitchen to bring him the extra mayonnaise he almost never requested.

Concerned they were getting off the subject uppermost in her mind, Nan turned toward Lyman and asked, "So have you solved the women's disappearances yet? Or is it still all just a mystery to you?"

"Still a mystery, I'm afraid," Lyman replied. "And I'd like it to go away. It's become burdensome."

"I suppose after two years, the thing does begin to get a bit old," Nan said.

"And yet I'm sure everyone wants a satisfactory resolution," Marley said.

"Is there one?" Lyman asked. "There seems to be a lot of talk and many suspicions but no solid answers to all the questions."

Marley looked up at the waitress, who had returned to their table. Once again, she asked her, "How about you? Have you solved these disappearances yet?"

"Solved them a year ago yesterday," she replied swiftly.

Lyman tossed back his head and laughed, and to Marley's dismay, the waitress once again walked away.

Marley and Nan glanced at each other, and each

resolved to allot time in the near future to further question the waitress, June.

Marley decided to broach another subject and said to Lyman, "I wonder if you might know of someplace where I might have access to the internet. I brought my laptop in order to keep up with my email, but unfortunately, Eagle's Cove Resort doesn't have the best internet connection."

"It doesn't seem to be the Chapmans' top priority," he replied. "Either that, or they're waiting until the season starts to put out the money for a good connection. What cabin are you staying in?"

"Number eight. The large one that's farthest from the resort's office. Why do you ask?"

"Well, it just so happens that my property is on the other side of the ravine next to your cabin. In fact, the bridge to the left of your cabin crosses the creek and leads to my home. I'm on the other side of the woods."

"Oh?" Nan said. "So the path I spotted must lead to your house."

Lyman nodded. "Yes, that's right." He averted his eyes from hers, and Nan wondered what he was thinking. Then he once again leveled his brown-eyed gaze upon her to say, "By the way, did you know the cabin you're presently staying in is the same one the two women rented? I'm talking again of the two women who disappeared."

"Really? Well, that's a bit creepy," Nan said. She turned toward Marley and, feigning a slight level of anxiety, asked, "Do you think we ought to find another resort entirely?"

Marley shook her head. "Where would we find another cabin with all the amenities we are enjoying at this late date?"

Perhaps in the hope of a subject change, Lyman turned to look at Nan and asked, "Did you know that particular cabin was moved across the lake one winter to where it now sits? Can you imagine the ice being so thick a truck could actually drag a home across it?"

But Marley was not interested in the previous location of cabin number eight. From what Ed and Ione had revealed earlier, she wanted to know more about how the professor would describe his relationship with Lynn Parker and whether he had known or become friendly with Suzanne Engelmann. "How do you know our cabin was where the women stayed?" she asked. "Did the newspaper stories up here have all those details? I don't remember reading anything about a particular cabin in the metro papers."

"As I told you, I live just over the creek," Lyman said. "And I come over to the resort quite frequently. So I had ample opportunity to meet both of the women at one time or another. In fact, I allowed the last woman to access my Wi-Fi connection. She would use the footbridge and sit at my picnic table on the knoll. It's a nice spot to work. From there, it was easy for her to pirate my internet connection. You're welcome to do the same if you wish."

"We're neighbors then!" Nan exclaimed, looking pleased.

"We are," Lyman replied.

Marley, who always wanted more information, looked at him quizzically. "Is that how you first met her? Did you just come across her sitting at your picnic table one day?"

"No, I met her here, as a matter of fact. The same way I met you two. After we visited a bit, she complained of the poor internet connection at the resort, and I made her the same offer I just made you," Lyman said.

"That was kind of you." Marley smiled approvingly. She fingered the napkin on her lap and then asked hesitantly, "Did you say it was the younger of the two women who pirated your connection? My memory fails me."

"Yes. Her name was—er, is—Lynn Parker," Lyman said.

He ran a hand through his hair, and as he did so, Marley couldn't help but notice his long fingers. Being married to a musician, she appreciated the importance of an octave reach in a person's hands and wondered if he played the piano.

He continued. "And yeah, she was a writer and had been presently working on a book. She wanted to be able to use Google for research, among other things."

He looked uncomfortable with the questioning, and Marley told herself she would need to proceed with caution. "From what I recall, the first woman, Professor Engelmann, taught creative writing. Isn't it an odd coincidence that they were both interested in the same discipline?"

Lyman didn't answer, and Marley told herself he was hesitating to such a degree that their questioning might need to come to an end.

Nan, however, didn't see it that way. She leaned forward and asked, "Did you meet Professor Engelmann here as well? Like you did Lynn Parker?"

Marley held her breath, hoping they hadn't gone too far, not wanting Lyman to see them as annoyingly persistent interlocutors.

But Lyman simply shook his head. "No, I never met Ms. Engelmann formally. I did run across her on the resort path a few times, and we exchanged greetings. But that was all. From what I hear, she was a bit of a recluse."

Marley said, "Some news reports implied she had just left a bad marriage."

"Well, that would explain her need for solitude," Lyman said.

"Was Lynn Parker published?" Nan asked.

"No," Lyman said. "She had high aspirations, though."

"What did she write? Any particular genre?"

Lyman looked down at his plate. His voice, when he spoke, was tinged with considerably more emotion than he had displayed before. He seemed uncomfortable with their questions and with the sound of his own voice. Marley wondered if he wanted to hide the depth of his feelings for Lynn Parker or if he had another reason for his uneasiness. Regardless, the discomfort did not go unnoticed by either Marley or Nan.

"She seemed to be interested in people and history," Lyman said. "I think her writing was oriented toward mystery and crime. But that's just speculation on my part. All I know is, looking back, I now realize she asked a lot of questions about the first woman's disappearance."

Just then, June, their waitress, arrived with Lyman's dessert, a big piece of apple pie, and Lyman changed the conversation to the beauty of the surrounding countryside and the scenery that could be seen out the window during the daytime.

After Nan and Marley agreed with his assessment of the awesome beauty of the lake region, he then asked, "Have you two been introduced to the owners of the resort? The Chapmans?"

Marley shook her head. "No, not beyond checking in, and then we met only Mrs. Chapman. It would appear Mr. Chapman doesn't spend a lot of time at the resort."

"It's fair to say that," Lyman said. "He is gone a lot. But I ask because I feel I should warn you. The man who tried to wrestle his way in line at the Roadside Café, Buck Sykes, is a frequent visitor of the Chapmans. So you'll probably see him around the resort."

"I can't believe Mrs. Chapman is a friend of that bozo!" Nan said, hoping to gain more information on Buck Sykes.

Lyman nodded in agreement. "I don't know about Christy or how friendly she is with him, but I've seen Sykes with Dale Chapman in town a lot, as well as on the lake fishing."

"Thanks for the warning," Marley said, making a mental note of the fact that Lyman had called Mrs. Chapman by her first name, Christy. "I must say, I'm not looking forward to encountering that particular person again. Does he live nearby?"

"Yes. He lives on a farm a short distance from the resort. His farm is known as the 'old Baker place' and has been in his mother's family for generations."

"He didn't seem like a farmer to me," Nan said. "Farming is hard work and calls for patience. This guy couldn't even wait his turn in line."

Lyman laughed. "He doesn't do much farming anymore. Sykes's dad was the farmer, but he's been an invalid ever since his wife died a few years back. I think he had a stroke or something. Anyway, he stays inside and never goes anywhere. But as for Buck Sykes, if your car breaks down, he's the guy to call. Locally, he's known as a pretty good shade-tree mechanic, meaning he makes a living by working on folks' cars."

Marley, who was always loath to give the impression that she and Nan were pumping someone for information, began to make lighter and more general conversation. Nan followed her lead. At an opportune time, Marley slipped away from the table in order to pay the bill before Lyman could object.

When they had finished their coffee, Nan and Marley rose from the table. They cheerfully declined Lyman's offer to buy them both an after-dinner drink at the bar, pleading exhaustion after a long day. They said their goodbyes, and Nan was able to give him a little flirtatious flip of her head as they headed for the door.

CHAPTER 11

THE NEXT MORNING, MARLEY PLACED her phone on the table before her and then slowly rotated her head in order to stretch the tight muscles in her neck. "Well, that's that," she said. "Eva gave me the information we needed, including the bully's full name. It's William Baker Sykes, a.k.a. Buck, and she also gave us the correct coordinates for the old Baker place, so we can program our GPS to direct us there."

Nan glanced at her watch. "It's almost ten o'clock. Let's go now to check out one of the three casinos in these parts. There's one just outside Brainerd. We can ask around to see if anyone remembers Suzanne or Lynn ever being there. It won't hurt to look into it. On the way there, we can scope out Sykes's place. And on the way back, we can stop for a late lunch at Ojibwa Point and try to talk to that waitress again. What did Lyman say her name was?"

"He called her June," Marley said. "But if she's on the night shift like she was last evening, she might not start work until three or more."

"Right. I didn't think of that," Nan said. "Tell you what.

Let's get to the restaurant by two o'clock. We can order a late lunch and go to the bar afterward for a quick beer. That way, we should catch her whether she's on the day or the night shift."

"Sounds like a plan," Marley said. "But before we leave, I think we need to make a visit to the resort's bar and plant one of Sean's bugs. You never know when we may need to overhear a conversation taking place there."

"I know, and I've been thinking along those lines as well," Nan said. "But here's my question: Won't the two bugs, the one in the bar and the one under the Chapmans' dining room table, interfere with each other? What if we pick up multiple conversations? How will we ever be able to tell them apart and sort them out?"

"That could be a problem, but what other option do we have?" Marley asked with a frown. "I think it's worth the risk of the possibility of interference. Beggars can't be choosers. I just hope there's room under that bar for me to attach a bug."

Nan placed the brochure for the casino they would be visiting after their stop in her purse and headed for the door to the cabin. Marley placed Sean's hearing device in her right ear and tucked her hair behind her ear so the device was visible. Then she threw her purse over her shoulder and followed Nan out the door.

When they were sitting in the car and buckled up, Nan started the engine, and Marley asked, "What's the name of the casino we'll be visiting this morning?"

"First Nation," Nan replied. "It's farther from the resort than the others. I figured when it came to scouting out each of the three gambling joints, we'd start there and work our way back."

They continued on their way down the gravel road, and when they drove up to the resort's bar, Nan parked Agatha under a clump of birch trees. The women wandered into the combination bar and café.

Christy Chapman was behind the bar, speaking to several weary-looking fellows hunched over beers. She looked astonished to see Marley and Nan in the bar at noon, and they tried to take no notice of her as they walked toward the back of the room. Nan selected a cellophane-wrapped package of doughnuts off a shelf that also held a jar of instant coffee, bread, and a few other items, which must have constituted the so-called store Ione had mentioned. Then they slid onto seats at the bar.

Christy left the men and approached her surprise visitors. Placing a bar napkin in front of each of them, she asked, "What can I get you two?"

Nan, smiling brightly, replied, "We just had the best walk and are absolutely parched. Two tall glasses of something icy cold with no alcohol, please."

"Cola OK?" Christy asked.

"That will do nicely," Marley answered.

Mrs. Chapman turned her back to them for a moment, and Nan expected to see Marley slip a bug out of her pocket and place it under the bar. But to her surprise, Marley sat motionless. When Christy turned back to face them, she held two tall glasses filled with ice and two bottled sodas, which she promptly brought over. Nan and Marley each took a long sip of the cool beverages. Then Marley wiped her face with her napkin and said, "That was so refreshing. It was just what we needed after our walk."

"Have you always lived up north?" Nan blurted out to Christy, who seemed out of place in a rustic bar.

"No," Christy replied, giving no further information.

"I ask," Nan said, "because I'm such a tenderfoot when it comes to the wilderness. I'm a city girl myself. And I have to admit I don't know how anyone can live up here year-round. Especially when one considers the extremes of Minnesota weather."

The resort owner smiled slightly but still said nothing.

Marley decided to get down to business. "Do you ever visit the cities?" she asked. "Either Minneapolis or Saint Paul?"

"Nope," Christy answered shortly.

"Really? You mean you never go down for the theaters or restaurants or to a sporting event or anything like that?" Nan asked with a note of amazement befitting her city-girl self-description.

"Nope. Too busy and not that interested," their hostess snapped in reply. Then, with a gesture the women took to be clearly dismissive, she asked, "Anything else I can do for you?"

"No, that's fine. Thank you."

She left Nan and Marley and once again joined the men at the other end of the bar. The two sleuths finished their sodas and, after leaving some cash, slid off their stools and walked through the room toward the door.

When they were halfway to the door, Marley stopped Nan by grasping her elbow. "Don't you need to use the ladies' room before we go, Nan?" she asked, her voice a bit louder than usual.

Surprised, Nan quickly glanced toward the men at the bar and noticed two of them staring straight at her. Irritated with Marley at that moment for putting her in such an awkward position, she nevertheless cheerfully responded, "Yes, as a matter of fact, I do." Then, turning to face away from the exit, she said, "I won't be long," and she practically sprinted toward the restrooms in the back.

Marley moved toward one of the tables across from the bar. "I'll sit at this table and wait for you!" she called out. "Take your time."

Marley lowered herself into a chair at the center table of six that had been placed in a row along one side of the room. As she waited, she slipped a hand into her jacket pocket and took out one of Sean's bugs. Then she attached it firmly underneath the table.

Marley then saw a lone man enter the bar. After giving her a friendly nod and ignoring the men already there, he walked briskly to perch himself on one of the stools she and Nan had just left. Marley casually raised a hand to her right ear and turned up Sean's hearing device as far as it would go as Christy Chapman made her way toward the new arrival.

After a while, Nan returned from the restroom, and the two left and walked slowly to where Agatha sat in the parking lot.

Once seated in the car and strapped in, Nan quizzed her friend. "Were you able to plant a bug under that center table in the bar? I assume that's what you wanted to do when you sent me to the restroom."

"Absolutely!" Marley exclaimed. "You didn't think I only

had your comfort in mind when I made that suggestion, did you?"

"No, by now, I can read you pretty well," Nan said. "But why was I the one who had to use the restroom? It's you older women who have to use the biffy a lot, or so I've been told."

Marley threw Nan a harsh stare. "A few months, Nan," she said through gritted teeth. "That's all. I'm only a few months older than you."

At another time, Marley would have laughed at Nan's little joke, but that day, it was clear something was bothering her. Nan decided it would be wise to change the subject.

Marley must have made the same decision, because in the next breath, she said, "I was able to check out Sean's listening device while you were away. A man happened to enter the bar and sit on the exact stool where you were sitting. When Ms. Congeniality herself approached him, I'm happy to report I could hear every single word they said. No problem."

Nan shook her head in wonder. "That Sean is a wizard," she said. "Did they say anything interesting?"

"No. But at least we now know Sean's device works. And that's something."

"Yes, it is."

Marley fell silent, and Nan started the motor of her little green car, but before pulling out of the parking lot, she looked over at her friend and said, "Anything particular on your mind, Marley? You seem to be miles away."

Marley frowned. "It's the lying. I really don't like all the lying. For example, did you happen to notice the scent Christy Chapman was wearing in the bar back there?"

"Yeah, as a matter of fact, I did. It was nice."

"It was nice all right," Marley said. "It happened to be Roja's Aoud."

"I wouldn't know," Nan said. "Why? Is it important?"

Marley looked at Nan in surprise. "Nan, that perfume is priced at two hundred dollars an ounce."

It was Nan's turn to look surprised. "You're kidding me!" She snorted in befuddlement. "How can someone like Christy Chapman wear a perfume that costly? How could she possibly afford it?"

"Precisely," said Marley. "Do you know what I think? The fact that she sports an expensive haircut and wears a rich perfume only goes to confirm my suspicion that she and her husband have a lot more money than they want people to know about."

CHAPTER 12

NAN MANEUVERED AGATHA DOWN THE resort road and out onto County Road C.

"You know," Nan said, "I'm glad we picked up that map yesterday in Brainerd. I know Eva gave us the coordinates for Sykes's place, but I'm old-fashioned. Like you, I appreciate the bigger picture that a map affords. Besides, how much can we trust the GPS? I don't want us wandering about aimlessly and wasting valuable time because Google doesn't have a strong cell tower signal up here."

"According to Eva," Marley said, "Sykes lives just off County Road C, the road we're presently on. Actually, I think the road to the Sykes farm is the one just ahead."

Nan slowed Agatha to a crawl and then stopped along the shoulder as they came to a dirt road that entered from the left. "Is there a road sign? Yes, there is!" Nan shouted. "Oh, it's only a fire number. Well, what do you know? Sykes lives just up the road from the resort. No wonder he hangs around there so much. Should I turn in?"

Marley shook her head. "No, I think it's too soon. We'll try to examine Sykes's place later. For now, let's continue to the First Nation casino and then hopefully talk some more with June later at Ojibwa Point. I think we need more information before we even think of venturing onto Sykes's property."

Marley opened the glove compartment and took out the Crow Wing County map they had purchased the day before. She opened it and, running a finger along its surface, scanned it in search of County Road C. "Maps used to be plentiful," she said. "Every gas station had a rack full of them. Today they're as scarce as a witch's broom. Good thing I thought of going to the tourist information bureau in Brainerd. They had what we needed." She continued to scan the map and then let out a deep sigh and exclaimed, "Well, that can't be good!"

Nan turned her head sharply to look at her. "What is it? Bad news?"

Marley frowned. "It looks like the dirt road that goes into Sykes's farm has a dead end. It doesn't go through. I suspect that's why it's dirt and not paved."

Nan frowned as well. "Damn," she said. "It's never good not to have two exits, two ways out." Then, deciding to strike a positive note, she quickly added, "But we'll cope. We always do."

Marley didn't comment, and Nan was hoping to contribute another positive remark, when Marley suddenly blurted, "Did you happen to notice the egg sign?"

"The what sign?" Nan asked.

"The sign that was in the culvert. Didn't you see it? It was made of wood, with faded painted letters that said, 'Fresh Eggs for Sale.' It was on the side of the dirt road leading to Sykes's farm, just off County C."

"No, I didn't notice it. Sorry," Nan said. "I was looking at something else entirely and wondering how it might work for us later."

"Funny, but I was also thinking along those lines," Marley said. "Only I was wondering how that egg sign might work for us later."

As each became lost in her own thoughts, Nan steered onto the entrance ramp to Highway 371, which would lead them into the Brainerd and Baxter area.

After a while, she said to Marley, "Not to change the subject, but what are your thoughts about Professor Lyman's relationship with Lynn Parker?"

"You mean about him sleeping with her?" Marley said. "I don't know. Did you get any inkling that he was romantically involved with Lynn when he was talking to us about her last night?"

"Not really. But then, sleeping with someone, in my lexicon, doesn't mean the same as being romantically involved," Nan said.

"So you think Lyman is the type of man to bed someone he didn't care about?" Marley asked.

"I'm not saying that. I think he cared," Nan said. "He cared enough to want to engage in sex."

"I suppose, although he didn't seem to me to be that type," Marley replied.

Nan glanced over at Marley, wondering what type she had in mind. "Look," she muttered, "it's got to be lonely living by yourself up here year-round. What I'm saying is, I can't imagine a guy like Professor Lyman not taking advantage of someone who is attractive, young, smart, and as eager as he is to tumble into bed."

"And who doesn't happen to be one of his students," Marley said. "An important point if he wants to keep his job."

"Right," said Nan. "Besides, he is damn good looking—you've got to admit that."

Marley smiled. "Just the type an inexperienced woman would fall for. And an experienced one as well. Come on, Nan. Admit it. You found him attractive. I could tell."

"Well, of course I did," Nan said, sounding offended. "And I flirted with him too. Big deal. It was fun. With looks like his, a woman would have to be dead not to. And I'm far from being dead, my friend. Besides, I wanted to see how much of an ego he had. I'd say someone his age who'd flirt the way he did with a woman my age has a fairly gigantic ego. Wouldn't you agree?"

"I suppose," Marley replied. "That conversation also made me think there might very well be more than a sign of friendliness in the fact that he calls Mrs. Chapman by her first name. But on another topic, what did you think of the Grahams' information regarding Buck Sykes's friendship with Mr. Chapman?" Marley asked.

Nan said, "I found that interesting. But what we also need to know is what his relationship with Lynn Parker was, if any. I'd love to know what they were talking about in the bar when Ione said she saw them having a beer together. I don't see the two of them having much in common."

"I know what you mean," Marley said. "The man is such a jack-pine savage!"

Nan frowned. "A jack-pine what? Is that some slur on Native American people?"

"Good grief, I don't think so!" Marley replied emphatically. "Anyway, it's not how I meant it. I've always thought of it as a classic up-north phrase. It refers to people who live alone and off the grid and never rise to the level of civilization expected of one's neighbors."

"Off the grid?" Nan said. "But doesn't that mean no sewers and no electricity?"

"Listen, Nan," Marley said strongly. "He may live with plumbing and electricity, but in his manner and demeanor, Buck Sykes is a typical jack-pine savage as far as I'm concerned."

"Hey, you'll get no argument from me," Nan said, temporarily tossing her hands into the air before once again placing them firmly on the steering wheel.

"From what the Grahams said," Marley added, "Lynn had Lyman as a love interest. And you have to admit, comparing Lyman to Buck Sykes, Lyman is someone cut from an entirely different cloth."

"Right," Nan said. "But if, like Eva reported, Lynn Parker was planning to write a true-crime account of her professor's disappearance, then she must have considered the rough fellow she saw at the resort a possible suspect?"

"Correct," Marley answered. "But maybe she had an even deeper interest in Lyman than a good time. Maybe she found him a possible suspect as well. Have you ever thought about that?"

"I don't know. Have I?" Nan asked, turning to give Marley a quick glance. "Look, I don't like Buck Sykes. And for that reason alone, I'm placing him high on my list of suspects. But Lyman Haynes? He just doesn't seem the type to murder someone."

"You're biased," Marley said. "Because he's a fellow teacher, you don't want to believe it possible. But don't you see? He fits your profile perfectly. You've always it's the least suspicious person you have to watch out for."

"Yes, I know," Nan said. "But it doesn't always turn out to be the least likely suspect. Sometimes it's the one you thought was guilty all along."

"The thing is, at this point, we don't know who to suspect, so we must suspect them all. It can't be helped," Marley answered. "But we need to move with particular caution around this Mr. Sykes. The guy scares me."

"You're just feeling vulnerable because we don't have enough information on him yet," Nan said. "Let's see what the waitress, June, can tell us about both Lyman Haynes and Buck Sykes when we see her later today. Since these guys are both local, she should know quite a lot about each of them."

"Sounds like a plan," Marley said.

"Now," Nan said with emphasis, "I want to talk about something that's been on my mind. It has to do with Ione and Ed's comments about the eagles' nest on the island."

"What's your concern?" asked Marley.

"That question mark we found written in the book on divorce, the one written next to the word *Island*. You know, the one that keeps haunting us? There has to be some meaning for it. Some reason Suzanne wrote it."

"Maybe she was merely wondering what had happened to the eagles," Marley said.

"No, remember, Ed and Ione told us the eagles were still on the island when Suzanne was here."

"Oh, that's right. They hadn't left yet."

"I keep asking myself, what was it about that island that Suzanne questioned? And do you know what I tell myself?" Nan asked, turning her head, giving Marley a hard look.

"I can't imagine," Marley said.

Nan slapped the steering wheel hard and loudly answered, "I tell myself, damn it all, we're here to search and investigate. And if we're going to discover what significance, if any, that island held for Suzanne, we are not going to find it here onshore. We need to explore that island!"

Marley raised her hands in frustration. "And how are we going to do that? The last thing we want to do, Nan, is draw attention to ourselves. And I've given this a great deal of thought. We're on a gambling vacation, remember? Also, it's late April, well before fishing opener. If the two of us were suddenly to ask to use a boat, wouldn't people question it? Why would we want to go boating? Wouldn't it make people suspicious and draw unwanted attention our way?"

"Those are all good points," Nan said. "And I've thought of them as well. But why do we need to use a boat at all? Not when you could easily swim out to the island."

Marley couldn't believe what she was hearing. "Are you crazy?" she stammered.

But Nan continued, saying encouragingly, "C'mon. Don't underestimate yourself. It's not that far of a distance, and you did almost swim the English Channel, didn't you? Let's put all those trophies and honors lined up on the shelves in your den to good use! Skills such as yours don't fade away."

Marley shook her head. "The skills you speak of require daily training, and I haven't trained in years. Be realistic, Nan. My glory days in swimming are way past and far behind me now. Besides, even if I were to attempt it, I would need a wetsuit. The ice only recently went out on that lake, and the water would be frigid."

"Well," Nan said, "maybe you're right. But we can't get to the island by boat. Why would we want a boat? We already told Christy Chapman we don't fish. Besides, as you just said, it isn't even fishing season! A simple pleasure ride? Too risky. For the sake of safety, the Chapmans might very well offer to take us out on a cruise around the lake in their boat."

"Nan," Marley said, "I think it's wise to put searching the island aside for the present. I don't like the idea of acting in any way that might bring suspicion upon us. Remember, we're two women who traveled north for a gambling holiday and to maybe do a painting or two and nothing more."

Nan knew Marley's assessment to be correct, but she couldn't extinguish the strong feeling she had that a visit to the island was necessary.

Soon they arrived at First Nation casino, and they felt fortunate to find a parking spot about a block from the casino entrance. Once inside, they spent the next hour and a half among the flashing lights and ringing chimes, wandering throughout a large space filled with slot machines. They walked around while dropping quarters into various machines and chatting purposefully with fellow gamblers as well as employees.

Their interrogations, however, proved fruitless. Although some of the locals knew all about the women and the case, no one had actually ever met either of them, nor could anyone recall having seen them at the casino.

When Nan and Marley noticed they needed to move quickly if they were to get back to Ojibwa Point by two o'clock in order to catch June, they made a swift exit from the casino and across the vast parking lot to where they had left Agatha.

When they were once again driving along the highway, they seemed to mutually decide to forget about the case for the length of the drive; they just chatted aimlessly, laughing and joking with each other over a myriad of inconsequential things, until Nan needed to turn her full attention to steering Agatha into the parking lot at Ojibwa Point and then into the open parking spot she noticed close to its front entrance.

"I hope we get lucky," Nan said, putting the gearshift into park and turning off her engine, "and June isn't off duty or as unresponsive as she was last evening."

"You know, I was wondering about that," Marley said. "Do you think it's possible she was hesitant to talk in front of Lyman? That something about him made her decide not to talk further? After all, she did wink at me when I asked if she'd solved the mystery. What do you suppose that wink meant?"

"That she had more to say," Nan replied. "Lyman's presence could have caused her to have second thoughts about speaking at greater length the other night, but it's hard to know. If she's working today and we have a chance to speak to her, we'll need to try to draw her out. Hopefully, once we've been able to do that, we'll have a clearer read on it all."

The two entered the restaurant and came to a halt just inside the door, where they paused for a few moments to let their eyes adjust to the darker interior. As they stood in the entryway, they noticed a cork bulletin board with a patchwork hodgepodge of flyers that advertised art fairs, fishing contests, and even Mass and service times at local churches. The ads likely served as a time-saver that freed staff from having to answer commonly repeated questions from vacationers.

Nan and Marley took time to scan the bulletin board, looking for anything that might catch their eye or, over time, prove pertinent to the case. At the entrance to the dining room, they noticed a sign inviting them to seat themselves.

Suddenly, Marley gestured toward the bar. "There she is!" she said excitedly.

Nan turned her head and noticed June sitting by herself at the bar with a glass of what looked like a soft drink before her. "What say we get a glass of beer?" she asked her chum as she sauntered toward the bar.

Nan and Marley approached the handsome mahogany length of paneled wood, with its brass rail, and Nan didn't hesitate to plunk her backside onto the stool next to June. Marley quickly seated herself on the stool on Nan's other side.

"Well, hello there," Nan said. "Remember us?"

"Back again?" June replied. "I'm not surprised." Then, gesturing toward her glass, she added, "I'm sugaring up. I'm going to need the energy. Tonight's prime rib night, and that means I'm going to be running my tail off. You're coming back for the prime rib, aren't you? It's really good, and it comes with popovers."

Marley's eyes widened, and Nan quickly said, "We'll have to skip it tonight. We've been busy this morning and need to eat something now. We're starved. We thought we'd have a walleye sandwich as our bigger meal for the day. Last night's fillet was delicious. I assume you have a walleye sandwich on the lunch menu?"

"Sure do," June said. "And it's a favorite."

"But first," Nan said, motioning to the young man tending bar, "we could both use a glass of beer."

The bartender approached them, and Nan took it upon herself to order for both herself and Marley. "My friend and I would both like a Stella Artois." Then, thinking it possible they might get handed two bottles of beer and nothing else, she added, "And two glasses, please."

He placed cocktail napkins before Nan and Marley and set a pilsner glass filled with the chilled golden brew on each. The bartender, Nan noticed, was tall and young, younger than most, and she noted his various piercings: a silver stud in his nose, which was small and rather attractive, and one through each ear. Clad in a black bib apron over a black T-shirt, he had the look of someone who played in a band and perhaps chose the day shift in order to be free to pursue his evening gigs.

Marley turned toward June. "What time does your shift begin?" she asked.

"I start at three," June answered.

"I ask because the last time we were here, Professor Lyman, Nan, and I were discussing the missing women, and you mentioned that you had solved the entire mystery. After our discussion, Nan and I couldn't help but be curious about the case. And especially what your solution might be. Professor Lyman, who knew one of the missing women, the one named Lynn Parker, didn't seem to have any solution or any ideas about the disappearance at all, and he knew her quite well."

June nodded. "Yes, he did. He knew her quite well. But I

also knew her. She used to come in here a lot. And we would gab, and later, we began to hang out."

Hoping to encourage the waitress to say more, Marley asked her next questions in a way that made the information she was about to impart sound like a well-known fact. "So you knew she was a writer? And that she was working on a book about the disappearance of the first woman, Professor Engelmann?"

"Sure," June said. "I knew all about that. Lynn was always full of questions."

"Such as?" Nan asked.

"Oh, you know, the usual. Did Professor Engelmann know Lyman? Did she ever come to the restaurant, and if so, with whom? And did I ever see her with anyone around town?"

"Do these questions appear important to you now?" Nan asked. "I mean, since you said you've already solved it and all."

June blushed slightly. "Well, I've solved a great part of it but maybe not all of it."

"But that's wonderful," Marley said. "What part of it have you solved?"

June looked uncomfortable, and Marley gently added, "If you don't mind our asking."

When June continued to hesitate, Nan, deciding to weigh in, added, "It's just that it's such a fascinating mystery, isn't it? A real puzzler, and the fact that we're staying at the resort and everything—well, our curiosity has risen to a fever pitch. Especially given what you said last night about having already solved it. But if you don't feel you can trust us with—"

"Oh no," June said, her eyes growing wide. "No. It's not a matter of trust."

Marley leaned forward so she could look June square in the eye. "It's because you don't think we'll understand? Is that it? That we'll dismiss outright what you have to say?"

"You don't need to worry about that!" Nan added, briefly placing a hand on June's. "Believe me, we understand. At our age, people dismiss what we have to say all the time. We're used to having our thoughts and feelings treated as trivial and insignificant, but we'd never make others feel that way."

June took a long sip of her soda and then placed it back on the bar in a way that told Nan and Marley she'd made up her mind. "Well," she said, lowering her voice, "I know the women didn't leave the resort, like the police and witnesses said they did. In my opinion, whatever happened to them happened at the resort."

Nan and Marley glanced at each other and then back toward June.

"How can you be so sure?" Marley asked.

June smiled knowingly. "Because Lynn suspected Suzanne of never having actually left the resort on the day she disappeared. She told me so."

"Why did she think that?" Nan asked.

June, suddenly keen to tell what she thought, said eagerly, "Because in the course of her poking around, Lynn discovered some additional information that didn't come out." She swiveled to face Marley and emphatically said, "Such as the fact that Suzanne had booked the cabin for a full week and wasn't expected to leave the resort until

Saturday morning. Yet she left early Thursday morning. Two days early."

Except for the books left behind at cabin number eight, which told Marley and Nan another story, Marley thought Lynn could just as likely have considered it highly probable Suzanne simply got bored and decided to leave early, but not wanting to stop June's reporting, she decided to keep that thought to herself. Instead, playing into June's sense of discovery, she filled her voice with wonder and responded, "Now, that is strange, isn't it?"

June nodded. "Lynn thought so."

"Goodness." Nan, as had June, lowered both her head and her voice. "So let me see if I understand what you're saying. Are you saying that Lynn believed the eyewitnesses who said they saw Suzanne leave the resort that morning, the ones the police report having interviewed, were all lying?"

"No, they weren't lying. They were misinformed."

"How could they have been misinformed?"

Looking about, June leaned in close and said, "Well, Lynn thought the police had been looking at it all wrong." She swiveled to give Nan her full attention. "Think about it. They only have the Chapmans' word that Suzanne checked out of the resort that morning, don't they? Well, records can be altered, can't they? And who better to alter them than the owners of the resort?"

"But wouldn't they have needed to forge Suzanne's signature in their record book?" Marley asked.

June nodded and said with a dismissive shrug, "Easy enough to do since they already had her signature from when she checked in. All they had to do was trace and copy."

"And the eyewitnesses?" Nan muttered as her mouth curved into a small frown. "What about them?"

June laughed lightly. "Oh, they all saw Suzanne drive away from the resort that morning—there's little doubt about that. But who's to say she wasn't simply going into town or to the Y Store for a newspaper or some milk? Of course, some weeks later, when the police interviewed them, they believed Suzanne to have checked out of the resort that morning, because that's what they were told by the proprietors. So it only stands to reason that what they think they saw was not her going to Brainerd or on some other errand but the start of her journey back home to the Twin Cities. Lynn said it's not unusual for eyewitnesses to be mistaken. She said most people see what they are expecting to see."

"Which explains why no one mentioned seeing her return to the resort," Nan said. "Because if they had a memory of a return, they would have dismissed it, telling themselves they'd been mistaken, once the police gave them their official findings."

"Right," June said. "Lynn said they would have told themselves they must have seen her the day before and simply left it at that."

"Lynn sounds like a wise lady," Marley said.

June nodded. "She is. And she's smart too. I think she had a good handle on what happened to Suzanne Engelmann, and that's why she disappeared. She discovered something she shouldn't have—something that someone didn't want to get out."

Nan lowered her head and said slowly, "Do you think

it is possible she disappeared on her own? That she's in hiding?"

June looked down at her Coke and slowly shook her head. "I don't know," she muttered. "She could be. But I don't think she would have gone into hiding without telling me her plans."

"Why? Because you were a team? Because you were helping her?" Nan asked, deciding to take a chance that she could be right.

"Yes," June said. "In fact, Lynn was going to stop here that day on her way back to the cities, and she didn't show. That tells me she disappeared somewhere between the resort and this restaurant. Since there's less than two miles between, I'm betting on the resort, and that's what I told the authorities."

Nan asked, "Is it possible she simply forgot to stop?"

June's reply was strongly confident. "That's what the police asked me, and I told them no. No way. Lynn needed to get back to town for various personal reasons, but she was also going to do some further research concerning Suzanne Engelmann's disappearance. I don't know what else exactly she had to look into, but she told me I'd know once I read her notes."

"Her notes?" Nan asked in surprise. "What notes?"

"The ones she was going to drop off for me that morning," June said, lowering her voice even more. Glancing about, she said nervously, "Don't you see? Lynn was definitely planning on coming back. And in her absence, I was going to continue the investigation for her. I was supposed to watch certain people and report their actions back to her. On the day she disappeared, she was planning to drop off her notes so I could be brought up to date on all the information she'd discovered so far."

"But you don't know everything she discovered? And you never received her notes?"

June shook her head sadly. "No, and I never saw Lynn again."

Nan thought for a minute and then asked, "If Lynn did discover something about Suzanne's disappearance that put her in so much danger that she went into hiding and if you two were a team and you were helping her, do you think you might be in danger as well?"

"I've thought about that," June said. "And the problem is, I don't know. I don't know if Lynn is in hiding. I don't know what happened to her!"

"Who knew you were helping Lynn with her investigation?" Marley asked.

"No one. Only Lynn. I haven't told anyone else, because to be perfectly honest, I don't know who to trust. I mean, someone up here may very well be a kidnapper or, worse yet, a murderer. And I don't know who that person is. I don't know. And that frightens me. It could be anyone. The only reason I'm speaking to you is—"

"Because we're not from around these parts, and you can therefore trust us completely," Nan said. "Besides, look at us; to most people who don't think too deeply, we appear to be two harmless, grandmotherly women. The last people on earth anyone would take for cold-blooded murderers."

June laughed. "I'm glad you said it and not me. But yeah, I took all that into account. And I don't mind telling you. It feels good to be able to share all this with someone. It's kind of hard to keep it to yourself."

Nan again laid a gentle hand on June's. "Anytime," she said.

Marley, however, frowned. "You said Lynn disappeared the day she was scheduled to drop off her case notes with you. So that means, if you never received them, then—" For June's sake, Marley didn't finish the thought. Instead, she said, "Tell me—how did the two of you usually communicate?"

"By cell," June replied. "Lynn called me that morning super early. I'd just arrived at the restaurant for my seven o'clock shift. The phone call was short; she sounded in a hurry and somewhat breathless. She simply told me she was heading back into town and that she'd drop her notes off on the way."

"Had Lynn previously planned on leaving that day?" Nan asked.

June shrugged. "I don't know. I know she talked about leaving at some point and coming back after, so I didn't question her going that morning." She glanced at her watch and slid off the barstool. "I have to punch in for my shift now. If you want to talk some more, you could try to catch me later. I'll take my break about eight o'clock tonight."

Marley and Nan watched June walk away, and when she was out of sight, Nan said, "I don't know about you, but I have a lot more questions to ask her. I say we eat our lunch now and come back for her break."

"Good idea," Marley said. "I have more questions as well. Chief among them is whether she told the police Lynn was planning on dropping off her notes the day she disappeared. From what we heard just now, I have a strong feeling she didn't. That she kept silent about that."

"I know," Nan said. "I was thinking the same thing. If Lynn is in hiding because she has information that's a threat to someone or if, heaven forbid, someone did something to her to shut her up, then June wouldn't want anyone to think she knew what Lynn knew. It would put her life at risk."

"Exactly. So there's a good possibility the police were never told about the notes."

Nan downed the rest of her beer and slid off her stool. "We also need to ask June who the suspects Lynn wanted her to keep an eye on were."

Marley pushed her nearly full glass away and stood as well. "Let's get a table and eat something. It's almost three o'clock, and my stomach's telling me it's past time."

CHAPTER 13

WHEN THEY HAD FINISHED THEIR lunch and dealt with the bill, Nan looked at Marley and said, "Well, what do we do now? We have four hours before June takes her break this evening. Should we go back to the resort?"

Marley shook her head. "No. Let's move onward and try to accomplish something. Why don't we visit the second of the three casinos up around this area? What was it called? Sleeping Bear?"

"Was that it? I don't recall," Nan answered. "Do you have any idea where it's located?"

"No, but I'll look it up on my phone. It can't be far."

It turned out that the Sleeping Bear casino was only some twenty minutes away. By the time they had parked in another gigantic lot and entered the casino, they had more than two hours remaining to explore the possibilities of the establishment. After walking about aimlessly, they felt their luck take a sudden turn for the better when Nan spotted the woman who had waited on them at the Merrifield Y Store the day they first arrived. Being the good storekeeper she was, she recognized them as well and gladly turned her attention from her unrewarding slot machine, pulling out her rewards card, to give them her full attention.

"Did you just arrive?" she asked. "Or have you been here awhile?"

"We just walked in the door," Nan said.

"Are you both still stayin' at that Eagle's Cove Resort?" she asked.

Marley and Nan nodded. "Yes," they answered together. "Still there."

The woman laughed. "I would've thought you'd have hightailed it out of there by now. Especially after I told you about cabin number eight."

"Actually," Nan said, "we've become interested in trying to solve these mysterious happenings. We've been busy visiting the casinos around here, trying to discover whether either of the women was a frequent attendee."

The woman from the Y Store looked surprised. "Well, I don't know about that first woman. From what I hear, she never went anywhere. But the other one, the younger of the two, would've gone to Five Feathers if she went to any casino at all."

"Oh? Why is that?" Marley asked.

"'Cause that's the casino all the young folks go to. It's the biggest of the three around here and has the kind of hip entertainment young people like. As for the gamblin', the slots might sit empty, but the blackjack and poker tables are always full."

"We plan to visit that casino tomorrow," Marley said.

"Well, if you discover anything new on those two women, I'd appreciate you stoppin' in at the Y Store to fill me in."

"We'll make sure to do that," Nan said.

The woman laughed heartily and rose to her feet. "Now I need to move to another machine," she said, "before this one puts the loser hex on me."

Marley and Nan stepped out of her way. As she walked toward what she saw as a more promising set of machines, Nan called out, "See you at the Y Store!"

"Well, that was a worthwhile use of our time," Marley said, buckling her seat belt, after the two climbed into Nan's little green car. Even though the sun was about to set, it was still bright enough in the parking lot to be almost blinding after the dim interior of the gambling mecca. "And it wasn't even that bad from a financial aspect. I actually won forty dollars by just throwing in a quarter here and there."

Nan waited for the long line of cars to move from the casino parking lot out onto the road. When they were finally able to merge into traffic, she sighed deeply and said, "Who would have thought we'd run into the Y Store woman? But she gave us more information than we got at the First Nation casino."

"I can't believe we didn't ask for her name," Marley said. "That's twice now. How rude!"

"I didn't even think of it," Nan said. "What's wrong with us? Are we a couple of class-conscious snobs?"

"Of course not," Marley said. "We're just plain rude at times."

The flow of automobiles seemed to be zipping nicely along, and Nan glanced at the readings on the dash to make sure she wasn't going too far over the speed limit. "Are we going to make it in time?" Nan asked.

"It's just seven thirty," Marley responded absently as her

mind drifted back over the day's revelations. "We should be fine."

"I'll make sure to step on it a little," Nan said, pressing her foot down on the gas pedal. "We don't want to be late. June's break is probably no more than fifteen minutes since she expected such a busy night."

The two women walked into Ojibwa Point at precisely eight o'clock and immediately looked toward the bar, expecting to see June on her break. But the bar, although crowded, was devoid of June. Their hopes sagged, and they wondered if her schedule had been altered. Not knowing what to do, they approached the bar, and Marley gestured to the bartender, who came over and informed them that June was taking her break in the kitchen. He kindly pointed to a doorway.

"She's just on the other side of that door," he said. "And she's expecting you."

Nan and Marley entered through the swinging door and immediately saw June sitting at a small table situated against the wall off to one side of the room, with ample space between herself and the frantic, busier part of the kitchen.

Nan and Marley pulled out chairs and joined her at the table.

June smiled up at them. "So you did decide to come back," she said.

"Yup," Nan replied. "We still have a few more questions to ask you."

"Well, ask away," June mumbled, brushing a crumb or two from her shirt.

Marley began the questioning. "June, did the police question you about a man named Buck?"

"You mean Buck Sykes? Boy, what a handful he is! Have you two met him?"

"Unfortunately, yes," Marley said, scrunching up her face.

June laughed. "Wow, your facial expression says it all. The guy's a real dirtbag, isn't he?"

"Was he one of the people Lynn wanted you to keep an eye on?"

"Yes."

"And who were the others?"

"The Chapmans, of course, and then there was this other guy. Someone connected with one of the casinos. His name would have been in Lynn's notes. The ones I never received."

"Did she tell you anything else about this man?" said Nan. "A description? Anything?"

June shook her head. "No. But she talked about him like he was someone important, someone with influence."

"Was Buck Sykes ever involved with either Suzanne or Lynn?" Marley asked.

"Lord no!" June said. "Lynn wouldn't have touched that guy with a ten-foot pole. Not in that way."

"What about Suzanne Engelmann?" Nan said. "Could she have been interested?"

"From what Lynn told me, she'd just gone through a nasty divorce," June said. "I can't imagine she'd have been interested in hooking up so soon, can you? Especially with someone like Sykes. Besides, from what I heard, she was practically a nun."

"So you yourself never actually got to meet Suzanne?" Nan asked.

"No, I never did," June said. "But I got a lot of information about her from Lynn and also from Ed and Ione Graham. The Grahams come in here once a week for the prime rib. No fail. They've already been here and gone. Have you two met them? They're regular springtime visitors at the resort."

"Yes, we have," Marley said. "They seem like very nice people. In fact, they're the ones who mentioned Buck Sykes to us. They told us he hangs around the resort a lot and that they had seen him and Lynn together in the bar."

"Well, believe me," June said with a roll of her eyes, "it wasn't from any real interest on Lynn's part. It must have been part of her research. Don't get me wrong; I wouldn't put it past that guy to hit on her if she stopped in at the resort bar. But knowing Lynn, she would have used it to her advantage if he gave her half a chance."

"Why do you think this guy is at the resort so much?" Marley asked.

June took a sip of her pop before answering. "I don't know. Maybe because he lives just down the road from there, so the resort bar is the closest to his house, and he likes his beer. He doesn't like to drive much once he's been drinking. He wouldn't want to risk getting any more DUIs. Besides, I think he and Dale Chapman are fishing buddies. Anyway, that's what Ed Graham says. He's seen them out in a boat together."

"So he lives right off County Road C?" Marley asked.

"Yeah. He lives on the next road or two up from the resort. I think it's a township road called Highland Road. It doesn't go through and only has two farms located on it: Sykes's place and the McNair farm."

"Only two?" Nan asked. "And one of them is the McNair farm? Can you tell us anything about the McNairs? For example, where is their property along the road, and what do they farm?"

"Anne and John McNair?" said June. "They're in the house at the far end of the road. They raise pigs and chickens. John is the pig expert, and Anne takes care of the chickens. She's known in these parts as the Egg Lady. She also has a large berry patch and sells fresh berries, jams, and pies during the summer. And she supplies a few of the local restaurants with her goods year-round."

Marley said, "What can you tell us about the Sykes place. Is Buck Sykes married? Does he have a family?"

"I think he was married once or twice before, but that was a long time ago," June said. "He's been single for a while now. The farm belongs to his folks. His mom was born and raised there. She passed a few years back, but his dad is still alive, although we don't see him anymore. He's an invalid and pretty much confined to home."

"What about Professor Haynes?" Nan asked, leaning in more toward the waitress, who was now shifting a bit, as though serving duties would soon require her attention. "Was he one of the people Lynn wanted you to watch?"

"Lyman?" June replied. "Well, Lynn was certainly interested in him but not in that way. At the time, I didn't think she saw him as a threat or a possible suspect. But since her disappearance, I'm not so sure. They were pretty close. He may have had something to do with her disappearance. Anyway, that's why I try to be careful about what I say around him. I feel like I can't be too careful. You know?"

June's break time had come to an end, and as she headed

back to work, Marley and Nan said their goodbyes and left the kitchen. On the way to the restaurant's exit, they came across Lyman Haynes, who was just leaving after, in all probability, enjoying a prime rib dinner. After an exchange of greetings, the three walked out into the parking lot together.

"Did you enjoy the prime rib?" Lyman asked.

"Actually, we didn't have any," Marley told him. "We had a fairly large and late lunch earlier and simply thought we'd stop in for a drink before going back to the resort."

"If we had known about the popularity of their prime rib, we wouldn't have had such a big lunch," Nan said, noticing Marley's grimace as she did.

"How have you been getting along with your Wi-Fi connection?" Lyman asked.

"Actually, so far, we've been relying on our phones to stay in touch with family and friends," Marley said. "But don't be surprised to find me sitting at your picnic table one of these days. I assume I'll need your password if I do go across the creek?"

"Just put in *LH2cove*," he said. "It stands for—well, I'm sure you can guess."

Nan began to chat about nothing in particular, and they all joined in until they said their good nights. The professor then turned and walked toward his car. When Marley and Nan were in Agatha and securely buckled up, Marley turned to Nan and said, "Did you happen to notice the right sleeve on his jacket?"

Somewhat perplexed, Nan said, "Uh, no, his sleeve went entirely unnoticed by me. My attention was focused elsewhere entirely."

"There was a certain button missing. It was the second of the four buttons on his right sleeve."

"Not unusual for a bachelor to have a missing button," Nan muttered. "Or is that a sexist statement?"

"It is, but I'll ignore it for now. Because what I did find unusual was its close resemblance to the button I found in the bedroom closet at cabin number eight. I'm sure it was a perfect match."

CHAPTER 14

THE NEXT MORNING, NAN DROVE down the resort road and onto County Road C. After a leisurely breakfast and time on the deck, they had decided to visit the McNair farm and have a look at the area surrounding the old Baker place, where Buck Sykes was supposed to live. After a short drive down County Road C, Nan swung onto the dirt road that led to the Sykes and McNair farms. She carefully steered Agatha down the deeply rutted, bumpy, rough gravel roadbed until they came to a rusty mailbox tilting unsteadily to one side with the barely visible name of Sykes printed on the side.

"We've located the beast's den," Nan said.

"I believe you're right," Marley replied. "No doubt this is the Sykes place."

Nan slowed the car to a crawl, and both women were disappointed when all they could see was a long driveway that eventually disappeared, curving behind a dense grove of trees.

"Can't see much from the road, can you?" Marley asked. "The next farm along here must belong to the egg people.

What was the name June used? The McNairs? Let's pull in to buy some eggs and see if we can gather any further information."

"Good idea," Nan said.

The McNair farm was farther along the road, on the right, at the end of a rustic cul-de-sac, and was in considerably better condition than the Sykes place, if the mailbox proved to be any indication. The driveway opened wide before a two-story, many-windowed typically white farmhouse with an inviting front porch that had been furnished with tables, chairs, and lamps, presumably for evening enjoyment, as the farm appeared to be a working one and not a country retreat. Attached to the back, they could make out a one-story addition that seemed to extend behind the full width of the house. At an ell, the obvious summer kitchen was more of a screen house, and through the screens, Nan and Marley could see two women just barely visible among billowing clouds of steam that carried the sweet scent of simmering grapes.

"Jam making," Nan said. "Unless I miss my guess."

"Mmm," Marley said. "If that's also for sale, let's make sure to buy a jar before we leave."

Marley raised her eyes and noticed, behind the summer kitchen by about five hundred yards, a pigpen with three pudgy black pigs, one of which was pushing its snout against the fence, trying to gather in the smells coming from the steaming kitchen. "Do pigs like grapes?" she asked.

Nan rolled down her window. "Look at all the chickens! They're all over the place. They must be free-range. It looks like they have four or five different breeds."

"Be careful. Don't hit any," Marley warned, reaching over Nan to tap the car's horn.

"Now who's the silly city girl?" Nan chuckled. "Chickens know how to scatter and make room for whatever's coming through. They're not turkeys, you know."

"This place is great," Marley said, rolling down the car window on her side as well. "I don't even mind the pig smell. I find that jam and pig make an interesting, farm-like juxtaposition."

Nan shut off the car, and the two of them got out. Nan practically sprinted to the two low steps leading to the door of the summer kitchen as she called, "Hello! We're looking for Mrs. McNair?"

A young girl of about fourteen swung the door open and gave them a wide, friendly smile. She was clad in blue jeans and a pale yellow sweater. "C'mon in," she said. "My mom's busy stirring the jam. My name's Elizabeth. Are you looking to buy something? Jam? Eggs? Bacon? Sunflower seeds?"

Nan and Marley stepped inside the screened room and noticed a stove up against a partially bead-boarded wall. A woman in jeans and a white T-shirt, who was wearing a bright yellow plastic bib apron, stood before the stove and a large, tall stainless-steel pot. In her right hand, she held an implement that neither Nan nor Marley had ever seen before. She was rotating it in a slow, circular motion. They also noticed that she was standing on a stool that elevated her about twelve inches off the floor.

Marley, curious as always, said to the women, "What are you stirring that with? And why do you need height to do it?" She asked her questions quickly without thinking, and as she heard herself, she blushingly said, "Please excuse me for asking, Mrs. McNair, but I've never seen this before; I find it fascinating."

The woman laughed. "Fascinating? Is it? All I know is, it's a lot of work." She directed her attention away from the pot and toward Marley and Nan. "I am Mrs. McNair. But please call me Anne. Everyone does." Turning to the young girl, she added, "Elizabeth, will you take over for me, please?"

The girl stepped in, hopping onto the stool while continuing to stir the pot with slow, rotating motions.

Anne McNair turned toward Nan and Marley, wiping her hands with a wet, purple-stained towel. "I gather you've never made jam yourself?" she asked.

"Never!" Nan and Marley replied in unison.

"Well, the tool Elizabeth is now using is our hand blender, because it saves your arm from wanting to fall off. Usually, the jam takes half an hour to come to a full rolling boil, and even then, you have to stir it until it can't be stirred down."

"In other words, it takes a lot of stirring," Marley said. She noticed two shelves loaded with small jars of ruby-red jam aligned in a row. Each jar was topped with a shiny golden screw top that seemed to glow with the sheen of a sweet promise. "We'd like to buy a jar or two of those," she said, suddenly hungry, pointing to the jars. "What sort of fruit are they?"

"Strawberry," Anne replied. "I make small-batch jam only. It's my preference. I think it tastes better. Like my grandma used to make. Those jars are from last year's summer harvest. Thank the good Lord for freezers, or we would not be able to make this jam from last fall's grapes during this cooler springtime weather. It's not fun to work at this in the heat of the harvest season, I assure you."

"That I can well imagine," Nan said. "And we love the notion of small-batch jam. Don't we, Marley? Let's get a few jars! And we'd like a dozen of your fresh eggs too, please."

Anne placed a jar of jam in one of the paper bags piled on the counter and then raised a questioning brow toward Marley.

"Make it three, please," Marley said. She turned toward Nan to explain. "One for each of us to take home and one to enjoy while we're at the resort."

Anne excused herself to go into the house for the carton of eggs. When she returned, Marley asked, "Do you and your husband both farm this land?"

"Well, I take care of the chickens and the gardens," Anne said. "But my husband farms the land with my eldest son, whose land is adjacent to ours."

"Oh, does your son live in the house we passed on the way here?" Marley asked, knowing that he didn't. "We may have met him. A tall, broad-shouldered fellow?"

"Good Lord no!" Anne replied in dismay. "You're describing Buck Sykes. We don't have much to do with him. My son Scotty lives across the field, on the other side of the woods that front our road. You can't see his house from here because of how dense the woods are, but it's not far, especially if you take the path that runs straight through the woods to his house."

Nan said, "Well, I, for one, am glad to hear that Mr. Sykes isn't your son. To be honest, he didn't make a very good impression on either of us."

Anne smiled. "I don't think that man cares two hoots what kind of an impression he makes."

"Does he live in that big house all alone?"

"No, he lives with his father. But he might as well live alone, because we never see his father anymore. Of course, he's quite elderly and frail. We used to see quite a bit of his mother. She was a nice lady, very friendly in her way. But she died a few years back. I assume the father is still alive. I haven't seen any obituary in the local paper."

"Does Buck Sykes farm too?"

"Used to be an active farmer, I guess, alongside his father," Anne said. "But not anymore. John and Scotty rent and farm most of the Sykes land now. The son spends his time fixing things for people. I guess he's real handy. With whatever money he brings in, his dad's railroad pension, and Social Security, they seem to do all right."

Nan put the bag containing the jam and eggs in the crook of her arm and said, "Well, it sure is nice to know where we can get fresh eggs and jam, Anne. The two of us are staying at Eagle's Cove Resort, so I'm sure we'll be back."

"How long will you be staying?"

"A week at least," Nan replied. "But we might stay longer."

"We enjoy this part of the state," Marley added. "Even though the water isn't yet warm enough for me to want to go swimming. Nan and I plan to visit the casinos, and Nan, who is an artist, is looking forward to doing a few landscape paintings."

"Are there many people staying at the resort?" Anne asked. "I would have thought the numbers would be down. Especially now, in the spring."

"Because of the disappearances, you mean?" Marley said. "Actually, it is rather vacant. From what we can tell, there is only one other cabin being rented at present."

"Were either of the two women who disappeared customers of yours?" Nan asked. "Or did you ever meet one or both of them?"

"No, I didn't," Anne said. "But I've heard about them, of course. It's the biggest mystery that's hit this area in ages. People are still talking about it. And likely always will— until it's solved, that is."

"Do you think they will eventually solve it?" Marley asked.

"My son Scotty is the sheriff here in Crow Wing County, and he has connections with the Brainerd Police Department; he says they definitely have strong suspicions. Of course, they can't say anything at present, but I'm sure they're working hard behind the scenes."

"The common problem, I believe," Nan said, "is acquiring the proof to back up your suspicions."

Anne nodded. "That's true. Scotty says whoever took those two women has to make a mistake somewhere along the line. And when he does, the police will be ready."

"So they think it's a sole man behind these disappearances?" Nan said. "Seems a bit complicated for one person."

"Maybe. I don't know," Anne replied. "What I do know is, every woman around here will sleep a whole lot more soundly once this is all over with and someone is behind bars."

Anne's daughter, Elizabeth, suddenly let out a long groan. "Mom, can you take over again? I can't stir down the boil."

Anne practically ran to Elizabeth and took the blender from her hand. "It's time to jar the jam," she said. Elizabeth moved aside as Anne added, "All the jam jars are ready to go. They've already had boiling water poured into them. Grab one for me, won't you?"

Marley and Nan stood transfixed as Elizabeth took a gripper and used it to lift one of the jars standing on a long wooden table. She hefted the jar above a sink, poured out the steaming water, and then carried the jar to her mother, who carefully ladled in the hot, sweet-smelling jam. Then Elizabeth dropped the gripper, picked up a pair of metal tongs to grasp a flat lid from a pan of steaming water, and placed the lid on top of the jar of fresh jam. She used the same tongs to go back into the boiling water for the twisting lid and tightened it around the flat cover with an oven mitt. As she went back to the table to get another jar for Anne, Marley and Nan heard the first jar ping.

"Get the other pre-sterilized jars from the kitchen, please. Did you finish your chores in the living room? And have you called Clarise about choir practice at church tonight?"

As mother and daughter became more engrossed in their tasks, Marley and Nan took the opportunity to move toward the screen door. "We won't keep you from your work any longer," Marley said, opening the door and stepping through. "It was so nice to meet you both," she added heartily. "We hope to see you again."

Once they were back in the car, Nan made a slow U-turn in the drive, scattering the chickens as she did so, and then drove onto the road, heading back toward the main highway.

CHAPTER 15

NEITHER WOMAN SPOKE A WORD until their car approached the entry to Sykes's place, when Marley said, "Slow down. I want to see if we can catch sight of any part of the house from the road."

Nan slowed the car to a crawl, and they both peered down the long, winding drive. What they could see wasn't encouraging. The house must have been close to a hundred yards down the driveway, and the only part of it they could see above the tree line was a third story with dormers. The rest of the house was obscured behind compact old-growth woods that made it difficult to even discern which way the entrance to the house faced.

"Can't tell much from here, can we?" Nan asked.

"No," Marley said. "We're going to have to find a way of scoping out the territory. I don't like the idea of going in blindly."

"How about the path that runs through the woods that Anne just told us about? You know, the one that connects her house with her son Scotty's? Could we somehow survey the Sykes house from there?"

Marley thought for a moment and then shook her head. "I don't like it," she said dismissively. "If we took the path, we'd still have to go to the edge of the woods to try to view the Sykes place, and we can't be sure what we'd find. It might be an open field, for all we know. We might even run straight into that big lout or, worse yet, be seen by him. We have no idea how many outbuildings there are or anything about the lay of the land on his property. No, I think we are just going to have to go in blind. We only need to be absolutely certain that Sykes has left the property before we do any investigating."

"What about his father? He'll still be there, won't he? He never leaves."

"Yes, but I've given that a great deal of thought. What we need to do is make any approach to the house and outbuildings on our part look entirely innocent, and I think I know how we can do that, Nan. We can use that egg sign alongside the road as our excuse. Don't you see? We become two addle-brained elderly women looking to buy fresh eggs who just happened to turn into the wrong driveway."

"That's a great idea!" Nan said. "After all, the sign only says, 'Fresh Eggs for Sale.' It doesn't designate any particular farm."

"No, it doesn't," Marley said. "So we'll need to do a good job of selling ourselves as confused older women and making it seem nothing more than a simple mistake when we show up in Sykes's farmyard looking for eggs."

"Is there a way we can make our visit when Sykes isn't there?" asked Nan. "At a time when he's away from the farm?"

"That would be ideal," Marley said. "We would be able

to do a lot more poking around if he were off the premises. But I don't see how we could pull it off. We would have to watch his every move. And given the lack of traffic along these roads, we would look pretty silly parked along a shoulder for any length of time. It's not like in a big city, where, at least before some of these recent carjackings, you could sit in your parked car for hours, and no one would bother with you. Up here, people would stop their cars continuously to ask if we needed assistance."

They had come to the end of the dirt road, where it entered County Road C. Nan was just about to turn onto the highway that led back to the resort, when she slammed on the brakes, bringing Agatha to an abrupt stop.

Marley, expecting to see an animal crossing the road, looked up. She was surprised to see the way was clear. "Nan, why have we stopped?"

Nan turned to give Marley a wide, silly grin. "Because I think I know how we can make sure Mr. Buck Sykes is off his property when we do our egg-buying stop," she said. She pointed to the field on the other side of County Road C. "I'm going to set up my easel in that field right over there and paint that beautiful old barn in the distance. That way, I'll be able to watch Sykes coming and going."

Marley squinted to peer out Agatha's front windshield toward where Nan was pointing. The field on the other side of the highway was open, lush, green, and dotted with tiny wildflowers. But its most important feature was what stood along its back rim: a tall, slightly leaning, paint-peeling, weather-beaten old barn. "Perfect."

"Isn't it, though?" Nan said. "So here's how it will go down. I'll be painting in the field—a good cover, right? And the minute I see Buck Sykes's truck head into town, I'll call you, and we'll make our egg visit to the Sykes farm. I'm sure he goes into town every day, probably in the early morning."

"I'm sure you're right."

"So what if I set up my stool and easel in the field early tomorrow morning and keep watch?"

Marley wrinkled her brow. "I don't know, Nan. You could be sitting on that stool for hours."

"It wouldn't be the first time," Nan said. "Besides, it's not as if I'd really be pouring myself into the painting. If I were to do that, I wouldn't stay more than two hours, because the light changes, and the shadows shift. Painting straight from the subject while outside is called plein air. But that's beside the point. I just want us to finally be able to step foot on the Sykes farm and—"

Marley finished the sentence for her. "Snoop where the police can't?"

"Right," Nan answered with a smug expression.

"OK then, this is definitely a plan," Marley said firmly. "What do we have to lose?"

When the two friends drove into Eagle's Cove Resort a little later, they noticed Ed and Ione Graham walking along one of the paths. Ione waved, and Nan stopped the car and rolled down her window.

"Come visit us tonight after you've had your dinner!" Ione called out to them. "Ed and I bought a yummy cake. We're going to have it with some ice cream and would love to have you join us."

"Thanks for the invitation, but we're expecting a few phone calls this evening," Nan said. "But we'd appreciate a rain check."

"Anytime!" Ed called out. "You know where to find us."

Nan pressed her foot against the gas pedal once more and continued down the winding road. They came to a stop at cabin number eight.

While walking toward its back door, Marley stopped and let her gaze fall upon the whitecaps that filled the small bay between the resort's shore and the island with the three pines. "I keep thinking," she said, "about what was written in that book you found. That reference to the island."

Nan lifted a hand to shade her eyes and looked out toward the island. "You agree that the island is a key to the women's disappearances?"

"I don't know," Marley replied. "But I have a question for you. What happened to the eagles' nest? I mean, what really happened to it?"

Nan pursed her lips. "I've thought about that as well. If I were doing something on that island that I didn't want anyone to notice, I don't think I'd allow an eagles' nest to stay there for long. It would attract far too much attention."

Marley tilted her head to one side. "Great minds think alike."

"We could be totally wrong, you know," Nan said. "With our imaginations, we tend to overdramatize. Maybe it was destroyed by a storm or some such thing."

Marley shook her head. "But in that case, wouldn't those eagles have rebuilt? Something had to have happened to that nesting pair and their nest for them to have made such a change in their habitat."

"How can we find out?" Nan asked.

"Let's grill the Grahams again when we can to see if they have any ideas."

Once inside the cabin, they placed the eggs they'd bought at the McNair farm in the fridge and the jars of jam on an open shelf over the sink.

"A quick cheese omelet for dinner tonight?" Nan asked. "With toast and jam?"

"Sounds good," Marley replied. She opened a cupboard door and lifted two wineglasses off a shelf. "Grab that open bottle of wine, and meet me on the deck. Eva will be calling soon. It's almost six o'clock."

Both women left their jackets on as a precaution against the brisk and, at times, chilly April breeze blowing across the lake and bluff.

Nan collected the opened bottle of Napa Valley cabernet and followed Marley onto the deck. "I can't wait to talk to Eva," she said as she stepped onto the planks of the deck and squinted into the fading sunshine.

"Nor can I," Marley replied, settling into an Adirondack chair and stretching her long legs out before her. "I'm sure she's come up with a lot of helpful information by now. It doesn't take that woman very long to accumulate data."

"She is truly great at that sort of thing," Nan said, lowering herself onto a deck chair.

The two fell into a comfortable, calm, and relaxed mood in which neither spoke; both were lost in thought while slowly sipping their wine as they waited for Nan's cell phone to ring. At two minutes to six, the somber tones of Beethoven's Ninth Symphony filled the air and wafted up and across the deck and along the tips of the trees that bordered the resort.

"There she is," Nan said, placing the phone to her ear. "Right on time."

"You must have been sitting on your phone," Eva said with a laugh. "I don't think it rang more than once."

"We're counting on you, Eva," Nan replied. "I don't mind telling you we're at a loss up here. We don't know what to think. Marley is with me, and I'm going to put our conversation on the speaker setting."

To ensure privacy, Marley and Nan moved into the cabin, shutting the sliding glass door behind them. Nan plopped onto the sofa, and Marley drew a chair close to her. Suddenly feeling chilly, Marley pulled her jacket close about her shoulders.

"Well, you'll know what to think once I tell you what I've discovered," Eva replied. "Are you ready?"

"Shoot."

"Bad choice of words, Nan, when you're trying to solve a mystery," Eva said.

Knowing her friend as well as she did, Nan was able to envision the disapproval that she knew was clearly exhibited in the pursing of Eva's lips. "Sorry. Proceed then," she said.

"Much better. Here's what I know to date regarding timing and finances. The Chapmans left Kansas City a week before they showed up in Brainerd and bought Eagle's Cove Resort. And the thing is, from what their neighbors reported, they were as poor as church mice. He hadn't worked in years, from what they could tell, and Mrs. Chapman worked at a nightclub in Kansas City called the Strip Stake. She was a waitress or something. Anyway, she met a woman at the club, a stripper named Randi Sykes, and they became fast friends—inseparable, from what I've been told."

"Did you say Sykes? There's a character up here named Buck Sykes."

"That must be Randi's ex-husband," Eva said. "She used to be married to Buck Sykes. They divorced a while back, and from what my bloggers tell me, Randi left the state where her ex lived and moved back to the Kansas City area for a while before leaving there to go out west. I guess she has a sister living somewhere out there. I have a few bloggers working on exactly where that might be."

"So there's our connection between the Chapmans and Buck Sykes. They definitely knew one another before arriving at Eagle's Cove?" Marley said.

"Yes, it looks as though that's been confirmed," Eva answered. "I have a lot more information regarding the armored-car holdups. It took me hours of research in the public library and the morgue at the *Kansas City Star*. My bloggers also helped out there too, of course. I discovered there were two robberies, not just one. And the armored cars were held up within minutes of each other, on opposite sides of town."

"Wow," Nan said. "That took some coordinating."

"From what I was able to ascertain," Eva said, "each holdup was accomplished by one masked man with an automatic weapon fierce enough to put the fear of God into the security guards and any observant citizens who might have been standing by with concealed-carry privileges. The holdups took the entire city by surprise. The police chief said it had never happened in quite that way before. That probably accounts for the lack of response on the part of the security guards—that and the early morning hour and the rather isolated locations."

"Any witnesses?" Nan asked.

"A few, but the descriptions were vague because the men

were masked. The witnesses did give good descriptions of the getaway cars the robbers used, though. Good enough so the police discovered them in very little time, both ditched in alleys a few blocks from where the armored cars were held up."

"They made a switch," Marley said. "Which means each of the robbers had someone waiting for him in another car. So there had to be two other people involved. Four in all."

"Yes. That's what the police think as well."

"And let me guess," Nan said. "Both ditched cars were discovered to have been stolen."

"Right again," Eva said with a sigh. "One from an impound lot and the other from a charity drop-off location."

"So Buck Sykes and Dale Chapman could have each robbed one of the armored cars," Nan said, "while Mrs. Chapman was standing by to pick one of them up a few blocks away. Two different locations, so we need a second getaway driver. Do you have any idea who that might have been?"

"No, but a blogger of mine told me she thinks Randi Sykes was in town during the robberies. In fact, she'd swear by it."

"Could it have gone down that way?" Nan asked. "It sounds like Randi and Buck had been divorced for quite some time by then."

Marley piped up. "Besides, would Randi Sykes have risked going to prison for her creep of an ex?"

"I don't know," Eva said. "She might have if she were hard up for money. I'm trying to learn where and how well she's presently living. If she took away part of the take, she should be fairly comfortable wherever she is."

"Not necessarily," Nan said. "Maybe, like the people up here, she's keeping a low profile and not living high on the hog. If they actually did snatch that money and had a part in those robberies, how much do you think they got?"

"The amount was never disclosed. They never give out that type of information, Nan. But from what I can determine, it was a considerable sum," Eva said.

"OK then," Nan said, "so why aren't they spending like crazy? What are they waiting for?"

Eva said, "My thought is, they might need to launder the money. There would be a record of serial numbers."

"How long could that take?" Marley asked.

"It depends on where and how you launder it, I suppose," Eva said. "Can you think of a place near Brainerd where they might be doing that?"

Nan and Marley looked at each other and cried out, "The casinos!"

"Casinos? You mean there's more than one? How many casinos are there?" Eva asked.

"Three, all owned by the same Native American tribe and located within a seventy-mile radius," Nan said.

"Sounds perfect," Eva said.

"How exactly would you launder money?" Marley asked. "How would they go about it?"

"I don't know exactly," Eva replied. "But they probably take a portion of the money, small amounts each time so as to avoid attention, and exchange it for chips to gamble with at the various tables. It would help if they had a connection with one or all three of those casinos. And that connection would need to have some authority."

"I assume you mean by that it would help them win

more consistently," said Marley. "Because the winnings would be laundered."

"That's my thinking," Eva said.

"It sounds like we have some further investigating to do," Nan said.

"You two do what you can up there, and I'll keep working with my connections and doing my own research down here," Eva said. "I have one of my bloggers connecting with some of Randi Sykes's old Kansas City friends, so maybe I can find out precisely where she's living and be able to give you an address the next time we talk."

"If you do discover her address," Marley replied, "and need to fly out there, call my travel agent. I told her to give you carte blanche."

"It must be nice to have money," Eva said with a laugh.

Marley laughed as well. "I've always thought so."

Later, Marley and Nan were busily chopping peppers and chives and whisking eggs for their omelet dinner. Nan, knowing Marley to be far more knowledgeable about wine than she, asked, "What's the best wine to go with an omelet?"

"Neither of the wines we bought earlier," Marley said. "But after the day we've had, we're having wine anyway. Let's open that just-okay pinot grigio, even if it lacks the necessary delicacy a good omelet calls for."

After dinner, the two women made themselves comfortable on the sofas in the living area. The once picturesque scene outside the floor-to-ceiling doors to the deck had long since disappeared, with just enough light at present for them to barely make out the lakeshore and water's edge. As they lost themselves in the calm of the moment while absorbing all the information Eva had just given them and reflecting on its significance, the heavenly sound of a harp rang out, alerting Marley to an incoming call.

Marley reached for her phone and, recognizing the calling name and number, said cheerfully, "Hello. How are you, Sean?"

Sean Finnegan's robust voice replied, "That's what we were going to ask you two."

"We?" Marley said.

"That's right. Ray is with me. We have you on speakerphone."

"Oh perfect," said Nan. "The four of us can talk, and we can bring you up to date."

"Have you narrowed down your persons of interest yet?" asked Sean.

"Yes, we have. We've narrowed them down to four."

"Good!" Sean said excitedly. "Who are they? What're their names?"

"Well," replied Marley, "they're the owners of the resort."

"Christy and Dale Chapman?" Ray asked. "Of course, they would be the number-one suspects, seeing as both women disappeared after staying at their resort. So what are they like?"

"Well," Marley said, "we've learned since coming that they're not at all interested in retaining their resort clients. This property is being neglected, and they have lost practically all of their formerly loyal long-term clientele."

Nan cut in. "I swear, you guys, Christy Chapman is like someone out of central casting for a strip joint. I'm not kidding—she would fit perfectly in some boozy urban locale but certainly not in an establishment like this in northern Minnesota. Besides, I mean, she doesn't have even the rudimentary social skills required."

"They sound like a couple of fish out of water, if you'll excuse the pun," Sean said with a low-throated chuckle.

"Sounds like a couple of owners who couldn't care less about their business," Ray said. "I'd say they had other things on their mind than running a resort."

"I agree. In fact, we have yet to meet Dale Chapman," Marley said. "The man is never around. And given the poor state of maintenance around here, I'm not sure he'd impress me much if he were here."

"Makes you wonder what their plans are."

"That's right," replied Marley. "And our job is to discover those plans and why they exist."

"How are you two doing in terms of your safety? Have you run up against anything threatening?"

"As a matter of fact, yeah, we have," Nan said. "We came across a big lout who practically floored Marley at a café up here. We found out later his name is Buck Sykes. And unfortunately, he's our third person of interest. From what we can tell, he has some kind of close relationship with the Chapmans."

"Just how loutish is he?" Sean asked.

"He's a mean one, Sean," Nan said. "We've already been warned to stay as far away from him as possible."

"Which you can't very well do if he's a person of interest," Ray said.

"Do you want us to come up there?" Sean suddenly asked with a rising level of anxiety apparent in his voice. "Just say the word, and Ray and I could book a cabin today."

"No need," Nan said hurriedly. "Really, Sean! There is no need! Marley and I can take care of ourselves. Besides, if a couple of guys who obviously didn't come for the fishing suddenly book one of the cabins, that might look suspicious."

"In more ways than one," Ray said with a low chuckle before adding, "Not that I have an issue with that."

"Don't let him make this into something less than it is, Nan. I'm serious," Sean said sulkily.

"I know you are, Sean. And Marley and I appreciate your concern. But we have to be reasonable. We don't want anything to jeopardize our work, do we?"

"And the fourth person of interest?" Ray said. "Tell us about that one."

"He's a professor named Lyman Haynes. He lives across a creek bed from Eagle's Cove Resort. No more distant from us than a ravine with a small bridge spanning the creek and then a woodland path leading away from our cabin. He knew Lynn Parker and seems to have had an intimate relationship with her."

"Is that it? Anything more on the guy?" Ray said.

"Not yet, but we've only just begun," Nan answered.

"He's a big flirt—I'll give you that," said Marley.

"Well, that's something. I take it this Lyman fellow is a looker in more ways than one?" Sean said with his usual levity.

Nan laughed. "That he is. He's a looker all right."

"Listen," Ray said, "if that Buck Sykes is as big and as dangerous as others say he is, if you ever find yourself up against him and things get anxious, don't hesitate to use those knockout drops I gave you if you have an opportunity.

For a guy his size, two should either put him out cold or render him sleepy enough to push over."

Nan knew the opportunity to deposit two drops into some liquid that Buck Sykes would later drink was practically nil; nevertheless, she appreciated Ray's concern over a potential future plight involving her and Marley.

"We'll be sure to do that, Ray," Marley said. "You two keep in touch."

"Don't worry; we will," Sean said. "And you guys also call us if there's anything more we can do."

Everyone wished everyone else a good night, and when Sean hung up, Marley laid down her phone. Turning toward Nan, she said, "You know it's going to take all the ingenuity we have to keep those two guys from coming up here, don't you?"

"I do. But I also know that for Sean and Ray, the offer of assistance is everything. They know better than to actually come unless it is an absolute emergency. But bless them, they have to offer, don't they?"

Marley rose from her chair. "Well, this has certainly been a night for phone calls. Do we expect any more?"

"No."

"Good. Then I'm off to bed."

CHAPTER 16

THE NEXT MORNING HAILED MISTY and damp. A light rain was falling, and the sky was a dull and boring gray. Nan and Marley agreed it was not an ideal day for painting a picture of an old barn, so the two were forced to reschedule their earlier plan of checking out Sykes's farm. Instead, they decided to set out for the Grahams' cabin, with the intention of inviting them for breakfast and also hoping they would find the older couple as eager as they were for a nice long chat. They were optimistic when they spotted the Grahams' car beside the cabin, but their repeated knocking went unanswered.

"They can't be far," Marley said. "They're on foot."

"Let's walk up toward the resort office and see if we run into them," said Nan.

As they walked along the narrow road, they noticed a large lilac hedge on their left. A rough, shaggy dog with floppy ears suddenly appeared around one side of a bud-bedecked lilac bush, barking sharply at them, before backing off, seemingly more afraid of them than they were of him. When they came to the bend in the road that led to the resort office, they spotted Buck Sykes's white pickup truck pulling in next to the office. Its door opened, and Sykes stepped out. They stopped where they were and watched him enter the small bar and café adjacent to the office, slamming the door behind him.

"What's he doing here so early in the morning?" Nan said.

"Good question," Marley replied, walking up to the truck. "Look at all the announcements he has plastered on his vehicle."

Nan began to read aloud the numerous stickers with ill-tempered warnings displayed on Sykes's back bumper: "If you have something to say to me, say it to my Smith and Wesson." Balanced on the other side of that notice was its snarky twin: "If you can read this, you're too damn close!"

"A man after my own heart," Nan said.

"My thought exactly," Marley replied. "Such a sensitive, caring modern-day male."

Just then, they spied the Grahams ambling toward them down the long driveway that led out to the main road. Nan and Marley smiled, waved, and waited for them to approach.

"Just the people we wanted to see," Marley said. "Are you two ready for some breakfast? We picked up homemade jam and fresh eggs at the McNair farm yesterday, and we'd love to repay you for treating us with those muffins the other day."

"Why, how sweet of you," Ione said. "Ed was just saying how good a cup of coffee would taste about now." Smiling, she went on. "We decided to have a little walk before breakfast this morning, but then somehow, time got away from us. We must have gone five miles or more."

"Good. Then you likely have worked up a good appetite," Nan said.

"That we did," Ed replied eagerly. "Breakfast sounds real inviting."

The four of them fell into step and continued walking slowly along the road to cabin number eight.

"I notice that fellow whose name shall not be mentioned is here again," Ione said, looking at Ed and gesturing toward the white pickup truck in the office parking lot.

"Yes, we did as well," Nan said with a nod. "And guess what. We discovered what his name is. Anne McNair told us. It's Buck Sykes."

"Well, may the angels in heaven pray for Anne McNair," Ed muttered, smirking.

"Now, stop that, Ed. Buck Sykes seems to be here most days, so they'd find out his name sooner or later," Ione said.

"Well, all I'm saying is, I warned them not to ask," Ed said. "Knowing that man's name isn't going to do them one bit of good."

"Do the Chapmans have many other friends?" Nan asked.

"Not that I know of," Ione answered. "The Sykes fellow is the only one who comes and goes around here regularly. Although that isn't really true, because the bar at the office does get quite a few regulars every night. I know Professor Lyman and Lynn Parker used to tip back a few beers there every so often."

"Do you think Professor Lyman and Dale Chapman are friends?"

"They certainly would know each other by now. But I can't see where they would have much in common."

"How about Mrs. Chapman? How well do you think Lyman knows her?"

"He knows her, but then again, she's here about as much as Mr. Chapman. I swear, she's away a lot. I suppose she could be visiting friends, but I wouldn't know. Why do you ask?"

Nan shrugged. "Oh, we're just curious. Christy Chapman gave us the impression she rarely left the resort because she was so busy running things."

Ione tossed back her head. "Running things?" She snickered. "That's a good one. If you want to know who runs things around here, it's Madge Sims. She's the head housekeeper, and she's been here for years. In fact, it's likely she's forgotten more of the ins and outs of running this place than Christy Chapman will ever know."

"Madge Sims?" Nan said. "I assume she's here most days? Or does she only come when a cabin is turning over?"

Ione nodded. "Madge comes when she's needed. And as you can plainly see by the lack of folks here, she certainly isn't needed much at present."

They had reached cabin number eight, and as Marley opened the door and held it wide, the other three entered the cabin. Ione immediately began to gush over the expansiveness of its layout. She liked what she saw of the view; the rustic furniture; and, most of all, the number of amenities. After a quick tour of the entire cabin and an even quicker investigation of the deck, Nan and Ed disappeared into the kitchen to whip up some scrambled eggs, toast, and Thielen's-made breakfast sausage.

Meanwhile, Ione and Marley busied themselves in the dining area. Once they'd finished setting the table, they wandered into the kitchen and found Ed pouring fresh coffee into a carafe as he kept a watchful eye on the toaster. Nan, wearing an apron about her waist, stood by the stove before two round stainless-steel pans, one filled with golden scrambled eggs dotted with mushrooms and fresh chives and the other filled with fresh, sizzling Thielen's sausage.

Nan raised her eyes from her cooking duties and motioned toward the kitchen counter. "Grab the strawberry jam, butter, and any cream or sugar that may be needed. I'm ready to fill this serving platter with eggs and sausage."

Everyone took part in transferring food and condiments from the kitchen to the dining table. When they were all seated and the coffee had been poured, Ed opened Anne McNair's jar of strawberry jam, scooped a hefty spoonful onto his toast, and said, "I've always said that jam tastes best at breakfast. I don't know why. It just does."

"These eggs are incredible," Nan said, reaching for a piece of toast. "In fact, everything is tasting divine."

Everyone agreed with Nan's assessment, and after a few more comments on the food, including how beautifully balanced the spices were within the breakfast sausage, Marley figured enough time had gone by to ask the question uppermost in her mind. Glancing toward Ione, she said, "I wonder if you might advise us how, if Nan and I should want to ask her a few questions, we could go about finding Madge Sims."

"Oh, that's easy," Ione said. "I can tell you where she lives. Her home is near the old paper mill in Brainerd. It's a small house with a big vegetable garden right next to it. You can't miss it. Madge has the biggest garden in that part of town."

"Is she approachable?" Marley asked. "I mean, we haven't been formally introduced."

Ed laughed heartily. "Introduced? Are you kidding me? We're up north, and Brainerd is a friendly town. It doesn't matter if you're a stranger or not; if you know how to say, 'Hey there,' you're approachable. No introduction necessary." He made an inch sign with his thumb and forefinger as he said, "Believe me, in this much time, you'll be gabbing as if you were lifelong friends."

Marley and Nan looked at each other and hesitated. Ione, noticing their reluctance to ask questions of someone they didn't know, added tentatively, "If you don't feel comfortable simply approaching Madge to chat, you could always stop by her house, saying you were hoping she might be open to selling you some of her tomato jam or marinara sauce."

"Tomato jam?" Marley said in surprise. "I've never—really?"

"That's right," Ed said with a grin. "And if you've never tasted it, you're in for a real treat. Madge Sims makes the best tomato jam there is. Everyone around here says so."

"Ed and I always make sure to buy a few jars of Madge's jam each and every year. Of course, because we usually visit Eagle's Cove in the spring, well before the peak of tomato season, what we buy is always from Madge's previous year's harvest. But it doesn't matter. Her jam and marinara sauce always taste the same from year to year. Both are a real treat."

Ed broke in. "Madge is a great gardener. Every summer, she grows tons of big, beautiful tomatoes and other vegetables in that garden of hers. Also, flowers of various kinds. She runs a little vegetable stand in the fall, where she sells what she harvests. She's been selling her tomato jam and marinara sauce for years now."

"If you like, you can tell Madge you tasted some of her jam at our cabin and that we sent you to her," Ione said.

"I don't think I've ever tasted tomato jam," Marley said.

Ione looked over at Ed and frowned. "We have an open jar of Madge's jam at our cabin. Ed and I have been enjoying it on toast in the mornings. We would have brought it over with us if we'd known you'd never tasted it."

"That's all right, Ione," Nan said. "We'll be sure to purchase our own from Madge. And thanks for the tip. It will make it easier for us to knock on Madge Sims's front door."

Ione smiled. "I thought the two of you might need a reason or some purpose for stopping other than to simply inquire about Dale and Christy Chapman or Buck Sykes."

Marley was taken aback by Ione's sharp intuition. "I'm afraid Nan and I have begun to develop far too curious an absorption with these people," she said. "I'm sure it's due to all the time we have on our hands; discussing them fills blank stretches that would otherwise be completely idle. Still, we wouldn't want anyone to think we're two nosy parkers bent on starting gossip or trouble."

"Right," Nan added, "but how can we not be intrigued by the fact that the Chapmans appear to be the exact opposite of a typical resort-owning couple?"

"I know. They do seem rather strange," Ione said. "Not like other resort owners we've known. They certainly aren't anything like the previous owners, the Tillers. Now, there were people who knew how to run a resort."

"How long did the Tillers own this place?" Nan asked.

"For as long as Ed and I have been coming here. And we've been coming a long time now. Back then, the resort was bigger than it is today. The Tillers decided to sell off some of their land prior to retirement a few years back. That was when they sold the land across the creek."

"You mean the land that Professor Lyman Haynes's house stands on?" asked Nan.

"That's right, only Professor Lyman didn't always own that house. Buck Sykes and his wife bought the land and built the house some years back, just after they were married. Lyman enlarged the place considerably once he moved in."

"Buck Sykes was married?"

"He sure was," Ione said. "His wife wasn't from around here, though."

"Where was she from?" Marley asked.

"I can't recall," Ione replied, swiveling toward her husband. "Ed, do you remember where that big guy's wife hailed from?"

Ed, who had risen from the table to fetch the coffeepot was presently in the process of filling his cup, answered, "Sure do. I remember because she used to sing that song all the time. You know, the one that goes"—he tossed back his head and began to warble—"'I'm going to Kansas City. Kansas City, here I come.'"

Ione burst out laughing. "Oh, that's right. And she'd do that slinky dance."

"Yeah," Ed said, shaking his head. "She was a real number all right."

"Where is she these days?" Nan asked. "Are she and Buck Sykes still married?"

"Good Lord no!" Ione said. "They divorced. She's been gone a good long time now—too long to remember. Just after she left, he sold the house and land to Lyman Haynes and then moved back in with his father following his mother's death."

"I understand Buck's father is an invalid," Nan said. "So then I guess Buck is his primary caregiver?"

"I sure hope not," Ed answered. "That fellow doesn't have a caring bone in his body, from what I can see."

"His father is old—that's true—but he's not really an invalid," Ione added. "He's extremely hard of hearing, I know, but other than that, I think he can take care of himself. He just doesn't get out anymore. Not since his wife died. Never leaves the farm, from what I hear."

The conversation paused as Ed, with his breakfast finished, rose and walked across the living area to gaze out the glass doors. "You have a great view of the lake from up here," he said. "And of the bay."

"I know," Nan said. "Believe me, Marley and I have been enjoying it."

"You also have a great view of Three Pine Island," he added.

"Is that what it's called?" Nan asked. "Yes, it's a great view. And I'm sure when an eagles' nest was still perched at the top of that tallest pine, Suzanne Engelmann thought so too."

Ed nodded. "No doubt. You know, I've been thinking about those eagles and what you or Marley said earlier about not thinking a storm damaged their nest."

"I've been thinking about that too," Ione said. "Eagle

nests are strong. They're built to withstand storms, aren't they?"

"Not necessarily. Although perhaps," Ed said. "It would depend on the storm."

"But even if the nest did suffer some damage," Ione said, "wouldn't the eagles have rebuilt?"

Ed turned his head to look at his breakfast companions. "That's the question that continues to haunt me: Why haven't the eagles rebuilt? They, or another pair, have nested on that island for as long as Ione and I have been visiting this resort. Actually, for as long as many of the locals can remember. So why would they abandon the island now? Why are there no longer eagles in Eagle's Cove?"

"I would think," Marley said with a shake of her head, "that there may be any number of reasons. Perhaps they left because of an overabundance of activity. The island may have become overused by fishermen or picnickers, and that made the eagles decide to leave. Have you seen more activity there lately than in the past?"

"No, not that I've noticed," Ione answered.

Ed walked over to the table and sat down. "I remember," he said pensively, "hearing Mr. Chapman mention more than once the fact that fishermen are using the island as a porta-potty. He supposed it saved them a trip to shore, but in his opinion, the entire island was beginning to become a health hazard."

"How disgusting!" Ione snorted with an unpleasant scrunch of her face.

"Do you think that's true?" Marley asked.

"I've never seen anyone putting in there myself," Ed

replied. "But I suppose it could be happening when there are more people fishing the lake."

"And do you think that would be enough to discourage the eagles?"

He shrugged. "Can't say."

Ed once again reached for the carafe, and Marley exclaimed, "No more for us! We've had enough coffee, Ed."

Surprisingly, when he steadied the carafe over Ione's cup, she placed a hand over it, also saying no to another cupful. "I'm going to slosh all the way to our cabin as it is," she said, rising from the table.

Ed carried the carafe into the kitchen and then came back and helped to clear the table. When the dishes were all rinsed and the dishwasher was packed, Ione and Ed said their goodbyes and made their way out of the cabin toward the resort's road out front.

Nan and Marley, having donned jackets, walked with them out onto the driveway and then stood on the back stoop, watching their steady and easygoing amble down the hill to their own cabin. The air was still misty and moisture-laden, and the temperature had fallen somewhat, giving every indication there might be a cool April evening ahead.

Nan turned to go back inside, but Marley stopped her. "Let's not go back quite yet. It's still early. What do you say we head to the resort office to talk to the Chapmans for a bit?"

"Anything in particular we might want to ask them?" Nan asked.

"No," Marley replied. "I just want to get a better feel for them. What we have so far is primarily from Ione's and Ed's observations."

"It couldn't hurt," Nan said. "It's not as if we don't have the whole day before us."

They started off and took their time, walking slowly toward the resort office. At one point, Marley reached into her jacket pocket and took out the plastic compact that held her fake hearing aid. She made sure to place it in her correct ear and then slipped the compact back into her pocket. They continued to ramble on.

To Nan, the resort grounds seemed eerily quiet and deserted. She glanced over at the playground and thought of the many children who, in all probability, played there in high season. "Look at the smooth sand in that box," she said to Marley. "Look how neat it is. It's sort of sad how it has yet to be disturbed by a single little footstep."

As they approached the office, they noticed that the inner door stood open, with only the screen door facing them. Nan reached out to grasp its handle, but Marley swiftly put out an arm to stop her. With a finger to her lips, Marley motioned for Nan to step away from the door. Within the office, Nan could hear Mrs. Chapman's voice. She was talking to someone, and since the conversation appeared entirely one-sided, Nan thought it likely she was speaking to someone on the phone. Both women listened intently.

"I was planning to get down to the cities today," Christy Chapman said, "but Dale had business at Five Feathers again. It's so frustrating, especially since I made a hair appointment, but he said he'd be gone most of the day, so I'm stuck here, minding the few losers staying in the cabins. God, why anyone would want to do this for a living is beyond me! It's torture to have to cater to their every want, as if we don't have anything better to do. I can't wait for it to end."

Marley and Nan glanced at each other with interest, and Marley whispered, "Dale Chapman is at Five Feathers? Let's see if we can find out why."

Nan nodded, and Marley boldly stepped right in front of the screen door, swung it wide open, and entered the office. Nan followed at her heels.

Mrs. Chapman's smooth and shiny hair swung to one side as she glanced up and quickly ended her phone conversation. "Gotta go. Talk to you later," she said to whomever was on the other end. Placing her phone on the counter, she turned toward Nan and Marley and forced a smile. "Is there anything I can do for you ladies?" she asked.

"Yes, thank you," Marley said. "We came for a bag of ice."

Mrs. Chapman turned toward a freezer behind the counter. "Five or ten pounds?"

"Oh, I think five will do," Marley answered.

As Christy opened the lid of a chest-style freezer that stood behind the counter and leaned over it to take out a five-pound bag of ice, Nan said, "It looks like it's going to be a delightful day. I'm rather partial to rainy days when they're misty like this one. I mean, having far more mist than rain. We thought maybe we'd stroll along the many paths here at the resort before going to the casino later." She paused and then asked, "Is Mr. Chapman anywhere around the property? We were both just commenting on the fact that if we were to come across him on our walks, we wouldn't even recognize him, because we have yet to meet him."

"I'm afraid Dale isn't here right now," Christy replied.

"He had a business appointment in town. I expect him back this afternoon."

"I don't think we'll be here. We plan on visiting the Five Feathers casino. We haven't been there yet, and I understand it's the largest of the three."

"Yes, it is," Christy said. "But you might want to rethink your visit. I'm told it isn't paying off as well as another casino is these days. According to a few of the guys who hang around our bar, the Sleeping Bear casino is hot right now."

"Well, maybe we should reconsider and go there. What do you say, Marley? Are you up to winning a little money?"

Marley laughed. "It would be a nice change from always losing some."

Nan leaned on the counter and gave Mrs. Chapman an excited smile. "Sleeping Bear casino it is. Can you please give us directions on how to get to Sleeping Bear? You said it wasn't very far from here, right?"

Mrs. Chapman began to write out directions to Sleeping Bear on a piece of paper, and when she finished, she slid the paper across the bar toward Marley. "Here's to Lady Luck," she said before turning away dismissively.

Nan hefted the five-pound bag of ice onto her shoulder, and she and Marley left the office. They took no notice of the screen door as it slammed shut on their way out.

Once they were a safe distance away, Marley said, "I don't know what you picked up from that conversation, but I'd say she definitely did not want us to go to the Five Feathers casino."

"I agree," Nan said. "Did you see that wide-eyed look she gave us when she thought we might be going to that particular casino? I don't know what you thought, but it told me something important is happening there. Something she doesn't want us to see or know about."

Marley went on. "We have an entanglement that we need to unravel, Nan. Like, who exactly is Dale Chapman meeting with at Five Feathers?"

Nan nodded. "And isn't it interesting that she mentioned on the phone her husband was attending a business meeting at Five Feathers, but she told us his meeting was in town? She outright lied!"

"It's not the first time," Marley said.

When they arrived back at their cabin, Nan popped Agatha's trunk and quickly deposited the bag of ice into an Igloo cooler. "Do you think Mrs. Chapman wondered why we were asking for a bag of ice, when our cabin has a modern refrigerator that makes perfectly good ice?"

"Who cares?" Marley answered dismissively. "I only wanted to give her some plausible reason for our appearance in the office."

Nan slammed the trunk shut and said, "Let's jump into Agatha and do some investigating."

When they were both seated in the car, Marley turned toward Nan. "About her many lies," she said.

"You mean when she told us she never visits the Twin Cities yet was complaining to someone on the phone about missing her hair appointment there?"

"Precisely," Marley said, nodding for emphasis. "The question is, why is she lying? What is she trying to hide?"

"Plenty, I'd say," Nan responded.

"I agree," Marley said. "I only wish I knew what it all amounted to."

"Me too," Nan replied. "However, the important thing is, where we're concerned, she's been exposed."

"Yes, she has," Marley said.

Nan started the car and drove down the resort road, making sure to brake and pull over when they came to Ed and Ione's cabin, where they made a quick stop in order to acquire a detailed description of their invisible host, Dale Chapman. After they received what they'd asked for, they continued on their way toward the Five Feathers casino.

CHAPTER 17

FIVE FEATHERS WAS THREE STORIES high, with an eight-story adjacent hotel surrounded by a multi-football-field-sized parking lot. Nan and Marley walked through the front doors into an entry hall, beyond which they saw row upon row of slot machines, with a sensory overload of flashing lights and repetitive pinging sounds emanating from each. Rotating bars of fruits and varied icons whizzed along on large screens, feeding the addictions of zombielike figures sitting on high-backed chairs, who moved little except for constantly punching buttons.

Primed with Ed's detailed description of Dale Chapman, once inside the casino proper, the two separated, with Nan heading toward the northern end of the casino and Marley heading toward the southern end, with its high-roller lounge.

Nan walked toward the buffet restaurant, noting that the menu for that evening featured an endless crab-leg feast. She smiled sweetly at the person at the cash register and asked, "Could I just check to see if my friend is here?"

"Sure, go ahead," the woman answered. "Not much of

a crowd right now, and it looks like the same for the rest of today. Your friend should be easy to spot."

Nan rushed into the restaurant and did a quick survey of the people inside as she walked among the rows of tables, looking for anyone who fit Ed's description. When she was convinced Dale Chapman wasn't eating at the buffet, she reentered the main floor of the casino.

As she continued to amble about, Nan realized the constant computer-generated sounds were beginning to disorient her. She was not a born gambler by any means, and all the different themes displayed on the upper screens of the machines made her dizzy. The names displayed, such as Weird Mouse, Neptune's Treasures, Salome's Dance, and Wild Wonders, made her feel as if she were on a merry-go-round, with none of the benefits of open air or cotton candy smells. On the contrary, the lights and sounds were oppressive to her, and the entire place, despite the flashing numbers and rolling images, seemed dark, with no access to natural light or anything even remotely wild.

She passed the first of the pull-tab booths and began to walk up and down the many rows of slot machines. Although she didn't think slots were Dale Chapman's bag, she nevertheless craned her neck while searching for him among the close-packed machines. When she had walked more than a few rows, she spotted the second pull-tab booth and, just beyond it, the Grey Duck restaurant. She was able to see at a glance that Chapman wasn't inside, and she continued on her way, passing the roulette wheel and three blackjack tables, all of which were also Chapman-free.

Nan had walked what seemed like a three-block stretch, when she suddenly heard a shrill shriek, followed by the tinny clatter of coins falling into a metal pan. The sounds told her someone had won a jackpot of considerable size.

At the upcoming corner turn, she spotted Marley walking toward her.

"Any luck?" Marley asked once they were side by side.

Nan shook her head. "No, you?"

Marley sighed. "No. If he's here, he's somewhere where we can't see him." She drew a hand through her hair in frustration. "Did you notice how people playing the slot machines seem to prefer the end machines over those in the middle of the rows? A lady actually told me they believe the end machines pay out more often because the win is more visible, and therefore, it benefits the casino. Do you think that's true?"

"Sure, I believe it; any number of tricks of the trade are likely to be employed in order to draw more people to the machines and encourage them to keep on feeding bills into these contraptions. Casinos are businesses, after all. And gamblers have all sorts of superstitions and gaming theories," Nan answered.

Marley shook her head. "Strange, but I think I saw a woman constantly feeding twenty-dollar bills into a machine. If what I think I saw was true, that would indicate a serious player."

"And here I am, trying to stay in the middle class on a professor's pension!" Nan said with an indignant expression and a toss of her curly red hair.

"She's probably an addict," Marley said. "Poor dear."

Nan gave Marley a nudge. "Well, there's a familiar face. Isn't that June from Ojibwa Point?"

Marley turned in time to see June just rising from the

poker table, pocketing a handful of chips. Marley motioned to her, and they made their way over to one another.

"Hi, June," Nan said. "How's your luck going?"

June smiled widely. "I'm doing OK!" She chuckled, patting her pocket. "Funny running into you two here. This must be Eagle's Cove Day at Five Feathers."

"Oh? Why do you say that?" Nan asked.

"Because I just saw your genial host Dale Chapman and his sidekick, Buck Sykes, a little bit ago."

"Really? We came over on our own," Marley said, "but it does seem odd that we're all here at the same time. Do you know where Mr. Chapman is now? Nan and I have yet to meet the fellow, and I have a few questions to ask him."

June looked over the heads of the people sitting at machines, toward the elevators. "The last I saw of them, they were getting into the private elevator of the guy who runs this place. They might be in his office. They seemed to be having quite the discussion."

"Oh?" Nan asked, cocking her head to one side. "And who is the manager of this casino? Do you know him?"

"Not personally. But I've seen him a lot at the restaurant. He comes in quite often. All I know is, he's a big spender and tipper. He must have a high limit on his credit card, because it's nothing but the best for that guy. He likes to show off. His name's Braun. Trevor Braun."

"You don't think they were conversing about either Dale Chapman or Buck Sykes being a big loser, do you?" Nan asked.

"No, they didn't look unhappy—the opposite, in fact. These guys seemed pleased with each other."

"By the way," Marley said, "I thought the casinos were

all owned by Native American tribes. Trevor Braun doesn't sound like any sort of Native American name."

"The thing is," June told her, "it seems people have to come from Atlantic City or Vegas with inside knowledge to run these places. It's a pretty complicated process. Believe me, the Indians may own them, but other experienced folks are brought in to help run things. At least that seems to be the case in the beginning."

"I see," Marley said.

Suddenly, Nan grabbed Marley's shoulders and spun her around. "We hate to run," she said to a startled June, "but we've got to go! See you later."

June followed Nan's gaze, and when she noticed what had put the look of panic on Nan's face, she said knowingly, "I don't blame you. I run from him too." Then she turned on her heel and headed toward the cashiers to turn in her chips.

In the meantime, Nan had pulled Marley behind a row of slot machines. Marley, now hidden and crouched low behind the contraptions, could finally see for herself the reason for Nan's unusual behavior. Peeking around the corner of one of the nearby machines, she spotted the large, bulky shape of Buck Sykes crossing the room with two other men. One of the trio looked to be the person June had described as the manager of the casino, Trevor Braun. The other man, tall and thin, wearing jeans, a denim jacket, and boots, was an exact match for Ed Graham's description of Dale Chapman.

"The last thing we want," Nan hissed in Marley ear, "is for those three guys to see us."

"Why?" Marley whispered back. "Only one would be

able to recognize us, and the first time we encountered Buck Sykes, he hardly gave us a second look."

"Nevertheless, we don't want them to be able to remember us if we should happen to meet them again. We need to be careful and follow them at a safe distance to try to hear what they're saying without them taking any notice of us."

Since the three men were deeply caught up in their conversation, the two friends were able to walk behind them at a discreet distance directly to the casino's front entrance doors without being seen. Just before the wide expanse of doors, six of them across the entry, Chapman and Sykes stopped suddenly and turned toward the third man in order to continue their conversation. That forced Nan and Marley to quickly lower their heads, pivot on their heels, and scan the enticingly decorated window of a conveniently located gift shop.

Since the shop window was filled with a mishmash of objects designed to gather back winnings from any type of casino visitor, it was perfect as the sort of thing any woman might find attractive. As their eyes took in rows of fine pieces of jewelry, many-colored silk scarves, and assorted knickknacks and coffee cups, Marley noticed that the shop window was so clean and highly polished that she could, from a certain angle, see the three men's reflections in it. She fastened her attention on their reflected images just as the third man, whom she took to be Trevor Braun, said, "I plan on being right here at the casino until about two in the morning."

"We'll let you know how it goes," Chapman said.

"See that you do. And make sure there's no problem this time."

"Don't worry," Sykes told the tall and authoritative figure. "There's practically no one staying at the resort. Just two cabins are rented, and both have old folks in them who hit the sack by ten or even earlier."

"They'd better," Braun said forcefully. "There's been enough hitches already. Like I keep telling you guys, I manage things, damn it, and what I can't manage I fix."

"Don't worry," Chapman replied, raising both hands in an attempt to calm the other man. "We don't plan to hit the island until twelve or later. No one will notice anything. Not a problem."

"Why do I have the feeling we already have more than one problem?" Braun asked.

Neither Chapman nor Sykes replied to Braun's comment. Instead, Marley watched the three split up; two of them headed toward the entry doors. She and Nan continued to stare at the many offerings on the shelves of the shop until they heard the front doors open. Taking a peek over her shoulder, Nan caught a glimpse as Chapman and Sykes stepped out into the parking lot. She also noticed Braun turn and walk back into the casino.

Marley and Nan hesitated for a few more minutes, letting the guys they were concerned with distance themselves a bit farther. When she thought enough time had gone by, Marley asked, "Should we follow any of them?"

"No," Nan said. "I found that stressful enough. I think we have all the information we need for today." Then, in a voice that was more snarling than melodic, she added, "Can you believe that creep Buck Sykes? Calling us old folks? Where does he get off?"

"I didn't even hear that remark," Marley responded. "I was far more interested in their plan to report to Braun after what's going on at the resort."

"Do you think they were speaking of meeting tonight? And what was that bit about hitting the island by twelve or later? Are we going to need to stay up until two in the morning or so?"

"I don't have the least idea. We'll just have to stay up to find out," Marley said. "What other option do we have? However, since we don't want to nod off, we should probably go back to our cabin now and take a nap."

"That sounds good. But still, we have plenty of time for that. Before we lay our heads down, we might want to stop in Brainerd since it's on our way. I think this would be a good time to pay Madge Sims a visit to inquire about buying a jar or two of her tomato jam."

"Good idea," Marley said. "Might as well try to get her view on Dale and Christy Chapman and their methods for running the resort. Let's hope she's someone who likes to talk. Can you think of any subject we might broach if she should turn out to be a person of few words?"

"Not offhand," Nan said. "But I'm sure we'll come up with something if that should prove to be the case."

Marley nodded. "And whatever one of us comes up with, the other has to back her up."

"Of course. That's our standard operating procedure."

It wasn't difficult to spot Madge Sims's house once they had located the now-shuttered paper mill on Brainerd's east side. Her small house was neatly tucked next to what looked like a full fourth of a block of tilled garden space surrounded by a cyclone fence with two gates. As Nan and Marley approached the house's front door, they could imagine the upcoming rows of lush green future bounty breaking through the garden's dark, loamy, well-tilled soil. The garden appeared to be fully prepared for planting in May, when the weather would allow.

Their knock upon the door was answered almost immediately, which told Nan that Madge Sims had been observing them from somewhere inside as they parked the car and strolled the length of her front walk. Nan was reminded of how conspicuous a person always felt in a small town, especially if he or she was a stranger.

At that moment, however, Madge Sims stood before them with a look that, Nan was pleased to notice, radiated a deep and abiding interest rather than suspicion. Nan was also pleased to see that the sturdily built woman, whose hair was caught back in a ponytail, did not hesitate a bit to step to one side and invite them both in, where Marley quickly introduced them before broaching the purpose of their visit.

"We've been staying at Eagle's Cove Resort," Marley said, "and as we were having breakfast this morning with Ed and Ione—"

"Lovely people, don't you think?" Madge said, cutting in. "I just love them. I really do."

"Yes," Marley said. "Although we've only recently met them, we've grown quite fond of them as well."

"I suppose they told you," Madge said, "they've been coming to Eagle's Cove every summer for some twenty years or so. I worked at the resort as a teenager the first time I met them. Can you believe that?"

"Ed and Ione told us you are the head housekeeper."

Madge shrugged. "Yeah, I was head of housekeeping for the Tillers. When the Chapmans came, I stayed on. Is that why you're here? Something to do with the housekeeping at Eagle's Cove?"

"Oh no," Marley said. "Nothing like that. We were very satisfied with the cabin. It was whipping-cream clean and very well stocked."

"Well, I run a tight ship if I do say so myself," Madge said, smiling.

"Actually, we had some of your tomato jam on our toast this morning," Nan said, "and we absolutely flipped for it. So Ione gave us directions on how to find you and told us you might have a few jars to sell."

"You'd like to buy some of my jam?" Madge asked.

"Yes, please. If you have a few jars to spare."

"I'll have to check the fruit cellar, but I'm sure I can come up with one or two jars for you."

"That would be lovely," Marley replied, "and perhaps we could purchase a jar or two of your marinara sauce as well?"

Madge tossed back her head and laughed. "Boy, that must have been some breakfast if you were also able to taste some of my marinara sauce."

"Actually, we haven't tasted that," Nan said. "But Ione and Ed told us it was fantastic, and we see no reason not to trust them."

"Have a seat in the living room," Madge said. "I'll be right back."

As Madge made her way to the root cellar, Marley and Nan seated themselves in Madge's comfortable living room. As they sat quietly taking in the many curio objects about them, which spoke of Madge's various interests, a cat, sleek and stately, holding its tail high, ambled into the room. Nan, who always missed her two boys something dreadful when she was away from them, kept her eyes glued to it. At its slow approach, she put out a clenched hand in the hope that the cat might touch its nose to it and perhaps end up on her lap. Instead, the cat stopped, rubbed a cheek against Nan's knuckles, and then gracefully jumped onto the arm of her chair. Nan gently stroked the cat while telling it how beautiful it was. The cat gave every indication that it agreed with the assessment.

Madge entered the room, holding a paper bag. "I got you three jars of tomato jam and two jars of marinara sauce. Will that be OK?"

"Wonderful," Marley said, reaching for her purse.

As Marley drew out her wallet, Nan continued to talk nonsense while gently stroking the cat.

Looking over at Nan, Madge said, "I see you've taken to the Bean."

"The Bean? Is that her name?" Nan answered in surprise.

"The Bean, Beaner, Bee-bee, or just plain Bean. She goes by many names and answers to them all," Madge said. "I found her when she was just a wee little kitten. Someone had obviously dropped her off in the garden. I suppose they thought anyone who had a garden like mine would be sure to give her a good home."

"You found her in your garden?"

"Yeah, she was hiding among the pole beans. So naturally, I called her Bean."

"Poor little thing," Nan said. "How can anyone be so cruel as to abandon a kitten?"

"It looks to me as if everything turned out for the best, though," Marley said, marveling at the smooth sheen of the cat's fur under Nan's stroking fingers.

Nan smiled up at Madge. "I have two cats of my own," she told their hostess.

While Marley and Madge took care of the bill, Nan regaled Madge with stories of her two cats. When she was through, Madge continued with more Bean stories of her own. For her part, Marley simply sat back and took it all in, thinking Ed had been right. They had been in Madge Sims's home for no more than ten minutes, and it already felt as if they had known the woman for years.

Once the stories were all told and cat oddities, idiosyncrasies, and favorite toys had been discussed, Marley decided it was safe to try to, in a roundabout way, bring up the subject of the Chapmans. "I don't know if you've heard or not," she said, addressing Madge, "but Ione and Ed told us they might not come back to Eagle's Cove next summer."

"That's sad," Madge said. "It really is. But it doesn't surprise me. A lot of the old regulars have left."

"I have to admit the resort does look rather desolate," Nan said, "but we just assumed that was due to it being so early in the season."

"That's part of it," Madge said. "But only a small part. The fact is the two women's disappearances from the resort, which I'm sure you've both heard about, along with the total incompetence and lack of care on the part of the current owners, have driven the resort's past business away. Actually, I'm leaving myself. In fact, I've already given notice."

"Wow," Nan said. "So you're leaving too? Will it be too late for you to find other work this coming summer?"

Madge shook her head. "Not at all. I'm well known in these parts, and my reputation precedes me. I can get a job tomorrow at any of the area resorts, even the bigger and pricier ones, if I want it."

"Well, that's good news anyway," Marley said. "However, it doesn't bode well for Eagle's Cove Resort, does it? I doubt any resort can survive a loss of good help and repeat business at the same time. What's wrong with those Chapmans? Why are they so hard to work for?"

"I don't think they give a damn," Madge said. "And that's the honest truth. If you ask me, they're just biding their time."

"Biding their time? For what?" Nan asked.

"Who knows? But whatever it is, it has nothing to do with the resort."

"So you see a lack of commitment?" Marley asked.

Madge threw Marley a look filled with surprise. "I see a total lack of commitment!" she said. "In fact, I really don't know why they bought the place or why they stay. I have a feeling they'll sell before the year is up, and we'll never hear from them again."

"They're not from around here, are they?" Nan said. "Perhaps they were just naive?"

Madge hesitated before speaking. "Perhaps," she answered with a look of disgust.

"They do seem to have one loyal friend, though. We've noticed a certain fellow hanging around the resort quite a lot. His name is Buck Sykes. Do you happen to know him?"

"Everyone in and around Brainerd knows Buck Sykes," Madge said.

"Marley had an unfortunate incident with him. He

practically knocked her down. It scared her half to death," Nan said.

"He's been known to knock women around," Madge said. "I'd stay away from him if I were you. He isn't safe to be near at all."

"We know," Marley said. "Ione and Ed warned us. They also told us he'd been married at one time. I think they told us her name was Randi. Knowing how powerful he is and what I went through, I can't help feeling sorry for her."

"She had it rough for a while," Madge said. "I'll give you that. He used to beat her hard and often. But she finally got her act together and enough strength to walk away in one piece."

"So you know Buck Sykes's ex-wife?" Nan asked.

"Yeah, I do know Randi Sykes. We were good friends. Still are," Madge said.

Marley suddenly shifted in her chair. "I wonder," she said to Madge, "if I might use your restroom?"

"Of course," Madge answered, smiling. "It's down the hall, next to the kitchen. Let me show you."

Marley rose to her feet and, holding her purse, said, "No need. I'm sure I'll find it. You two just continue your conversation. I won't be long." Marley threw Nan a look that told her she would be doing far more than visiting the restroom and to make sure Madge Sims was kept busy and didn't leave the living room.

Since Nan took Marley's directives seriously, once her friend had left the room, she leaned forward in her chair and asked in a concerned, soothing voice, "Is Randi Sykes safe now? Please tell me she is."

"Well, she's twenty-two hundred miles away from here,"

Madge said with a laugh. "That should be a safe enough distance."

"She's living in California?" Nan said, deciding to risk that she'd guessed correctly.

Madge nodded. "Yeah, she lives with her sister. That way, they can split expenses."

"So she's doing all right?"

"Well, things are tough financially," Madge said. "California is expensive as hell, but they're getting by. The thing is, Randi doesn't have any real training. She's always worked at the sort of jobs that don't pay very well."

"Still, her life is better than it was when she was here and still living with that brute," Nan said. "As you were a close friend, you must miss her. Do you ever go out to visit her?"

"I've gone once. And I plan on visiting her again next winter. Winter is a good time to go to California."

"It's the best time if you're from Minnesota. Is she on the coast and close to the ocean?"

Madge smiled and nodded. "She's in Alameda and only a short walking distance from the bay. It's beautiful. They live in a small rental, and they put me up on their sleeper couch. A bit crowded, but we spend a lot of time outside, of course."

"I've slept on plenty of sleeper couches in my life so far," Nan said, "and have never once complained."

"How can you complain when you're in California in the winter and only blocks from the beach?"

"Exactly!" Nan exclaimed, throwing her arms into the air. "A person would have to be out of her mind to complain."

"Or a regular prig."

At a sudden sound, Nan looked up to see Marley, with

her purse slung over her arm, reenter the room. Marley flashed Madge a wide smile and said, "Nan and I are going to have to leave, I'm sorry to say. Until just now, I didn't realize how late it is. It's almost three o'clock, and I promised my husband I'd call him."

Taking her cue from Marley, Nan gently lifted Bean from her lap and placed Madge's beloved companion animal beside her on the sofa cushion. Then she rose from the couch and, along with Madge and Marley, walked toward the front door of the house, where a number of farewell greetings were exchanged.

Out on the walk, Nan and Marley made their way toward Agatha, and once they were inside the car, Nan started the engine, turned toward Marley, and said, "You have no intention of calling Dan, so what's up? What were you doing all the time you were away? I know damn well you didn't visit the bathroom. You never do."

Marley shook her head. "No, I didn't. I went into the kitchen. I wanted to search it. I was looking for an address book that might have Randi Sykes's address in it. But although I opened every drawer there was, I could see nothing that even vaguely resembled an address book."

"People don't use address books today," Nan said. "They keep all their important numbers in their phones."

"I know. But I thought it was worth a try."

"Oh, it was," Nan said encouragingly. "Everything is worth a try."

Marley's smile was radiant. "But then guess what!" she cried. "I got lucky!"

Nan's eyes widened. "You don't say!"

Marley, looking like the cat that swallowed the canary,

replied, "Just as I was about to leave the kitchen, I stopped and took one last look around, and that was when I spotted a three-slot letter holder hanging on the side of one of the cabinets. It was stuffed full of bills, seed packets, letters, and whatnot. And among everything else was a recent letter from Randi Sykes, with a lovely return address in its upper left-hand corner."

"Did you take the letter?" Nan asked.

Marley frowned. "No. Unlike you, I don't take readily to thievery. I simply copied it down." She opened her purse and withdrew a small notebook. Opening it, she said, "The address on the letter was 655 Logan Lane, Alameda, California, and the zip."

It was Nan's turn to smile. "Well, believe it or not, I can confirm that address as being current," she said smugly. "Because while you were out of the room snooping, I was able to get Madge to disclose the fact that Randi is presently living in Alameda, California. She lives there in a small rental with her sister."

"Great work," Marley said. "We're making good progress. I'll be sure to give Eva Randi's address when we talk to her this evening and suggest she pass it on to Gretchen."

"Absolutely," Nan said. "But before we head back to the resort, I feel pretty certain that a glass of something cold, a sit-down, and a warm meal would be a good idea. It's almost three. We need to find a place to eat. I'm hungry. Aren't you?"

Marley nodded. "Yes, now that you mention it. I could eat something. It's been hours since breakfast. Should we stop at Ojibwa Point on the way back to the resort to have a late lunch?"

"Sure, I'm OK with that."

The parking lot of the Ojibwa Point supper club was nearly empty when Nan maneuvered Agatha into a spot close to the side entrance and turned off the car's engine before slipping her keys into a pocket. "Looks like the only people here at present are those whose cocktail hour starts well before five."

"Fine by me," Marley responded. "If you count a glass of Stella Artois as a cocktail, I'm going to be starting the cocktail hour early myself."

The two women entered the restaurant and waited for the hostess to notice them.

As her eyes adjusted to the dark interior, Marley noticed the familiar bearded face of Professor Haynes sitting at a table, and she turned toward Nan. "There's someone we know. Professor Lyman."

"Looks like he's just finishing a late lunch," Nan said. "Unless I miss my guess, that's a piece of cake on the way to his table."

The hostess approached them. "Table for two?"

"Yes, thank you."

As they followed her to their table, Lyman, spotting them, called out, "Hello there! Come let me introduce you to June's little sister."

The hostess turned to Marley and Nan and waved a hand toward a table snugged into an alcove. It looked to be a highly desirable table, from what they could see of the glorious scene outside the many-windowed bump-out. Views of water and woods displayed a classic northern pattern that, if not for the movement within it, could have been a painting, with its sailboats, trees, and lake frosted with whitecaps. With a hospitable smile, the hostess said, "Go ahead and greet your friend; I'll just set you up by the windows over there."

"Thanks," Marley answered. "We shouldn't be long."

As Marley and Nan walked toward Lyman Haynes's table, Nan turned toward Marley and whispered, "I'm surprised he wants to interrupt his flirtation. Don't you think she's a bit too young for him?"

"A bit?" her pal whispered back.

Just then, the waitress, a shapely young girl who appeared to be in her late teens and who was presently leaning over the professor, straightened her back, tossed back her wavy blonde hair, and giggled. "Oh, Lyman," she squealed, "you're so funny. Thanks for the invite. I'll let you know if I can get over there or not."

When Marley and Nan reached the table, Lyman wiped his mouth and beard with his napkin and, tilting his head toward the waitress, said, "I don't think you've met June's sister April. April, meet Marley Phillips and Nan Abbott. They're staying at Eagle's Cove. They've already met and visited with your sister June."

"April?" Marley said, wondering at the reason behind Lyman's sudden reference to Nan's and her visiting with June. "Why, how very creative of your parents to want to name their children after the sunniest times of our year; I suppose they wanted to celebrate the times in Minnesota when the sun doesn't darken the day at four in the afternoon?"

April made a face and said, "I also have a sister named May. Can you believe that? There are three of us in all: April, May, and June. I think it's crazy."

Lyman Haynes picked up his fork, cut off another bite

of his cake, and popped it into his mouth. Marley and Nan took that as a signal that they could continue on to their own table.

"Have a good lunch," Lyman said as they turned to leave. "The walleye sandwich is always good. But so are most of their offerings."

When the two were seated at their table, Marley opened the menu and said, "I think I'll try something other than the walleye sandwich. As good as it was, I feel a yen for something different."

Nan said, suddenly bringing up a thought that had just occurred to her, "Besides talking to Eva, don't you think we should call the rest of the Finders? To catch them up on what's going on? You know how Sean and Ray are about staying informed."

"Absolutely," Marley replied. "Besides, I want them to know that something big may be going down tonight."

Nan frowned. "Well, just don't make it sound too ominous or dangerous," she said grumpily. "The last thing we need is for them to jump into a car, thinking they need to come to our rescue."

Marley looked down at the napkin spread across her lap and smiled softly. "They would never actually come, Nan. They know better than that. They realize when it comes to sleuthing, two works perfectly, but three or more is just a crowd. But don't you see? They want us to know they would come if needed. And they need to reinforce that conviction to themselves as well. And for that, I say bless them both."

After a short wait, the waitress named April came over to the pleasantly situated table, drawing their attention from the natural beauty outside, so she could take their order.

When she left, they noticed Professor Lyman slide a few bills under his plate, rise from his table, and walk across the room. At his wave, Nan and Marley each raised a hand and waved back.

Just then, a man stepped into the doorway of the room. Nan and Marley were surprised to recognize Mr. Braun from the Five Feathers casino. As Professor Lyman approached the newcomer, he put out a hand, and Braun grasped it. The two men leaned into each other, and Nan could see Braun's mouth moving mere inches from Lyman's ear. Then, just as quickly as they had come together, the two men moved toward the bar and out of the dining room.

"Well, would you look at that?" Nan said. "Professor Haynes and that Trevor Braun fellow seem to know each other."

Marley pushed her chair back from the table and pulled her handbag up off the floor. "Excuse me, please. I need to use the restroom." With that, she was off, following the route the two men had taken.

Nan turned in her chair to face the windows overlooking the front side of the dining area and craned her neck in an attempt to see some part of the parking lot, but the only view she had, even in that direction, was of the lake and the boat docks.

Just then, April came bearing a tray with their two glasses of beer. Setting them on the table, she said, "Your orders will be here shortly."

"Thank you, April," Nan answered. Then, looking at the waitress's cheerful and youthful face, she added, "I wonder if you might help me. I just saw Professor Haynes leave with a man I think I should know, but I can't remember where I might have seen him. Perhaps you know who he is. The man I'm speaking of is quite large—broad-shouldered and about six feet tall. Middle-aged, with a sweep of distinguished gray at his temples. He was dressed in a dark blue pin-striped suit?"

"Oh yeah, that's Trevor Braun," April replied. "He's a big wheel around here. He manages our casinos."

"All three of them?" Nan frowned, and her voice reflected surprise.

April shrugged. "I don't know. I couldn't say for sure. But I think so. Yeah."

"I thought he might have been at a conference I attended but not if he's a casino executive. The conference was on education. And well, I did just see him chatting with Professor Lyman. I suppose they know each other well?"

"Oh, Lyman Haynes knows everyone around here. So it's not surprising that he knows Trevor Braun. All I know is, I've seen them together more than once."

"Well, thank you, April," Nan said. "I seem to have been mistaken. I don't know anybody named Braun, so I obviously mistook him for someone else."

April left, and Nan saw Marley reenter the dining room. Once seated at their table, Marley said, "I don't have much to report. The two of them walked into the parking lot together. The casino guy walked the prof out to his car, and Lyman got in and drove away. Our Mr. Braun is still standing in the parking lot, talking on his cell. I decided since I couldn't hear a single word he said, I would give up my spot by the front window to a sweet little old man who was waiting for his grandson to come pick him up."

"Well, at least you tried," Nan said. "You didn't think it

wise to enter the parking lot? You might have been able to overhear that conversation."

"I thought about pretending I'd left something in the car as an excuse, but then I remembered that we locked Agatha, and you have the keys."

Nan noticed an empty table not far from them, by the next window over, and said, "Well, if Braun returns, let's hope he's seated next to us. Maybe we can still get lucky and overhear a phone conversation or two."

But Trevor Braun did not return to the restaurant, and in a short while, April brought their food. The two ate quickly, paid their bill, and then hurried from the restaurant, eager to return to the resort and formulate their plan of action for the coming night.

"My sense is that we are coming to an important junction point in this investigation," Marley said. "I can feel it in my bones; tonight's activities may disclose what we've been waiting for."

Nan nodded. "I agree. I'm running through a list in my mind of the equipment Sean sent up here with us. There's no doubt we're going to need the night goggles."

"Yes, those are going to be vital," Marley replied.

"And," said Nan, "I think Sean's periscope might prove useful as well. It will allow us to look in a window without being seen."

"Right," Marley said. "We'll wear the black shirts and pants we packed, so we blend into the dark."

"And I brought plenty of black grease paint from the theater to darken our faces," Nan added.

"Is that going to be absolutely necessary? It's not as if we're James Bond or Laura Croft, for heaven's sake."

"Listen," Nan said firmly, "we're dealing with a nearly full moon tonight, and we don't want to take the chance of our faces shining like two headlights when everything else is dark."

"I suppose you're right. Better to be safe ..." Marley let the thought dangle in midair, not wanting to add the words "than sorry," because she refused to consider the possibility that a carefully constructed plan, which they would surely form, would have any flaw in it. She rubbed her hands together in anticipation. "I'm getting excited," she told Nan. "I absolutely love this, don't you? I just hope we can stay awake."

Nan laughed. "Are you kidding? I can't picture myself falling asleep. Not with all this adrenaline coursing through my veins. I've never felt more alive."

When they reached the turn into Eagle's Cove, Nan steered Agatha around the corner by the big sign, which, like almost everything else at the resort, was sagging at an angle, signaling neglect. She then continued along the long, vacant drive.

Marley looked out her side window and sighed. "Just think, Nan. Further into the season, this driveway would usually be lined with RVs, and that entire space over there would be a regular RV campsite. It would be surrounded by grills and lawn chairs under little striped awnings, and beneath the protection of that shade, any number of chattering guests would visit with people they knew from previous summers. Each would be holding a tall, sweating glass of something cold that contained clinking ice cubes. All classic elements of a Minnesota summer well spent would be on display here. Not to mention that every cabin would have people sitting at the picnic tables out front; there would be a big community bonfire; the playground would be filled with squealing kids; and the dock would rumble its aluminum tones, signaling the return of fishermen with their catches."

Marley stopped talking to take in the vacant, empty scene before her. "But now, at this time of year, it's so quiet it's almost creepy, like a set in some Alfred Hitchcock movie. And this is the exact time of year when those two women disappeared. It kind of gives me the willies."

"The willies?" Nan replied. "I haven't heard anybody use that phrase in quite a while. I wonder where it comes from."

"It's British," Marley answered, turning with a smile, more than ready to move on from ruminating on the countless dreary aspects of the resort. "It comes from the word *woolies*, which were long underwear made from some material that was very itchy and aggravated people's skin. Wool, I imagine."

"You mean people got the willies from their woolies?" Nan asked.

"That's the gist of it, yes," Marley responded with a chuckle.

"Well, we won't be wearing any woolies tonight," Nan said. "So no willies. Let's count on that, OK?"

"Agreed," Marley said. "No willies tonight."

"No, not tonight. Tonight is the night to focus, not fidget."

CHAPTER 18

BACK AT CABIN NUMBER EIGHT, Marley called Eva and gave her all the information they had garnered from Madge Sims, along with Randi Sykes's address.

"I'm sure you're keeping Gretchen up to date on all the information your bloggers have been giving you," Marley said. "I'm speaking now of the possibility that Randi was with the Chapmans and Buck Sykes in Kansas City when those armored cars were held up and, therefore, might very well also have been involved."

"I've filled her in on everything," Eva said. "But up until now, it's all speculation. However, if you two should discover something more concrete, something Gretchen could actually move on, this address of Randi's you just gave me could prove very helpful."

Marley drew in a deep breath and said, "I think something big is going down tonight, Eva. Nan and I are going to stay up most of the night to keep watch. Let's hope we get something both Gretchen and the authorities up here can use."

"Can you tell me what you think is about to happen?" Eva asked.

"No, it would be pure guesswork. I'd rather wait."

"Well, make sure you two focus on staying safe."

"We always do."

"Listen," Eva said quickly, "Sean and Ray are here as well, and they want to talk to both of you. They have a few ideas they want to share with you. Can you put your phone on speaker?"

"Sure," Marley said, punching a button on her phone and motioning to Nan.

"Hi, Sean! Hi, Ray!" Nan hollered.

"Hi, you two," Sean said. "Is that whopping-great fellow who practically mowed Marley down the first day you arrived up there involved in this something big that you say is going down tonight? You know who I'm talking about. What's his name?"

"Sykes," Ray's voice suddenly said. "His name's Buck Sykes."

"Yeah," Sean said. "Buck Sykes."

"Yes," Marley answered briskly. "He's involved in what's going down this evening. But Nan and I aren't going to be doing anything other than observing him. That's all. So you don't need to worry."

"That's right," Nan added. "We don't plan on searching his farm until tomorrow."

There was a slight pause, and then Sean said, "I see. And I take it you've figured out a way to search it when he's not there?"

"We have."

"Well, that's what Ray and I want to talk to you about.

We were thinking about the two missing women, and all of a sudden, it dawned on us that something else is missing: the women's cars! They both left the resort driving a car, didn't they? So where are their cars? What happened to them?"

"We've given that some thought as well," Marley said. "We think they might be buried somewhere or at the bottom of one of the many lakes hereabouts."

There was another pause, and then Sean muttered, "Not likely. It's not easy to bury one car, let alone two. A lake bottom is a possibility, but we think we have a better idea. Ray and I think since this Sykes fellow is an auto mechanic and known around Brainerd as someone who fixes cars, he could very well have stripped both women's cars—taken them apart piece by piece and either sold the parts or simply spread them around. Have you run across any auto salvage yards up there?"

"No, but then again, we haven't looked for any."

"No need at present," Sean said. "But when you search his farm tomorrow, be sure to look in any outbuildings big enough to hold a stripped-down car. You should look for a car floor or chassis that's around one hundred eighty inches long, or about fifteen feet in length. That's the length of a Honda Civic, the car the younger woman, Lynn Parker, was driving. The car of the older woman, Suzanne Engelmann, would be longer."

"The thing is," Ray added, "Eva says Gretchen could match any particular chassis with one of the victims' cars if she had a serial number. And serial numbers are etched on the chassis of some cars. So if you could look for a number, that would be a big help in connecting the stripped-down car with one of the victims."

"We'll do what we can," Nan told their concerned allies. "As of now, we don't know what's on Sykes's farm. You can't see anything of his property from the road. It's all too far back."

"That's bad," Sean said. "I don't like the thought of you two going in blind. You're sure you have a plan?"

"Yes," Marley and Nan said strongly.

The next voice they heard was Ray's once again, and it sounded troubled. "How about a script?" he asked. "Do you have a script?"

"We do," Marley and Nan said.

"Good," he said. "Because from the sound of that Sykes fellow, you're going to need one if he happens to arrive on the scene unannounced."

*   *   *

That evening, in order to pass the time, the two excited pals decided to play Scrabble in the back bedroom. They sat on the floor with the game board between them and only a small flashlight no brighter than a night-light for illumination. They'd lowered the blinds and made sure the slats were pulled tightly together. The rest of the cabin was in complete darkness, giving the impression that the so-called old folks were in bed and fast asleep.

"I don't think you have to worry about using your *U* and *Q*," Nan said in a low voice. "My watch says eleven thirty-five. I think we'd better get into our positions."

Nan moved toward the living area while Marley said, "I was thinking that the bar will be closed, so we don't have to worry about that particular bug interfering with the one I placed under the Chapmans' dining room table. I'd say the stars are aligned, wouldn't you? Now I just pray I actually get to hear something."

Nan reached into her pocket and drew out a jar of black grease paint. She opened it, covered her face and neck with paint, and then passed the jar to Marley, who mimicked her, briefly reaching forward to smear a bit on a spot Nan had missed on her chin. When they were through, they moved toward the places they were to occupy for the first stage of their surveillance.

Nan positioned herself on a cushion she had pulled from an armchair, and using the same chair as a support for her back, she lowered herself onto the floor. She'd already made sure to open the glass doors at the front of the cabin, so they would not make noise if she needed to go out onto the deck. From there, she could see a wide view of the lake and the island beyond. Marley, meanwhile, perched herself on a tall stool in front of the small side window in the kitchen, which allowed a clear view of the path leading down toward the resort office and the office's back parking lot. Since neither could see the other, they had decided to use their cell phones to text about anything they observed.

Time passed slowly, and the cabin filled with a deep silence that was patterned with fragmented shapes of long shadows from the oak trees outside as the moon cast their quivering outlines onto the floor and walls of the cabin. The adrenaline that had surged through them so powerfully before was beginning to wane. Now only the metallic *tick-tick-tick* of a clock kept them awake, and with each passing minute, they knew they were getting closer to the time when some sort of activity would take place.

Both women had to concentrate intently to keep their heads from growing heavy and falling forward into a sleep-induced nod.

Marley was just about to shift her weight from her right hip to her left, when a sudden beam of light from a vehicle flashed across her field of sight. "Car. Back of office," she quickly texted Nan.

Marley held her breath as she heard a door slam. She practically pressed her nose against the window glass as she peered out into the night, hoping that would allow her vision to penetrate the darkness. She texted, "Truck. Sykes?"

When she received no reply from Nan, she texted, "What next?"

"Wait," Nan replied.

For her part, Nan squinted, continuing to look out the front doors to the deck. She could see only the streak of light the moon spread onto the calm surface of the lake. After some time, movement caught her eye, and she reached for her phone. She texted, "Something moving by dock."

"Night goggles. Go onto deck," Marley replied.

Nan hurriedly slipped on the goggles and slithered through one of the glass doors. She made sure to stay low, crawling toward the outer edge of the deck on her stomach. Sean's night goggles gave her a clear view of two men moving on the dock, where a small fishing boat stood waiting. She watched as they got into it and began to row out onto the lake. Their rowing was soundless, causing nary a ripple, as they moved slowly toward the island.

Nan was about to text Marley again, when she felt her friend close by her side. She turned to see Marley beside her, also lying flat on her stomach. Nan texted, keeping her phone under her jacket the entire time so its blue backlight wouldn't show: "Small boat rowing to island. BS & DC."

Marley looked down at her phone, nodded and placed a finger to her lips, and they remained motionless, close together, in silence as they watched the boat move across the lake and then disappear around the other side of the island. More than a few minutes passed, and finally, Nan felt it safe to whisper, "I can't stand the suspense. What do you think they're doing?"

"They're up to something," Marley whispered back. "That's obvious. Why row when you could use a motor? And why go out at this time of night? If we're lucky, we'll be able to find out exactly what they are up to."

"Sh," Nan said. "I think they're coming back. Yes, there they are. They're rowing back toward the dock."

"They can't hear us," Marley whispered. "They're too far away."

"Sound travels across water," Nan cautioned.

The two fell silent again as they watched the rowers head for shore. The boat reached the dock, and one of the two men, the heavier and taller of the two, wrapped a rope around one of the pilings and jumped onto the dock, steadying the boat. The other man stepped out of the tipping and teetering rowboat, lifting a large, square grip of some kind. They walked the length of the dock and then continued up the path toward the resort office. Once they had entered, the two watchers squirmed back through the glass door and into their cabin.

"That bag that one of them clambered out of the boat with—did you notice either of them carrying it when they started their trip out to the island?" Marley asked.

Nan shook her head. "No, but one of them could have been holding it in front of him. I was only able to see their backs."

Marley fell quiet, and Nan knew she was thinking. "What do you think is in that duffel?" Nan asked.

"I don't know, but I'm going to find out," Marley said. She rushed to the kitchen's side window and looked out. "There!" She continued to whisper, pointing a finger. "Do you see it? A light just went on in the office. Right in that east-facing window. I think I could peek in with Sean's periscope. I only hope there is some sort of hiding place around it. Do you think I could risk kneeling directly under it if I don't find cover?"

Nan shook her head. "No. I think you should use camouflage of some kind if you can. Besides, Sean's periscope is designed so you don't have to worry about whether you're directly under the window. It's flexible, remember? And it extends, so you can use it at an angle. All you need to do is place the moth against the window and look through the periscope's lower end. It's all done with mirrors. Just don't tap the moth against the window. We don't want them to hear anything. Although it probably wouldn't matter if they did, seeing as that's what moths do."

Marley grabbed the slender and extendable telescopic device Sean had designed for them and headed for the door with Nan close on her heels. "You keep an eye out, and give me a signal if they head back outside," Marley whispered.

"What kind of a signal?"

"Can you hoot like an owl?"

"Not convincingly. How about I toss a stone at your feet?"

"Fine. Just keep it low. Don't aim for my head."

Nan inched forward away from cabin number eight in the direction of the resort office and its lit window. She positioned herself behind a large bridal veil bush, where she leaned over, picked up a few landscape stones, and shoved them into her pocket. Then she watched as Marley crept slowly toward the resort office and the light that sent a streak out into the gloomy, shadowy night. Since there wasn't a place to hide directly beneath the window, Marley was forced to position herself behind an arborvitae, where she knelt on the ground. She then silently angled the periscope into position at a near-horizontal angle, placing the moth a mere quarter of an inch from the window.

Nan continued to observe Marley, who was now bending her head in order to gaze into the lower portion of the periscope. Nan's heart skipped a beat, and her eyes peered through the darkness as they scanned the surrounding area for the slightest movement from either the front or the back of the building.

Clouds had rolled in to cover the moon, effectively eliminating its light, which had concerned her at the beginning of their watch. All was quiet, almost hypnotically so, with only some slight ruffled movement of waves, which were now once again responding to a breeze and washing up upon the shore.

Not far off, Nan could hear the low-grade buzz of an insect, and its insistent drone seemed intent on breaking the night's hypnotic spell. Time passed, and Nan's left foot was beginning to twitch for want of movement, when the back door of the office flew open with a loud bang, and someone stepped out. Nan's head and shoulders went into a crouch as an overhead light flooded the parking lot, causing her to shove her left fist into her mouth to stop from screaming. Her right hand had gone instantly into her pocket at the sound of the door's bang, and her arm was already drawn back in order to pitch a stone at Marley's feet, when, as the first wash of light illuminated the night, she noticed Marley drop onto her stomach on the ground and slither farther back behind the arborvitae. Realizing Marley was now completely concealed, Nan took her eyes off her friend and kept them glued to the man now standing in the parking lot, whom she could plainly see under the light from above the door.

There was no question it was Buck Sykes hoisting himself into the driver's seat of his beat-up white truck. To Nan's relief, he didn't seem, in his haste, to have spotted Marley or her, although she was only partially concealed behind the bridal bush. Nan had to stoop even lower to keep herself from becoming a human-shaped shadow as the beams from the truck's headlights raked across the lawn. Then Buck Sykes backed up his truck and drove it down the drive toward the highway. Nan watched as the truck's red taillights grew smaller and smaller.

When she noticed Marley rise to her feet and, while still crouched, run toward their cabin, Nan followed suit, reaching the cabin just moments later. Once they were inside, only after they closed the door securely behind them did either of them feel free to speak, and then they both spoke at once.

"What did you—"

"You won't believe—"

Nan and Marley both stopped talking and took a deep

breath. Then, holding up a hand, Marley said, "Let's go into the kitchen. Pour us some wine. And I'll tell you everything I saw and heard."

Nan trotted into the kitchen. Her eyes were so well adjusted to the dark that by feel, she could grab two wineglasses, put them side by side on the counter, and quickly take out a twist-topped bottle of chilled chardonnay from the fridge. Then, using the refrigerator light, she poured the libation liberally as Marley positioned herself on one of the stools at the counter.

As they sat in the dark, Nan grabbed a flashlight, turned it on, and slid it against the napkin holder in order to illuminate the counter somewhat. Then she took a swallow of her wine. Decisively, she leaned all the way forward and turned to Marley, wearing a no-nonsense look, and sternly asked, "OK, what did you see?"

"Money."

"Did you really?"

"Yes, money! Bundles of money."

Nan drew back her head. "Are you telling me that entire bag was filled with money?"

Marley nodded. "Yes. From what I could tell, there were bundles of fifty- and hundred-dollar bills. There had to have been fifty thousand dollars or more stuffed into that suitcase!"

"And they got the money off the island?'" Nan asked, her mouth twisting with a look of satisfaction.

"It would appear so. And I doubt they brought it all back on this trip."

"So you think there could be more money on the island?"

"Well, if the money comes from the two Guardian security trucks held up in Kansas City that Eva told us about, fifty thousand dollars would be only a small part of what was stolen. On the other hand, we don't know how many trips to the island they've made or how much money they've already moved."

"Or if they were actually involved in the Kansas City holdups."

"I'd bet my life on it," Marley said, "given what I just saw. Where would a couple of losers like Dale Chapman and Buck Sykes get that kind of money? And where else but the casinos would they need Braun's help in laundering it?"

"Do we have proof that's what they're doing?" Nan asked.

Marley nodded. "I heard them talking," she answered in a satisfied tone. "The window was open a crack, and they were standing around the table where you placed one of Sean's bugs earlier. With the listening device in my ear turned up all the way, I could just make out their ongoing plans. I heard them say that this latest stash was close to the end and that they'd have only one more pickup left."

"That tells me we need to work fast," Nan said.

Marley nodded. "They talked about their recent instructions from Trevor Braun. The casino they were going to visit next was First Nation, and Chapman told Sykes he was to play poker while Chapman gambled at the third blackjack table. Braun would make sure they both won big. Just as Eva told us, that's exactly how they launder the money."

"Yeah, I can see how that would work," Nan said. "But why stash the money on the island? For security purposes?"

"Sure. When you think about it, what better place is there to hide it? Even if the police were to somehow get a warrant to search the entire resort—and as we know, they did search parts of it—would they ever think to search that island? It's not as if it's a popular place or has a lot of visitors; it's not big enough for a picnic, and there isn't a beach, from what I can see from here. Fishermen would be the only ones to frequent that island, and our host Mr. Chapman has already taken care of lowering the chance of that happening by spreading the rumor that the place is a virtual Urine Town."

Nan grinned. "You're right. He did spread that rumor, didn't he? But that eagles' nest? Now, that would attract certain people's interest, wouldn't it? Certain people like Suzanne Engelmann, the first victim."

"That's right," Marley said, smiling back. "I'll bet she had her binoculars raised more than once toward that island while she stayed here. In fact, I'm absolutely convinced she did."

"But she wouldn't have been watching the eagles at night, would she?" Nan asked.

Marley shook her head. "I wouldn't think so, but maybe Sykes and Chapman didn't always go over there in the middle of the night. Because of the early season and lack of resort clients when both Suzanne and Lynn were staying here, those guys may have felt perfectly safe to venture out in the early morning hours, thinking they wouldn't be seen."

"Only they didn't count on the fact that the crack of dawn is a typical time for a birder to begin her watch with notebook in hand," Nan said. Then, blinking hard in a way that told Marley she was thinking, she added, "We really need to get over to that island. Are you sure you can't swim over there?"

"Let's not start down that path again," Marley answered, taking a sip of her wine.

Nan wrinkled her nose at Marley. "But don't you see? We have to search it! We need to find the rest of the money. Where do you think they're keeping it? It's got to be hidden somewhere."

"I'm sure it is," Marley answered. "And I'm also sure Chapman and Sykes have built themselves a hiding place as dry and secure as Fort Knox somewhere on the island. But, Nan, we don't have to visit the island. Remember, we aren't here to solve a Kansas City robbery. Our mission is to solve the disappearances of two women, one a teacher and the other a writer, neither of whom deserved to disappear off the face of the earth."

"I know, but surely you think this Chapman guy and that brute Sykes are involved in their disappearances?" Nan asked.

"Yes, I do. And from what I saw and heard tonight, I now believe that our mystery turns on what those two women likely discovered about the robbery and the money."

Nan nodded. "Yeah, they both must have stumbled onto information that proved to be dangerous. Perhaps more dangerous than they realized."

Marley looked away before saying, "Has it occurred to you at all that we are placing ourselves in the exact same position now that we hold the same information?"

Nan didn't answer right away. When she did speak, she used a tone that told Marley she was ready to move along. "So tomorrow we're going to try to get a better look at Sykes's place," she said. "What time should we begin our stakeout?"

"Something tells me Sykes isn't a real early riser," Marley replied. "I think we'll be safe to wait until eight o'clock to set you up in that field with your easel."

"So I'm going to get to paint that old barn at the end of the field?"

"Yes, and whatever you do, don't forget the reason you're there. I know how easy it is to lose yourself in your work when you're painting. But you've got to keep focused on maintaining a steady lookout for Sykes's truck. So when he heads into town, which he will at some point, call me on your cell, and I'll come pick you up. It might take a while, you know. You might have to be out there for hours."

"No problem," Nan responded. "I'll wear a hat."

*   *   *

The sun was just beginning to rise high enough to be seen over the evergreen windbreak when Nan put down her brush and squinted at the painting in front of her. After grabbing a palette knife, she applied smears of a dark shade to the left-hand side of the canvas, where the impression of a low row of bramble bushes demanded a heavier layer of paint. She was just about to smear the knife with a lighter color with which to add highlights, when she heard the unmistakable sound of a truck's engine. She peered out from under her hat and was pleased to see Buck Sykes's white truck turn onto the highway, heading toward town. She felt a rush of excitement course through her body as she somewhat reluctantly placed her palette knife on the easel's tray, noticing as she did that her hand was shaking with nerves. She reached into her pocket, pulled out her cell phone, and called Marley.

It took her pal a mere three minutes to pull up at the side of the road to collect her. By that time, Nan had folded the easel and snapped shut the lid of her wooden paint box.

Marley jumped out of the car to grab the painting and paint box, while Nan tucked the easel under her arm and deposited it on the backseat of the car. Marley clicked open Agatha's truck, carefully laid the painting on the tarp covering the floor of the trunk for just that purpose, and tucked the paint box securely beside the spare tire. Seconds later, the two women were on their way.

As Marley steered the car down the long drive toward Sykes's farmhouse, Nan felt her mouth go completely dry. "How long do you think Sykes will stay in town?" she asked.

"I have no idea," Marley answered. "For all I know, he may not even be going into town. He might be going no farther than the gas station two miles down the road."

Nan didn't respond, and Marley added reassuringly, "Don't worry. We'll be fine. As long as we stick to the script. So remember, no matter what happens, stick to the script."

Marley drove on to the end of the gravel driveway and turned off Agatha's motor. She and Nan hustled out of the car and took a few quick seconds to assess their surroundings. Sykes's farmhouse stood before them on their right. It looked abandoned, but they were aware that Buck Sykes's invalid father was somewhere within. Nan couldn't help sweeping her gaze across each of the house's windows to see if anyone was looking out. But there wasn't the slightest hint of motion to indicate someone watching.

A few hundred feet to the right of the farmhouse stood a long, narrow one-story building that could have housed chickens at one time.

"Hey, that helps our ruse," Nan said. "That looks like an old chicken coop." Directly in front of them and to their left, at the end of the driveway, rose a tall metal pole barn of considerable size that managed to look as dilapidated as what they took to be the old henhouse.

"If there are any cars on this property belonging to our missing women," Marley said, "they've got to be in that building."

Nan noticed a narrow entryway beside the large garage-type overhead door, which was likely to allow access for trucks and automobiles into the pole barn, and the two sleuths wasted no time before walking toward the narrow door and turning its knob. To their surprise, it easily swung open.

"Good deal," Nan said. "We won't need to use Sean's picks to break in. That'll save us some time and not involve a possible breaking-and-entering charge."

She and Marley stepped inside, stopping after a few steps so their eyes could adjust to the dark shadows. Nan wrinkled her nose at the stale smell of dust, mold, and rust that seemed to rise from the sandy floor and made her think of a thousand spiderwebs. She looked down, and the thought crossed her mind that it would be easy for a man to dig a grave in that dirt. "Place doesn't seem to be used much," she whispered to Marley.

Marley didn't answer. She was peering across the wide expanse at an old pickup truck parked next to what might have been the stripped-down chassis of a car. "Does that look like a Civic to you?" she asked Nan.

Nan squinted as she stared at what looked to her like a steel platform. "Are you kidding me? It barely looks like a car. It's only a frame."

"Oh, it was a car all right," Marley said. "At one time anyway. But now that I see it up close, that frame appears too long to have been the right dimensions for a Civic, which was the make of Lynn Parker's car."

Nan left Marley to check out the chassis further as she walked toward the back of the pole barn. Looking about her, she saw some tarps thrown over a few items, and she quickly lifted each one to see what it was covering.

"Hey, Marley!" she called out. "There're a few more car frames in the back of this old pole barn. And one of them still has its seats attached. I also see some farm equipment back here and even a few hay bales."

Once again, Marley failed to answer. But she was now walking swiftly toward Nan. "Where's the chassis with the seats still attached?" she asked eagerly.

Nan lifted the tarp. "Right here."

Marley tugged on the other end of the tarp, and working together, they succeeded in pulling it off entirely. "This one does look more promising," she said. "It's the right size. Help me search under and between the seats. Maybe we'll get lucky and find something."

Marley fell to her knees beside the frame and began to run her hands over one of the cloth seats, which appeared to be grimy, with oily dark splotches. Nan, after walking around to the other side, did the same. On opposite sides of the stripped-down frame of what once had been an automobile, they began their search.

"What are we likely to find?" Nan asked her friend.

"Anything that might help connect this chassis with the young writer Lynn Parker."

Nan peered under the front seat and then ran a hand gingerly under it, expecting to discover a dead mouse or, worse yet, a live one. "I can't see us finding anything," she said. "This car has been stripped pretty thoroughly."

"Pray, Nan," Marley muttered. "Pray."

As Marley began to recite the prayer to Saint Anthony, from whom she often requested help in locating lost items, the two continued to search the seats, both on top and beneath, slowly running their hands over the upholstery, making sure to pay close attention to any holes or rips large enough to hide anything. Neither of them had to remind the other of the time they had worked on a case in which an old man, preceding his death, had secreted into the top of a hollow pipe a rolled-up business card that had led them straight to his murderer.

From their past experiences, each knew those who experienced the indignities of an unnatural death had an almost instinctive way of doing all they could to further the march of justice they hoped would come about in the future. Neither Nan nor Marley ever wanted to overlook a victim's dying effort.

Moments went by, and then Nan saw Marley plunge her hand as far as it would go down into the crease between a seat's back and cushion. She ran her hand along the opening, and then Nan heard Marley let out her breath to release a deep sigh.

Leaning back on her heels, Marley drew out a grimy hand and waved it over her head. "I've got something!" she muttered in a hoarse whisper.

"I don't believe it," Nan whispered. "What is it?"

Marley smiled widely and held out her open palm. Within it lay a thin dark object.

"Is that what I think it is?" Nan stuttered, still squinting in the dark.

"*Flash* is part of its name," Marley said, rising to her feet.

"Is it really a flash drive?" Nan asked wonderingly.

Marley closed her eyes and nodded.

"Where? What?"

"It was tucked deep down into the crease between the lower and back cushions of the driver's seat."

They stared at each other as an image of a helpless, panic-driven woman fearfully shoving the thumb drive down into the crease behind her, where she hoped it would be found later, flashed before their eyes. They could feel the rise of dread and anxiety and her frantic hope that her attackers would not discover it.

At that moment, as they both looked at the flash drive cradled in Marley's palm, the connection they felt with Lynn Parker was so complete it resonated psychically within their minds.

The experience was so real Nan could barely catch her breath to speak. "Do you think it belonged to Lynn?" she finally said.

"We won't know until we see what's on it," Marley said. "But yes, I think it contains the notes Lynn was bringing to June." She rose to her feet and brushed the dirt off her knees.

"I think our mission is accomplished. Let's get out of here before Sykes gets back."

No sooner had the words left Marley's mouth than they heard the crunching spray of gravel under the tires of a vehicle on the driveway outside.

Nan held up a hand to stop Marley from talking further as she listened to the fast-approaching sound. She turned her head sharply toward the door they had entered. "He's back!" she whispered.

The two women hurried quickly toward the door. Marley arrived first and opened it a crack to peer out. Then she turned to face Nan, who couldn't fail to notice her friend's face had gone a sickly pale color.

"What are we going to do now?" Marley asked.

Nan placed a finger to her mouth and whispered, "Stick to the script."

Both of them peered quickly and anxiously around, looking for another way out, and Nan spotted another door at the back of the pole barn. Pointing to it, she grabbed Marley's sleeve, tugged hard, and mouthed, "Follow me." She and Marley then ran toward the back door and, upon opening it, stepped into the rutted field that backed the pole barn.

With Marley at her heels, Nan turned and murmured, "I'm going to circle around to the left and come at Sykes from behind, between the henhouse and the farmhouse. You circle around this barn to the right. Wait until you hear me talking to him. When you see that I have his full attention and that his back is turned away from you, take off across the field toward the woods and the path that leads to the McNair place."

Nan pointed left toward a row of thick woods that bordered a plowed field. "Whatever you do, don't look back! Once you're in the woods, find the path Anne told us about, and take it straight to their farm. I'll meet you there."

Marley shook her head stubbornly and hissed, "No. I won't leave you here all alone!"

But Nan was already running toward the henhouse and out of hearing range. Marley, knowing she had no choice but to follow Nan's revised script, turned in the opposite direction to edge her way along the back of the barn and then around its far side until she came to the farthest front corner. Once there, she crouched down low and took a quick look around the edge. She saw Buck Sykes get out of his dirty white pickup truck.

He stood still for a few minutes, looking at Nan's car, and then he slowly turned on his heel and looked straight at the pole barn. Marley, with heart pounding, drew back her head. She pressed her back against the barn and held her breath. Her ears strained fearfully as she expected to hear Sykes moving toward the barn. No more than a second passed, and she clearly heard the frightful thud of his boots crunching against the pebbles of the drive. He was on the move and headed in her direction. The sound of Sykes's boots grew ever louder, and Marley frantically tried to come up with a plan B to the already altered script, when she suddenly heard the artificial singsong sound of Nan's voice.

"Yoo-hoo! Hello there!"

Marley heard Sykes's footsteps stop their forward motion and then start up again, only this time, they seemed to be moving away from her. She took a deep breath and, as the sound of the footsteps grew fainter, hazarded a quick peek around the corner. Sykes now had his back to her and was swiftly moving toward Nan, who was waving her hands to get and hold his attention as she sauntered casually toward him from around the side of the old chicken coop.

Marley could tell Nan was pulling out all the stops when it came to her acting ability. She was using her vast theatrical experience to captivate her audience of one and switch Sykes's attention from the pole barn to the henhouse and, ultimately, herself.

Knowing they were at a critical juncture in the investigation, Marley took another quick look around the edge of the pole barn, and seeing that Sykes's back was still toward her, she took a deep breath and ran along the side of the aluminum building, heading in the direction of the woods. She then took off running across the field. She did not look back.

For her part, Nan gave Sykes a wide smile and, in a voice similar to the one she'd used when she played the duchess of Berwick in Oscar Wilde's play *Lady Windermere's Fan*, announced, "I knocked on your front door, and then I went around to the back door of your house, but still, no one answered. I would like to purchase some of your eggs. I saw your sign up the road. I thought you might have been in the henhouse, but it's empty. Where are the chickens? I don't see or hear any chickens about. How can you sell eggs if you don't have any chickens?"

The scowl Sykes gave her nearly took her breath away, but as she could now clearly see over his left shoulder that Marley was running frantically toward the woods, Nan steeled herself and approached him. She made sure to lock her eyes with his and hold him in what she knew was a controlling stare.

It seemed to work, for Sykes was now looking at her in such fascination she might have been a swaying cobra. When she was less than a foot from him, she came to a halt, looked up at him, and giggled like a crazed schoolgirl.

"You know, they used to say eggs weren't good for you." She chatted on. "Cholesterol, you know. Of course, I never believed it. Not for one minute. Nature's perfect food, I always said. And then I saw your sign, and it's been ages and ages—oh, oodles, really—since I've had a fresh egg. You know, there really is no comparison."

Nan took a quick breath and rattled on. "I mean, free-range eggs are so much tastier than eggs that have been laid in those small little cages where the poor birds can't even turn around." She then drew in her breath suddenly, widened her eyes, and placed both hands on her cheeks. "Oh dear, I do hope your chickens are free-range. They are, aren't they?"

As Sykes took a small, threatening move toward her, his six-foot-some-inch frame cast a fearful shadow that seemed to block out everything in sight. But Nan knew what she had to do and stood her ground.

With a steely glare, Sykes growled, "I ain't got no chickens. Never had no chickens. Never going to have no chickens!"

Nan changed her demeanor to one of pure innocence. In a voice both meek and apologetic, she said, "But I don't understand. Your sign says, 'Fresh Eggs for Sale.' It's right on the side of the road out there." She pointed.

At that moment, Nan saw Marley reach the edge of the

field and disappear into the thick woods beyond, and her flesh seemed to melt into her bones. She told herself she now needed to accomplish a hasty retreat. She only hoped her wobbly legs would accommodate her.

"Not my sign, lady," Sykes growled. Only now there was a difference in his demeanor. He was glaring down at her in a peculiar way, as if studying her and searching his memory for where or when he might have seen her before. It was enough to unnerve Nan, who decided that before anything could refresh his recollection, she'd be wise to begin inching her way toward Agatha.

"Not your sign? Well, what do you know about that? Silly me! What a fool I am." She prattled on, edging her way toward the car. "My mistake entirely. I assumed the sign would be for the first farm along the road. I'll just be on my way. Sorry to have bothered you."

She somehow managed to reach Agatha. As she stretched forth a hand to open the driver's door, she expected Sykes's powerful arm to suddenly wrap itself around her neck and grab her roughly from behind. But to her surprise and relief, no such scenario took place. Instead, she gingerly slipped behind the wheel of her car and started the engine.

Then she made a wide U-turn in the drive, and as she drove past Sykes, who was still standing in the driveway, she made sure to give him a smile and a friendly little wave.

Once out on the road, however, she was free to let loose, and as adrenaline surged through her, she exultantly threw back her head and shouted with relief. Now she could think only of getting to the McNair farm and checking out the flash drive they'd found in the stripped auto chassis. If it turned out to contain what she and Marley thought it contained, they might have cracked their case.

When she pulled into the McNairs' driveway, she half expected to see the back door of the farmhouse pop open and Marley come flying out. But that didn't happen.

Instead, the house appeared empty, and the side door to the house remained closed. Nan, drawing on inner resources to calm her nerves, slowly climbed out of her car and approached the door. She raised a tightened fist and knocked forcefully. Then she knocked again.

The door opened, and Mrs. McNair blinked at her in surprise.

"Hello, Anne," Nan stammered. "Is my friend Marley here?"

Anne McNair's brow wrinkled, and she shook her head. "Why, no. Is she supposed to be?"

A bolt of electricity shot through Nan's body as she opened her mouth to speak.

But before she could get a word out, a phone rang inside the house. Mrs. McNair opened the door wide and motioned for Nan to enter. "Come in," she said. "If you'll excuse me, I'll get the phone."

Nan followed Anne McNair through the side porch and into her kitchen, where a phone on the table continued to ring.

Anne picked up the phone and spoke into it. "Yes. Yes. She's here now. That's right. OK, I'll tell her." Anne smiled as she lowered the phone and turned toward Nan. "Don't worry," she said reassuringly. "Your friend is fine. She's at my son Scotty's house. His wife is on the phone. She says they've already called my son at the station, and he's on his way home. She wants you to drive over there and meet them. I'll go with you and show you the way."

Nan nodded. "That would be great. Is it possible for me to speak with Marley now? I have something to say to her."

Anne put the phone back to her ear. "We'll leave right away. But first, she wants to know if she can speak to her friend." She then handed the phone across to Nan. "Here she is."

Nan took the phone and let out all her pent-up fear in one mad rush: "You didn't follow the script! You were supposed to go straight to Mrs. McNair's house!"

"Sorry about that," Marley answered. "But once I came to the path in the woods, I was struck with a dilemma: *Do I turn right toward the McNair place, or do I go left and hopefully find the McNairs' son Scotty at home?* The fact that Scotty's a peace officer decided it for me."

"Well, OK, I guess that makes sense," Nan said. "But you practically gave me a heart attack when you weren't here. So for now, don't leave, OK? Stay right where you are. I'm on my way."

CHAPTER 19

SCOTTY MCNAIR RAN A HAND over his already tousled hair and slowly shook his head. "I just got off the phone with Commander Reichert in Saint Paul, and I don't mind telling you that I wouldn't be giving you guys the time of day if not for the accolades she recited to me. Did you really help solve the Austin case? And the lost emerald necklace case in Duluth?"

Nan and Marley nodded assent. Nan said, "Yes, but all of that is in the past. We want to focus on this case."

"Well, I can't just open my arms to any amateur encroaching upon my turf. I needed to know that you two were credible."

"Understood," Marley said. "And are you convinced?"

"I wasn't, but I am now," he mumbled. Then he turned his attention to his laptop screen, upon which Lynn Parker's notes were displayed. "It looks like she had more than a true-crime book going here. This is a collection of her jottings and a rough explanation of a lot of criminal activity she had observed."

"Yeah," Nan said, "all of which, sadly, got her murdered."

Scotty looked up. "So let me get this straight. You're saying that in your estimation, Lynn Parker's entire reason for booking into Eagle's Cove was to search for information about her missing professor, Suzanne Engelmann?"

Marley nodded. "Yes, she thought it would make a great true-crime book. And according to June Gunderson, who waitresses at Ojibwa Point, Lynn was going to drop these notes off to her on Lynn's way back to the cities."

Scotty scratched his head. "But why didn't June tell the authorities about these notes? From what I recall, she was interviewed, wasn't she?"

"Yes," Nan said with a nod. "But you need to remember June is young and inexperienced, and when her friend suddenly vanished into thin air just like the first woman, Suzanne Engelmann, she freaked out. She was afraid. If someone harmed Lynn, they might harm her if they suspected she knew what Lynn knew. So why would she tell anyone of her and Lynn's attempt to solve Suzanne's murder? Besides, who do you tell something like this? Who do you trust? In a town the size of Brainerd, word gets out; people talk. And that talk might get to the wrong person. I don't think June wanted to risk an attempt on her own life."

"That may be," Scotty said. "But she spoke to you two. She told you all about the notes."

Marley sighed. "Yes, she did. But really, you have to understand; we're not from around here. And whoever was responsible for Suzanne's and Lynn's murders, if it turns out they were murdered, in all probability, was someone local."

"Besides," Nan said, spreading her arms wide, "look at Marley and me. Who's going to fear two sweet little old ladies like us?"

Scotty placed a hand on his hip and gave Nan and Marley a quick look. "From what I can tell, you two are anything but a couple of sweet little old ladies."

"You're wrong, Sheriff," said Nan. "In most people's eyes, that's exactly what we are and will continue to be. And that's fine with us because that's our ace in the hole."

"But I still don't understand why Lynn was dropping off her notes in the first place," Scotty grumbled.

"The plan," said Marley, "was for June to continue the investigation while Lynn was away. According to June, Lynn was planning on coming back."

Nan, seeing the confused look on Scotty's face, hurriedly explained. "You see, June and Lynn met at the restaurant and became friendly. You know how two young girls have a way of making pacts? Well, at the point when Lynn disappeared, the two of them had been putting their heads together about this crime for quite some time, trying to solve it together. It was an obsession with them. At the very least, it appears to have been the mainstay of their relationship."

"And what I am seeing on this flash drive are those notes?" Scotty asked.

"Yes, that's what we think," Marley said. "Strange, isn't it? To think all that information could have been stuck deep within the crevice of the front seat in a stripped car all this time without Sykes noticing it."

"Who knows? Maybe he wasn't familiar with modern technology," Nan said. "Besides, he wouldn't have been looking for notes per se, because he didn't know she was working on a true-crime book. If he looked under the seats at all, which I think he probably did, he wouldn't have been looking for something as small as a flash drive. If it had been a notebook, even a small one, he would have grabbed that for sure. But as it is, the flash drive, thankfully, escaped his notice. All he was interested in was stripping the car of any documents or personal belongings connecting the car to Lynn Parker."

"I'll bet you think Suzanne Engelmann's car is in the shed as well?" Scotty said, looking first at Marley and then at Nan.

Marley shrugged. "I doubt it. Suzanne and her car disappeared two years ago. I don't know why I feel so strongly about this, but I think Suzanne and her car were both buried. There's so much land up here containing wetlands and swamps. And so many people, up north especially, use earth-moving equipment, like Bobcats, to clear their property; it would be easy for someone to bury a car with a body tucked inside. I think Suzanne's car was well hidden."

"Hidden so well, in fact," said Nan, "that as time went on and Sykes's worries began to subside, he became a bit careless. Maybe he thought he needn't go through the trouble of burying Lynn Parker's car. Or perhaps he didn't want to draw attention to himself by asking someone a second time to use their earth-moving equipment. But you never know. With Sykes's work as a mechanic, he may have simply thought it safest to spread parts of Lynn's car all over the county."

"We've been told that a car chassis can have a serial number on it," Marley said.

"If there is one," said Scotty, "and it's still readable, I assure you we'll find it. With this flash drive and Marley's testimony of what she witnessed regarding the money, we'll have plenty to begin a search of the island and Sykes's property."

"The thing is," Nan said in a concerned tone, "the information on this flash drive connects Sykes and Chapman with Lynn Parker's car and, therefore, her disappearance. But without a connection between Sykes and Suzanne Engelmann, you're only going to be able to charge Sykes for Lynn's murder."

Marley nodded. "However, if you are able to question Sykes's father during your search and he ends up telling you something important, something to connect Chapman with the women's disappearances, for example—"

Nan broke in. "He may well have seen or heard something. He might be an invalid, but from what we've been told, he still has his faculties. He isn't blind, and although we've been told he's hard of hearing, he's not completely deaf."

Marley agreed. "Knowing what I do of Buck Sykes, I think that poor old man could well be living in fear of his son. If you approach him right, you should be able to convince him to tell you everything he knows—if, that is, he actually does know something. The money and the Kansas City holdups will link Sykes with Chapman and give each of them a motive to kill the two women. Hopefully, in your search of his farm, you'll be able to find a connection to Suzanne on the premises. Perhaps you'll even come up with a grave or two. After all, Chapman and Sykes had to get rid of the two women's bodies somehow."

"So you think neither of the two women made it any farther than Sykes's farm on the day they disappeared?"

"That's right," Nan said. "We think Sykes and Chapman

set up a roadblock for each of them where the road to the old Baker place enters the main one."

"Yeah, they could have placed Sykes's truck there or something—anything that would force a stop in the middle of the road," Marley added.

"Then," Nan said, "either Sykes or Chapman approached the car; climbed in; and, probably with the threat of a gun, ordered her to drive to Sykes's farm. Once on the farm, she would have been killed, and her body would have been disposed of. One person couldn't have done this alone. It would have taken two people to pull it off."

Scotty said, "Well, at this point, it's all pure supposition. I'm going to have to take both of you down to the station with me. We need to get everything in writing. Especially what you two saw last night between Chapman and Sykes and the money from the island."

"What we saw was the self-same scene that Lynn Parker has in her notes," Nan said, "and I'm willing to bet Suzanne Engelmann observed that scene as well, given she was such an avid bird-watcher and had such a powerful pair of binoculars. So there's your motive. Once they realized what the women knew, Chapman and Sykes had to keep them quiet about what they'd seen."

"And there's nothing more silent than the grave," Marley said.

"Two women dead," Scotty said reprovingly, "and you two were foolish enough to go snooping around. What were you thinking?"

"But surely you must see," Nan answered with a flip of her head, "that we were the only ones who could snoop. I'm sure the police would have loved to search all the nearby farms after those two women disappeared, but the law wouldn't allow it. We have a wonderful system of justice in this country, Sheriff, but I know you will agree that in order to retain its integrity, you and your peers are very often necessarily restrained from acting. Whereas Marley and I are at perfect liberty to do all the snooping we want as long as we have a good excuse for doing so and look perfectly innocent and harmless while doing it."

"Nevertheless, you should have left it to the proper authorities to investigate. You could have ended up like the others," Scotty sternly responded. "Perhaps I should put an armed guard on you two? Or are you through with all your crime solving now?"

Nan glanced at Marley. "Are we through?"

Marley smiled. "Not as far as this case is concerned. I, for one, am not yet willing to pass the baton."

"Nor am I," Nan said. "We still have a few loose ends to tie up. For example, we still need to connect Trevor Braun and the casino operations with the island money. Is there enough to get him on?"

Scotty rose from the chair behind the desk in his den. "If, as you seem to think, they're laundering money from that robbery in Kansas you were telling me about through the casinos, believe me, we'll discover it. We have the professional resources and connections to get the job done. I already asked the station to place a call to the police department out in Alameda, California, to ask them to look into the whereabouts of Sykes's ex-wife."

Marley looked at Nan and said, "I gave Scotty the address I came across at Madge Sims's house."

"Her name is Randi," Nan said. "And from what Madge

told me, she doesn't seem to be living in luxury out there in California. We think she helped the Chapmans and Sykes with the armored-car robberies. She may have driven one of the getaway cars. We discovered from contacts within our group that she was in Kansas City during that time."

Scotty looked down and scratched the back of his head. "So Marley told me. But why would she help an ex-husband? It doesn't add up. Wasn't he a wifebeater? From what I hear, their divorce was anything but amiable."

Nan shrugged. "Some people will do almost anything for money. Especially if they're hard-pressed for cash."

"The way we see it," Marley said, "you can use Randi as the key to locking up the others. Once you determine how much money was actually stolen from those armored cars, you can tell Randi it was double, triple, or four times that amount. You have that right; you're the police. You don't have to tell the truth when you question someone; you can lie. You can make her think the Chapmans and Sykes duped her royally. Make her think they cheated her out of what she would see as her fair share. We know she already hates Sykes because he cheated her out of her divorce settlement, so it shouldn't take much convincing. If you do it right—and I know you will—you can have her eating right out of your hand. She'll turn on them. You'll see."

Nan didn't hesitate to agree. "I see her ending up being the weak link in their chain. She'll bring them down."

"Let's hope you're right," Scotty said.

"So what are we waiting for?" Marley asked. "Let's get down to the station and get the wheels of justice rolling."

They began to walk toward the door, when Scotty said, "I'm afraid I can't let you drive your car. You'll have to leave it here. For now, we'll go in the squad. I'll bring you back later."

"Can we drive with the siren blaring?" Nan asked.

"I don't think that would be wise," Scotty said with a laugh. Then, in a more serious tone, he said, "Listen, I'd just as soon keep you two under the radar for a while. At least until Chapman and Sykes are safely incarcerated. In fact, my second thought is to have my mother come with you and to bring the three of you into the station from the back, through the museum. I'll drop you off on the corner. It'll look to anyone observing us as if I gave my mother and two of her friends a ride to the museum. You three enter there, and follow the normal route of the tour until you get to a small kitchen at the back of the museum. Once you're sure nobody is noticing you, knock on the door that connects to my offices—Mom knows which one I'm speaking of—and I'll let you in. Either that, or you can call me on your cell. Just make sure in either case that you aren't being observed or overheard."

"Is all that necessary?" Marley asked. "It sounds rather cloak-and-dagger."

"You have to remember once again," Scotty said, "this is a small town, and nothing goes unnoticed around here. We don't want people asking, 'What were those two women doing when they were going into the station with Scotty McNair?' Until we make our arrests, we've got to keep both of you safe. You're the only living witnesses we have at present. And who knows? There may be others out there, perhaps connected to the casino, who would like to see you two vanish the way the other two ladies disappeared. At this point, we don't know how many characters may be involved in this business yet."

"In that case, why don't we be extra cautious and not even knock on that door?" Nan said with a roll of her eyes. "After all, someone might hear it. Give us your cell number, and we'll phone you. Should we use your code name?"

"The problem with you two," Scotty said, "is that you think this is all a game."

"No, we do not," Marley replied. "We never think of murder as a game. But after all we've been through, well, you can't blame us for wanting to have some fun."

Nan gave Scotty a warm smile. "Seriously, Sheriff, you've found out already, now that you've spoken to certain individuals in the Saint Paul police department, that these aren't the first murders Marley and I have helped the police solve. In fact, you'll eventually see that we are part of a group, the Finders, who share quite a distinguished and admirable history of crime solving."

"She said with a great deal of humility," Marley added with a certain flourish.

Scotty turned off his laptop, dropped Lynn Parker's flash drive into his shirt pocket, and turned toward the door. "Well, in that case, let's go have some fun."

CHAPTER 20

TWO WEEKS LATER, THE FINDERS found themselves once again gathered in Marley's back parlor. This time, however, the reason for their meeting was entirely different. Whereas they'd experienced an atmosphere of tension previously, when their discussion had held far more questions than answers, now they all sat comfortably in overstuffed chairs. Ray sat relaxed with his legs crossed, while Sean slouched across the cushions of a love seat, and Eva slowly sipped coffee from one of Marley's Belleek china cups.

All listened intently and with a great deal of satisfaction to the fascinating details being related by Nan and Marley—details they knew had contributed greatly to the final solution of what they had come to call the Eagle's Cove Case. They knew that each of their talents had contributed to its solving. It mattered little whether their individual contribution had been accomplished onstage or off; the Finders always thought of themselves as a team. Although they sported more than a few wrinkles on the outside, their team was seamless at its core, hence their first authorized team motto: "All or naught!" Which they had all agreed provided a proper bookend to their second authorized motto: "What? Me? Old?"

At the moment, Sean Finnegan was holding court. "You know," he said, leaning forward to pat Eva's tail-wagging Maltese on the top of his fluffy head, "we did a good and great deed in liberating that poor man from the clutches of his evil-hearted son. I can't help feeling sorry for him and what he must have been going through."

Nan nodded in agreement. "I know what you mean. It made me so mad when all the details came out. I wanted to kick Buck Sykes from here to some outer moon, and I would have too, if Scotty McNair hadn't been there to stop me."

"Where Buck Sykes's father is concerned, unfortunately, it's not an unusual story," Eva said. "Sadly, it happens far too often. With one parent critically ill in the hospital and the other an invalid at home, it becomes fairly easy to persuade the parent controlling the purse strings of the need for a special executor, a trusted guardian given power of attorney, in order to look over and safeguard their assets. And who better to sign over control of your finances, your entire life, to than your own child? In this case, unfortunately, the child happened to also be one of the devils—Buck Sykes."

"I still don't understand how someone can treat his own father that way," Ray said. "Keeping him a prisoner in his own home and forcing him to sign his Social Security check every month so you can cash it and use it for whatever? Stripping your deceased mother's inheritance to line your own pockets? How could you sleep at night?"

"Sleep at night?" exclaimed Nan. "The man's a murderer,

for Pete's sake. Didn't you hear? They found both of the woman's bodies buried under the dirt floor of his henhouse!"

"Yeah, and knowing Buck Sykes, such a move on his part was an attempt to make a snarky reference to where he believed all women belong," Sean said. Then, looking about the room sheepishly, he added, "And I'm not kidding this time."

"You most certainly are not," Eva said with an incredulous shake of her head. "Such a wicked, despicable mind!"

"Did you know Marley was the first to come up with the idea of looking in the henhouse?" Nan asked, once again feeling free to toot Marley's horn because she knew her friend wouldn't. "She suggested to Scotty that they might save some time if he had the people with the ground-penetrating radar equipment search below the surface of the pole barn and henhouse floor."

"It dawned on me," Marley said, "while Nan and I were in the pole barn investigating—"

"You mean snooping," Nan said playfully.

Marley, who chose to think of what they did as discreet explorations, ignored her and continued. "I thought the dirt floor would provide a perfect place to bury a body. When you think about it, a person would be able to dig a grave in complete privacy without feeling in any way rushed. But it was Sykes's father who became the incriminating factor in the matter. In his testimony, he said he saw his son go into the henhouse with a young girl, who, as far as he could tell, never came out again."

"And he gave a fairly decent description of her too," Nan added. "Enough to make the police feel secure in thinking the woman had been Lynn Parker. Of course, the DNA analysis will be the last word on the subject."

"It's strange he wasn't able to testify to any possible foul play where his son and Suzanne Engelmann were concerned," Ray said. "Like Lynn, she was also kidnapped in broad daylight. You'd think he would have seen or heard something."

Nan glanced at Marley and gave her a knowing look. "I know," she said, "and believe me, Marley and I have discussed the difference between the two deaths at length. The only solution we've been able to arrive at is that both Sykes and Chapman were super careful when it came to the death and burial of Suzanne Engelmann. They probably killed her on the road leading to Sykes's farm and then left her body stuffed in the trunk of her car. Sykes's father wouldn't have thought anything of seeing a strange car on the premises; after all, his son was a well-known mechanic who often worked on other people's cars."

Marley continued the story. "Later, under the cover of darkness, Sykes or maybe both of them carried her body to the henhouse and buried it. We think when it came to Lynn Parker, they simply became careless."

"Cocky, you mean," Sean said. "The one weakness of a serial killer is overconfidence. The police rely on it."

"I agree," Ray said, busily rubbing the lobe of his right ear. "Once people like Sykes think they've gotten away with murder, it's only natural for them to think they have a better-than-even chance of getting away with it again. Of course, it makes absolutely no sense when it comes to the laws of probability, but what do they know?"

Eva placed her coffee cup on a side table and sighed

heavily. "That's all fine and good. But the fact that they found both bodies on Sykes's property doesn't tie Dale Chapman to the missing women's murders. What about that? How are the police going to be able to hold him equally responsible for these horrible crimes? Or will they not be able to?"

Marley opened her mouth to say something, but Nan spoke first. "The fact that Marley's testimony allowed the police to search the island, leading to the discovery of the money, also allowed for a thorough search of the resort."

"Yes, but you said they found no forensics," said Sean. "No fluids, no blood—nothing to link the murders to the resort."

"But that's only because the women weren't killed on the resort premises," Eva replied, showing her frustration. "We now know they were both killed after they drove away from the resort. So as far as I can tell, it's a good bet the authorities can get Chapman on armed robbery and money laundering, but he's going to take a walk when it comes to these murders. And it just makes me sick!"

Marley was quick to share her thoughts. "He won't necessarily walk, Eva. The police already have a handwriting expert examining the resort's register to see if they can prove Suzanne Engelmann's signature was forged on the day she disappeared. Remember, she had told people that she planned on staying until that coming Saturday but left on the Thursday before. There's a more-than-fair possibility that she never actually signed out of the resort the day she disappeared and that her signature was forged later."

Eva frowned. "But I don't understand. There were eyewitnesses who saw her drive away from the resort the day she disappeared."

"Yes, but that doesn't necessarily mean she was leaving for good, does it?" Marley replied. "The Chapmans were the only people who knew whether or not Suzanne had checked herself out of the resort that day to head back to the cities. All they had to do was relay to anyone asking the lie that she had, to have it never be questioned."

"Of course, we always assume we're being told the truth, don't we?" Eva exclaimed. "It's a fault of human nature to trust unquestionably unless proven otherwise."

"One can hardly call it a fault of human nature," Ray said quickly. "Not when trust contributes so mightily to the building of strong communities."

Eva turned her adoring gaze in Ray's direction. "Good point, Ray," she said sweetly, "but you have to admit that murderers often take advantage."

Seeing an opening for a joke, Sean said with a flourish, "Well, they sure as blazes don't take advantage of Nan and Marley. When they're working a case, they don't trust anyone. Not even each other!"

Everyone laughed, including Nan and Marley. As Nan rose to her feet and began to gather cups, Marley went on. "I'm not so sure Buck Sykes won't eventually crack under pressure and implicate Dale Chapman in the murder. After all, he's being changed with armed robbery, money laundering, and murder! He's not going to let Dale get away with only two charges. Not if I read him correctly. No, he'll be looking for a deal that will help lighten his sentence, and I'm sure the district attorney will be more than happy to supply him with one."

"You're right," Sean said. "That's what he'll do. If, as

they say, there's no honor among thieves, then there must be even less among murderers."

For a few moments, the room fell silent as each undertook the unpleasant task of contemplating the mind and heart of a murderer.

Then Nan said softly, "Perhaps because I'm a woman and have experienced more than one divorce, the person I feel most sorry for is Randi Sykes. Like in so many cases of women who have been battered by men, she found herself in a situation she had no control over. All she could do—all she had sense and will enough to do—was make the best of a bad situation."

Eva looked sadly at Nan and said, "So you believe she really didn't know?"

Nan sighed heavily. "I do," she said, nodding firmly. "I believe the story she told the police in Alameda is the truth. That she was desperate to get out of Kansas City and start a new life with her sister in California, and when her ex-husband showed up in town and promised to give her enough money to get to California, she never questioned the favor he asked for. She said all he asked of her was to sit in the car and wait. Only after he approached with the bags, jumped into the car, and screamed at her to pull out and drive did she realize something criminal might have gone down. According to Gretchen, she told the police she thought it possible he may have held up a gas station or convenience store. It's not surprising that she had suspicions along those lines; after all, she knew the man. But she was shocked when they told her it had been an armored car. And once the shock left her, she became absolutely livid when told the amount of money that had been in those bags."

"I don't blame her for being angry," Sean said. "After putting her, an innocent stooge, through all the worry and anxiety of being implicated in a robbery, the brute ended up giving her only two thousand dollars!"

"Which she very happily accepted," Nan said. "It was enough to buy a ticket to California and have a little left over besides."

Marley yawned and stretched her arms above her head. "Well, unless someone has another question, that about wraps it up for now. We really don't have any more information to relay. The DNA analysis will answer the main question of what happened to the women and allow the grieving families to finally lay their bodies to rest." She rose from her chair, and the others followed suit.

"And now," Eva said, lifting Dewey and placing him back in his basket, "I believe a nice rest is what we each could benefit from. We need a relaxing vacation to get our minds off murder and mayhem. Because I've no doubt another case will come our way before long."

"Do you really think so?" Nan and Marley asked together.

"Of course. Why would any of us question it?" said Ray. "I mean, you have to admit, they do have a tendency to seek us out."

"So much so, in fact," Sean said boldly, "that although it's presently the end of May in Minnesota, I'm willing to bet a crisp Ulysses S. Grant that we have another case to solve before the snow flies. Is anyone here willing to take that bet?"

Few hands were raised.

CPSIA information can be obtained
at www.ICGtesting.com
Printed in the USA
BVHW042004210922
647677BV00007B/64